W9-CPF-724

Jordan stopped dead in his tracks at the sight of her

No. Way.

The rodeo queen? Something else he'd held in his brain without realizing it. The memory of high and mighty Shae McArthur's face—living proof that beauty was only skin deep. There'd never been one thing about her that he'd liked during the years they'd been on the rodeo team together...except for maybe that time she'd come on to him. He'd enjoyed her utterly shocked expression when he turned her down cold. She'd needed to be knocked off her high horse and he'd been glad to do the job. Literally, in fact.

"What are *you* doing here?" he demanded.

Shae blinked as he spoke, letting her hands drop a few inches. He could see when recognition kicked in, followed almost immediately by a look of horror. Of course. Beauty and the Beast. Face-to-face. As he recalled, Shae wasn't too fond of the imperfect. Nothing but the best for her.

"Good to see you, too, Jordan," she said huskily.

Dear Reader,

In the first installment of The Montana Way series, *Once a Champion* (Harlequin Superromance, June 2013), I created a monster—a Bridezilla, to be exact. In that book, Shae McArthur was an overachiever who'd been spoiled by her widowed father and stepmother. She was utterly self-absorbed and clueless as to the effect her actions had on other people.

I must be honest—it's a lot of fun writing clueless and self-absorbed people, and I had a ball creating Shae. The only problem was that Bridezilla Shae was to be the heroine of the third book in the series—this book—so I had to figure out a way to redeem her. The best course of action seemed to be to destroy her world as she knows it (sorry, Shae, but it's for your own good) and to force her to take a long, hard look at herself. So in a blink of an eye, Shae no longer has a fiancé or a job. She's struggling to pay wedding bills and fighting to convince her boss to hire her back. Things are no longer coming easily to Shae, and it's an eye opener.

Enter the hero. Jordan Bryan just wants to be left alone to heal. The survivor of a bombing while serving in the military, he's dealing with physical and emotional scars. He retreats to the Montana ranch he inherited during his convalescence, only to discover perfection-loving Shae McArthur working there. Well, he's not so perfect anymore, but neither is Shae, and he starts to feel a connection with the woman he'd written off as beautiful but superficial years ago...and he's not certain what to do about that.

I like writing characters with issues, and Shae and Jordan gave me a lot to work with. These two have ended up being some of my favorite characters ever. I hope you enjoy reading them as much as I enjoyed writing them. For more information about me and my books, or to contact me, please visit my website at www.jeanniewatt.com.

Take care and happy reading,

Jeannie Watt

JEANNIE WATT

All for a Cowboy

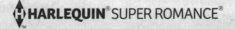

HARLEQUIN®SUPER ROMANCE®

If you purchased this book without a cover you should be aware that this book is stolen property. It was reported as "unsold and destroyed" to the publisher, and neither the author nor the publisher has received any payment for this "stripped book."

Recycling programs
for this product may
not exist in your area.

ISBN-13: 978-0-373-60852-2

ALL FOR A COWBOY

Copyright © 2014 by Jeannie Steinman

All rights reserved. Except for use in any review, the reproduction or utilization of this work in whole or in part in any form by any electronic, mechanical or other means, now known or hereafter invented, including xerography, photocopying and recording, or in any information storage or retrieval system, is forbidden without the written permission of the publisher, Harlequin Enterprises Limited, 225 Duncan Mill Road, Don Mills, Ontario, Canada M3B 3K9.

This is a work of fiction. Names, characters, places and incidents are either the product of the author's imagination or are used fictitiously, and any resemblance to actual persons, living or dead, business establishments, events or locales is entirely coincidental.

This edition published by arrangement with Harlequin Books S.A.

For questions and comments about the quality of this book, please contact us at CustomerService@Harlequin.com.

® and TM are trademarks of Harlequin Enterprises Limited or its corporate affiliates. Trademarks indicated with ® are registered in the United States Patent and Trademark Office, the Canadian Intellectual Property Office and in other countries.

Printed in U.S.A.

ABOUT THE AUTHOR

Jeannie Watt lives in rural Nevada with her husband, horses and ponies, and she teaches high school in a small combined school close to the Nevada-Oregon border. When she's not teaching or writing, Jeannie enjoys sewing retro fashions and reports on her new projects regularly in her blog, *Retro Sewing Romance Writer*. She also makes mosaic mirrors, ignores housework as much as possible and is thrilled to be married to a man who cooks.

Books by Jeannie Watt

HARLEQUIN SUPERROMANCE

*Too Many Cooks?
**The Montana Way

Other titles by this author available in ebook format.

To my editor, Piya Campana.
I liked The Montana Way stories when I turned
them in. I loved them after you shared your
insights and helped me tweak, edit and overhaul.
Thank you so very much!

CHAPTER ONE

WAS THERE ANY way she could wear sunglasses all day?

Shae McArthur tipped the dark glasses down and tilted the rearview mirror so she could see her eyes. Dreadful. As if she'd been crying all night. More like crying for a week, to the point that even if she wanted to cry again, she'd have no tears left. The last registry had been canceled, the last deposit surrendered, all the many details involved in calling off a wedding dealt with—to a degree. There was still the matter of informing friends and extended family.

And the embarrassment. No, make that the flat-out humiliation.

Shae lowered her head to the steering wheel, summoning strength. She wanted nothing more than to crawl into bed and shut out the world for... oh...ever, but she had a huge presentation that day, which she would give with swollen eyes. In an effort to distract, she'd slicked her long dark hair into a barrette at the back of her neck and worn a bright red dress and chunky jewelry, hoping to draw the eye away from her puffy face.

Shae pushed the sunglasses back into place and opened the Audi door. At least she could wear them until she got to her cubicle. Forcing her lips into a semismile, she crossed the parking lot and pushed through the front door of Cedar Creek Enterprises: Guest Ranch Division—not to be confused with Cedar Creek Enterprises: Real Estate Division one door over.

"Way to take surprise vacation days," Gerald Bruffett muttered as he crossed in front of her carrying a presentation board.

"It couldn't be helped," Shae replied.

"Floral emergency?" he called back to her as he disappeared into the conference room. Shae ignored him and walked on. Her part of the presentation had been completed before she'd left for her sister's wedding—and the worst day of her life—exactly one week ago. She was prepared. Sort of. The fine-tuning she'd hoped to do the past week hadn't been done, but if there was one thing Shae was good at, it was winging it. Heaven knew she'd done it enough over the past year.

"What happened to you?" Melinda Brody asked as soon as Shae walked around the cubicle wall. So much for red dresses and chunky jewelry—or sunglasses, for that matter—distracting anyone.

"Allergies."

"Since when have you had allergies?"

"Last Sunday," Shae said darkly as she shoved her purse into the bottom drawer of her desk. Mel had known her for far too long to be fooled by a lame excuse. She'd also been her only friend to decline the invitation to become a bridesmaid, because she spent every moment of her free time studying for a law degree. Shae sat and pulled off the sunglasses, surprised at how shaky she was—she who breezed through situations ordinary people hung back from.

She who had to tell her colleagues that the wedding was off.

"Allergies, my ass," Mel muttered as she returned to her keyboard. Shae swiveled her chair toward her friend, who was now focused intently on the screen in front of her, and moistened her lips.

"Mel?"

"Yeah?" her friend asked, still studying the screen.

Reed called off the wedding.

The words stuck in her throat. She was gearing up to try again when Gerald stuck his balding head around the wall, somehow looking both harried and smug. "Wallace wants to see you," he said.

Mel, who answered directly to the division manager, started to get up, but Gerald shook his head. "He wants to see Shae."

"Thanks," Shae said with a frown and Gerald disappeared again.

"Any idea?" Shae asked Mel. She hated going in blind if there was something she needed to know.

Mel shook her head, her eyebrows drawn together in a faintly perplexed expression. "Not a clue."

Risa Lewis, Wallace's associate, who, as usual, was wearing way too much makeup, smirked at Shae as she walked by. Risa always smirked at her, so that was no big deal, but this smirk seemed particularly self-satisfied, making Shae's stomach tighten as she approached the open door of Wallace's office. Something about this felt off, and when the division manager glanced up at her, all business, Shae's midsection tightened even more.

"Close the door, Shae, and have a seat."

Shae smiled, hoping it actually looked like a smile. "Thank you, Wallace." She sat on the other side of the cluttered oak desk, smoothing her skirt.

"Shae, there's no easy way to do this, so I'm just going to lay it out. We have to let you go."

For a moment Shae simply stared at him, very much as she'd stared at her ex-fiancé less than a week ago, trying to wrap her mind around what he'd just said. This had to be a joke, something he'd cooked up to drive home the point that she'd taken vacation days at an inopportune time for the company.

"I have a marketing presentation today for the new acquisition," she blankly.

Wallace gave his gray head a firm shake. "Risa has a marketing presentation today."

Shae's eyebrows shot upward. "You gave *her* my part of the project?"

"No. You did that."

"I don't understand." And the numbness spreading through her insides as she realized just how serious Wallace was about firing her was making it hard to breathe.

"For the past eight months your mind has not been on the job."

"I—"

He raised a hand. "You have been immersed in planning and executing not company business, but a wedding instead."

"I've done my job—"

"Not with your full attention." He leveled a hard stare at her over the top of his glasses. "You could have done better."

Shae swallowed drily, desperately trying to come up with a strategy, but her brain, which always came up with a solution—except with Reed—seemed paralyzed. *Do. Something.*

She cleared her throat and said in her most reasonable voice, "If you'd given me some warning... a chance to redeem myself... If you would perhaps consider this a warning?" She smiled at him hopefully. Wallace had always liked her; surely he'd change his mind. Give her just one more chance. After all, she was good at what she did—especially when she was focused on it, and damn it, she *would* focus on her job, and only her job, in the future.

"Miranda is adamant that we need to cut back." One corner of his mouth tightened ominously at the mention of the company owner's name. She was a woman people tended to tiptoe around, but Shae had always prided herself on getting along well with their demanding boss. So why had she now been singled out?

"I've spent the past four days going over employee performance," Wallace continued.

The four days she'd been gone. Things started to fall into place. "I took legitimate vacation days," she protested.

"With very little warning."

"I had a personal emergency."

Wedding related? He didn't need to say it. Shae could read it in his face. "I'm sorry about this, Shae."

"Reed called off the wedding," she blurted. "I needed a couple days to deal with it."

A look of dawning comprehension crossed Wallace's face. "I can understand that," he said after a few silent seconds. "But it doesn't change things." His voice softened as he said, "I know this is a shock, but it's not negotiable." He pushed a packet toward her. "I'd like to go over the severance package with you."

Shae didn't hear a word he said about the packet, but she must have nodded at the right times, because he continued to explain while she tried desperately to think of some way to save herself. She'd always been able to save herself. Finally he said, "Vera will

escort you from the building and be in contact in
case you have any questions regarding severance."

That got through to her. Shae's head snapped up.
"Escort me?" As in, she'd have to walk past Risa
and out the door with Vera dogging her?

"Company policy."

"I need my purse."

"Vera has already collected your things." And
sure enough, when she walked out of Wallace's office, the older woman was waiting near Risa's desk
with a cardboard box, Shae's Dooney & Bourke
purse balanced on the top of her other belongings.
Shae reached for the box, but Vera stepped back.

"I'll carry it, dear."

Shae tilted up her chin, inhaled as she focused on
the exit thirty feet away and started walking, wincing a little as her phone began buzzing from inside
her purse. Last week it would have been a caterer
or florist. This week it was probably her family,
checking up on her.

Well, now she had more bad news for them and
she had no idea how to tell them.

JORDAN BRYAN DIDN'T know how much longer he
could drive without finding a place to pull over
and sleep. His travel partner had been drifting in
and out for most of the day, but once it got dark,
the poodle had conked out for good.

The poodle.

Go figure.

Once he'd made his mind up to go, Jordan had tried to slip away while the dog was on his neighborhood rounds, but Clyde had come scampering around the Arlington apartment complex at the last minute, skidding to a stop at the curb next to the car, curly head cocked to one side as if to say, *Really, man? After all this you're running out on me?*

Yeah, he was. He was running out on everything and nothing. He was running and he couldn't even say why, except that every day he stayed where he was, doing the mindless job he'd been given, added to his raging sense of unrest.

The dog had then taken it upon himself to trot around the car to the driver's-side door and jump up, his toenails scratching the metal. Jordan had tried to harden himself, just as he'd hardened himself that morning when he'd abruptly told his supervisor he was leaving his mercy job and wouldn't be back, but at the last minute he'd opened the door. The homeless poodle had jumped in, scurried across Jordan's lap and settled himself in the passenger seat as if there'd never been any question of whether or not he'd be going.

Jordan only hoped that the dog knew what he was getting into traveling cross-country in a tiny used Subaru with no air conditioning. He snorted now at the thought and wiped a hand over his tired face, his fingers grazing the numb ridges of the burn scars near his ear before he reached over to turn the volume of the radio up. Hell, he didn't know what *he* was getting into—or going back to.

He just hoped Miranda hadn't screwed him over.

THE BLACK BUTTE PORTER that Reed had left behind wasn't working. Shae set the glass on the table and reached for the tequila, pouring a healthy shot before settling back against the teal-blue sofa cushions and staring out across the room. It looked barren without the boxes of wedding favors, her master-plan board...her dress.

The dress was listed on Craigslist for a price she'd never get but was still half of what she'd paid. The favors and master-plan board were in the trash, along with the tasteful ivory invitations embossed with indigo lettering inviting one and all to celebrate the joining of this man and this woman.

Shae socked back the shot and poured another.

She hadn't heard from Reed in two days, but even if she did, it would just be a courtesy on his part. Whatever they'd had was well and truly over—mainly because she wouldn't be with a guy who'd done this to her. A little notice might have been nice, before she and her parents had spent a fortune.

Shae reached for the bottle again. She probably should have had a clue that something wasn't quite right when he'd refused to move in together to save rent after she'd pushed the wedding date back for a second time so she had time to make everything perfect. He hadn't given a reason, but had said simply, "Let's wait." And since he'd seen things her way in all the other matters pertaining to their wedding, she'd agreed. It was only a matter of two months' rent, and her apartment had been jammed with wedding stuff, anyway.

Tequila dripped onto Shae's leg as she poured the next shot. At least he'd told her before the invitations had gone out. She'd organized her stunned bridesmaids into a phone tree, except for her stepsister, Liv, of course, who was on her honeymoon.

Liv, who was happily married.

Was she jealous?

Hell, yes.

Shae brought the glass to her lips, coughing as she inhaled the fumes at just the wrong moment. She wrinkled her nose, scowling as the doorbell rang.

What? What now? No doubt someone had just hit and totaled her new car where it was parked on the street. Fully expecting to see either a neighbor or her stepmother, she peered through the peephole to see Mel standing there, still wearing her work clothes.

Shae unlatched the door and pulled it open. Mel shoved her hands in her jacket pockets, shifting her weight uncomfortably.

Silently Shae stepped back, allowing her to come in. Once the door was closed, Mel turned toward her. "I heard the wedding is off."

"Yep."

"Were you going to tell me?"

"I was, but then the bad thing happened and I figured Wallace would pass word along," Shae said, going to sit on the sofa. Mel stayed where she was.

"He did," she agreed. She nodded at the bottle with the full shot glass sitting next to it on the coffee table. "I see you're coping."

"Just numbing the pain for a while. Getting fired came as kind of a shock."

"Really."

Since Shae had thought this to be a sympathy visit, Mel's flat tone surprised her. "Did *you* know?" she asked candidly.

"That Wallace was letting you go? No. But I understand why it happened."

Shae studied Mel for a moment, more than a little surprised at the answer. They'd known each other forever, and even though they were polar opposites in many ways, their friendship had remained strong since the first grade. There'd been times when they'd gone their own ways, lived their own lives without a lot of contact, but Shae knew she could count on Mel. Or she had. "Why can you understand it?" Shae asked.

"Because you were living and breathing that wedding. And when *Montana Skies* signed on for the photo essay, you spent the majority of your time in another world that had nothing to do with the job. Even when you were there, you weren't there."

"I did my job," Shae protested.

"You went through the motions. Gerald and Risa were forever clearing up loose threads you left."

"They're my assistants." And if there was one thing Shae was good at, it was delegating.

"You weren't doing *your* part."

"Well," Shae said briskly as she got back to her feet. "Thank you so much for stopping by. I feel better now."

"I'm not here to bury the knife deeper," Mel said bluntly.

Shae wrinkled her forehead. "Then why does it feel so much like that's exactly what's happening?"

Mel sighed. "Pretending you were fired for a bogus reason might make you feel better tonight, but it won't help in the long run." She nodded at the bottle. "Are you willing to share, or do you need the whole thing?"

"I'll let you have a little," Shae said, getting to her feet and walking into the kitchen. With altitude the tequila had more of an effect. She turned around.

"Maybe you'd better have *that* shot," she said pointing at the glass she'd left on the coffee table. Getting drunk out of her mind sounded good in theory, but was the aftermath worth it? Wasn't she dealing with enough aftermath as it was? "If you're not afraid of loser germs."

Mel smirked at her as she reached for the shot and sipped at it. Mel always had been a sipper, very much like Liv, while Shae was a tosser. She liked to have the whole thing. Now.

"Have you told Whitney and Bree and Heather—"

"No," Shae called from the kitchen, stopping Mel before she could name all seven bridesmaids. She turned on the faucet, filled a glass, thought about what she wanted to say. A moment later she walked back to the doorway, took a sip of water and faced the truth. "I don't think they're that anxious to hear from me." She'd run them hard for over a year. As the plans had escalated, so had their duties, and she had been sensing some rebellion close to the end. Besides that, there was the embarrassment factor. Dumped *and* fired.

Shae gave a sniff, feeling the ridiculous tears starting to surface. She was not going to fall apart. Not again. "How'd Risa's presentation go?" she asked as she came to sit beside Mel, who'd barely made a dent in the tequila shot.

"Not so well," Mel said. "Miranda was there, and you know the effect she has on people."

"I know the effect she's had on me," Shae said darkly. Hearing that Risa had crashed and burned wasn't as satisfying as it should have been. "And do you know what really fries me? I admired her. I thought that she was a tough, capable business-woman." She'd actually thought they were two of a kind, confident go-getters who said what they thought, went after what they wanted.

"I think she still is, Shae."

Shae hated hearing that. Hated thinking that she'd screwed herself here. Much better to feel the victim…except that Shae never embraced that sort of role. She changed things that needed to be changed until she was happy with them.

How was she going to change this?

"So you're saying I lost my own job," she finally said.

"It was like wedding planning possessed you."

"Planning a wedding is time-consuming and stressful," Shae said, once again eyeing the tequila bottle.

"I understand, but it was…" Mel made an odd face. "You were…" She shifted her position on the sofa, turning toward Shae with a frown knitting her forehead. "It was like everything had to be beyond perfect—bigger and better than any wedding anyone had ever seen."

"There's a problem there?"

"There is if you let the need to be the best rule your life."

"I like things to be…nice."

"Over-the-top nice." Mel exhaled and settled back against the cushions. "I'm just trying to point out what got you into this trouble. And until the wedding plans began, you poured that energy into the job, which was why Miranda loved you. And Gerald and Risa hated you."

"Gee. Thanks so much."

"You know it's true," Mel said. "And you know it doesn't bother you that they resent you."

"Touché."

"Do you have any leads for jobs?"

"I've only been fired for a matter of hours."

"Are you telling me you don't already have a plan?"

"I have a list of firms to cold-call," Shae admitted before sipping the water again. "I've posted my résumé on the job-search sites." Her mouth tilted down at the corners. "I want my old job back. I liked it. And Mel, I was ten months away from being vested in retirement. Ten months!"

Mel reached out to squeeze her shoulder. "If you need a reference, I can give you one."

"Meaning Wallace won't?"

"I don't know. Depends on Miranda."

"Yeah." Shae pinched the bridge of her nose for a moment. She'd get past this. Mel finally finished off the shot and set the glass on the table.

"I have a study session. Are you going to be all right here? Because I can cancel and stay."

"Don't do that," Shae said. She would have liked the company, but she was beginning to think some alone time wouldn't be bad, either. She'd had enough hard truths for one night.

Mel picked up her purse, then gestured to the tequila bottle. "Maybe you should do yourself a favor after I leave...pour the rest of that bottle down the sink."

Shae flashed her friend a frown. Damned if she was pouring good tequila down the sink. Shae picked up the bottle, putting the stopper back in and pressing it down hard before handing it to Mel. "If it makes you feel better, take custody. I really need to be alone."

"Are you sure?"

"No. I want you to stay and tell me about how I had my head up my ass for months."

Mel smiled. "Call if you need me?"

Shae closed her eyes. Mel was the best friend she'd ever had. And the most sensible. Maybe this was the time to tell her that her head had been where the sun didn't shine, while she was still reeling from shock. That way it didn't ruin yet another day. "I'll call," she said. "Will you be available to answer? I know how you are when you study."

"I'll leave the phone on." She gave Shae a quick hug. "Call."

"I will."

Once Mel's footsteps faded into the distance, the apartment was too quiet. So quiet that the lack of sound seemed to press in on her. Where were the noisy neighbors when she needed them?

The phone rang then, the vibration making it dance on the glass coffee table. Shae glanced at the number. Vivian calling for the second time since hearing Shae's most recent bad news. Shae wanted to ignore the call, but if she did, her stepmother would be there knocking on the door, probably with her father in tow.

The phone rang again. One more ring and it would go to voice mail....

Taking a deep breath and suddenly regretting the lack of readily available tequila, Shae picked up the phone, forced a smile and said hello. Her father's voice, heavy with concern, answered her.

"Shae, honey. We're in Missoula and Vivian wants to stop by, if it's not too late."

In Missoula? At this hour?

"Dad, I'd love to see you," Shae said. There was no way she could turn them away after they'd obviously driven in from their home a good hour away.

"We're right outside. I thought it might be too late, but we passed Mel as we turned into the cul-de-sac."

"Come on in," Shae said, picking up the shot glass and carrying to the dishwasher, where she popped it in out of sight. "See you in a few."

She hung up, raced into the bathroom and quickly gargled some mouthwash. If Vivian thought she was drowning her sorrows, no telling what steps she'd take. Seconds later the doorbell rang.

Vivian hovered for a moment, then said, "I can't help it," and threw her arms around Shae. "I'm so sorry, sweetie."

Shae tried to smile as she gently eased out of Vivian's embrace and then hugged her father.

"I called around," her father said. "Checked with some buddies to see if they've heard of any openings. No luck yet, but I'm sure it's just a matter of time."

"The problem is the real-estate market," Vivian

lamented, taking Shae's hand and leading her to the sofa.

"I know," Shae replied gamely.

"Of course, we'll help you with the bills until you get back on your feet," her father said. Shae started to say *thank you,* but he held up a hand. "No arguments."

"I appreciate that," Shae said. The bills were her big concern at the moment. She'd charged an entire trousseau and had yet to see the final damages. And then there were the living expenses, which were going to catch up with her soon, since she'd been living paycheck to paycheck, spending every dime she had, as well as several dimes she didn't have, on the wedding. "I'll pay you back, of course."

"Of course," Vivian said, shooting a glance toward her husband that Shae couldn't quite interpret. "Whenever you can."

Her father sat down on the sofa, pulling a list out of his jacket pocket. "Here are the guys I contacted for you. You should check back in with them periodically. Several of them owe me favors. The ones without check marks are people I couldn't get hold of."

Shae stared down at the list, a bit overwhelmed. Her parents were in full rescue mode, and even though a small voice inside her protested, it was soon overpowered by logic and necessity. These were her parents. This was what they did, and Shae wasn't about to stop them.

CHAPTER TWO

JORDAN MADE IT as far as Wisconsin before trouble struck in the form of a faulty alternator. Since it was impossible to travel without headlights, he'd stopped in the first town he'd hit at dusk. On a Saturday evening. When no garages were open, or even due to be open, until Monday.

The first night he'd slept in his car in a campground, putting the seat down to open up the cargo space and make just enough room for him to almost stretch out. The second night he thought, *Screw it,* and rented the cheapest motel room he could find, smuggled Clyde in and settled for the night. Less than three hours later he woke up fighting, his breath coming in short, painful gasps, his body covered with sweat.

Shoving the tangled sheets aside, Jordan stumbled out of bed, his head swimming as he regained his feet.

Whoa, shit.

Jordan wiped the sweat off first his forehead and then his upper lip with what was left of his now-healed hand, feeling the unwelcome scrape of overly dry skin across his damp face. He paced to the window and stopped, staring at the brown plaid drapes. Clyde shadowed his movement, keeping a distance away, as if not wanting to crowd him.

The dog understood.

Jordan tried to clear his throat, found it impossible on the first try. He hadn't cried out. Usually he woke up yelling, but not this time. This time he'd felt as if he was drowning. Suffocating as water filled his lungs.

What the hell?

He turned away from the window, scrubbing both hands over his face. It'd been months since he'd had a nightmare, months since he'd cautiously weaned himself off the prazosin, which had been prescribed to help him deal with the symptoms of post-traumatic stress and had stopped the dreams cold.

There was no point in going back to bed, so Jordan slumped down into the uncomfortable armchair next to the window and stared into space until Clyde jumped up into his lap.

The dream had to be stress related. The alternator. The trip home. Having no means of support except for his disability check. All of his instincts were still urging him to go back to Montana. He needed to go home.

But since his dad was dead, what was he going home to?

The question had niggled at him more than once on the drive and he had no answer to it. Maybe it was because the High Camp, the remote ranch he and his dad had co-owned, was one of the few places where he'd felt a modicum of peace after Miranda had come into his life; it was the one thing she hadn't poisoned. Not that she hadn't tried. When he'd proposed to Becky Christopher just before he'd gone into the service, Miranda was the one who'd suggested that he and his father create a formal lease, so that Hank could continue to farm the land if something happened to Jordan and Becky inherited. She'd referred to Jordan's possible demise so often that he'd gone overseas with the distinct feeling that Miranda hoped something did happen to him.

Well, Miranda had gotten her wish shortly after Becky had called it quits—and he was still suspicious about Miranda's influence with his former fiancée. Something bad had happened to Jordan, but he hadn't died. His father had, so now he owned the place outright and there wasn't one freaking thing she could do about it.

It took three days to get the alternator repaired, then Jordan made it as far as North Dakota before finally pulling off the highway and following the frontage road until he found a gravel lane leading off into the hills. He followed it for a ways, then pulled off. Clyde woke up as he slowed to a stop and they both stepped outside to pee before once again making themselves as comfortable as possible in the Subaru. Jordan debated before reaching for the bottle of pills in his jacket pocket. He'd hate himself in the morning when he couldn't wake up, but he'd hate himself more if he woke up in a cold sweat gasping for air in an hour or two. He'd wait until he got home, then wean himself off the pills once again.

SHAE CLOSED HER apartment door and let her designer bag drop to the floor with a thud. Would it have killed any of the people she'd cold-called to give her a smidgen of encouragement?

Apparently so, because even the people she knew well—come to think of it, *especially* the people she knew well—had been pretty damned blunt about the possibility of employment. True, her firm had been unique, combining real estate and guest-ranch management together, but as far as she could see, that gave her experience in two fields, which should have doubled the job opportunities. Not so. Three days of looking and not much hope. Meanwhile, bills for things she'd forgotten buying had started trickling in. She needed to find a job before the trickle became a flood.

The way people had reacted to her cold calls, even the ones on her father's list, made her wonder if word of why she'd been let go had spread through the small real-estate community. Had Miranda blackballed her?

And if so, why? It wasn't as though she'd done anything heinous.

Shae reached into the fridge to pull out her last

bottle of chardonnay. She'd just started working on the cork when a knock sounded on her door.

Opportunity, perhaps?

Her mouth twisted as she pulled the cork before abandoning the bottle and crossing the living room to look through the peephole. Her younger brother, Brant, stood on the other side.

Shae opened the door and without hesitation walked into her brother's arms, hugging him close. His arms closed around her and for a moment they just stood. The last time Shae could remember him hugging her was when she'd lost the Miss Rodeo Montana crown by one and a half points. She'd needed moral support then and she needed it now.

"How was Texas?" she asked as she eased out of his embrace.

"Flat and humid, but I won some money." He pulled off his hat as he walked into her apartment. "I hear you've had some life changes since Liv's wedding."

Shae nodded as she closed the door behind him. "Want a beer?" she asked.

"You know I do." He put his hat on the table, then took a seat on the sofa while Shae went to the fridge.

"Is Black Butte okay?" she called. She had two bottles left and once those were gone, yet another reminder of her three-year relationship with Reed would be history. After that she never wanted to see another bottle of Black Butte Porter again.

"Fine," he called. She popped the top on the beer, poured herself a glass of chardonnay—although at this point in the day she could have easily chugged from the bottle—and brought both out into the living room. Brant took the beer from her, lifting it in a salute as he always did when they drank together. Shae did the same, glad that he didn't feel the need to toast anything in particular. What could she toast right now? *Here's to all the sucky things that are happening?*

"Want to talk?" her brother asked.

"No," she said candidly. "But I will." She took a sip of wine, which was sweeter than she liked, but adequate for helping her through yet another recital of how her life had gone so terribly wrong. "I got dumped and lost my job."

Brant looked at her over the top of the bottle. "Anything else?"

"I can't find another job?" She sank back farther into the sofa cushions, staring across the room. "Bills I'd forgotten I had are starting to pile up?"

"What happened with your old job?"

"Reduction in force."

"I didn't think you were lowest in seniority."

"I'm not sure how they picked who got canned."

She shot him a sideways glance and could tell that he didn't believe her, but he let it pass. "So how's the…wedding canceling going?" he asked.

"Not good. I've lost all of the deposits. Reed paid for his half, though." Brant nodded over his beer and there was something in the way he was studying her that seemed...off. "Vivian is really upset, as you can imagine. She's put a lot into this."

"Yes, she has," Brant said slowly, and Shae's radar kicked up a notch.

"What's up?" she asked.

Brant met her gaze dead-on, his expression solemn. "Don't take any money from Vivian and Dad, okay?"

"What?" Shae asked, startled at the unexpected request.

"If you need money to tide you over, come to me, but not them. I know they'll offer—it's the way they are—but don't take it."

Shae closed her eyes. "Don't worry. I won't take their money." She thought of the check from her dad that was nestled in the bottom of her purse, the godsend she'd hoped to live on while she found a decent job, because the way things were looking, eight weeks of severance wasn't going to cut it. Not if she was going to keep making her car payment.

"Shae...you always land on your feet. You know you will this time, too. I'll help."

Her eyes snapped open and for a moment she simply stared at him, stunned. Really? He thought it was that easy? She'd just jump to her feet, dust herself off and carry on?

"I know no such thing."

"Tell me a time you haven't."

"Brant...maybe you don't quite get what is going

on here. My fiancé walked out on me six weeks before the wedding I've been planning for almost two years. Then my boss fired me—"

"I'm here for you, honestly I am. But Shae...I don't know if you realize how much you depend on other people to bail you out of your problems."

Again she stared at him, a slow burn starting deep inside of her. "First Mel and now you. Why are you adding fuel to the fire?"

"What?"

"Mel stopped by the day I was fired to tell me it was my fault, and now..." She didn't finish because there was no need. He knew where she was going with this. "Why are you doing this?"

Brant considered for a moment, then said, "Because it's something that needs to be said. And it's time."

"It's time. Now while I'm down is the time to give me another swift kick?"

"No. I'm not trying to kick you while you're down." He set down the beer and slid across the sofa to sit next to her, his voice earnest as he said, "If you need a loan, I'm happy to give it to you. Just...don't take anything more from Vivian and Dad, okay? They've dipped into their retirement for your wedding and they don't need to be dipping again."

Shae's head was starting to throb. "I'll pay them back," she muttered, putting a hand to her forehead. "They insisted that I take it. I told Dad that

Reed and I were paying for everything, but he insisted on helping with my half. He said it was his duty as a father."

"And maybe," Brant said softly, "Since you knew they were trying to save for retirement, it was your duty as a daughter to say no."

She set her wineglass down abruptly, sloshing chardonnay over the glass tabletop. "I care about my family," she said.

"Yeah, I know, Shae. But do you *think* about us?"

"Yes." Shae pressed a hand to her forehead. "Yes, I do. I've just… The wedding… Crap!"

Brant reached out to pull her hand away from her head and held on for a moment. "Like I said, Shae, I'm here for you. It's a rough time. If you need to depend on someone, depend on me."

Shae pulled her hand out of her brother's and reached for her wine. "Thank you. I appreciate the offer." But at that moment she was pretty damned sure that she wasn't going to depend on anyone to bail her out of her problems.

Brant hung around long enough to finish his beer and reiterate his offer of help, then took off to meet his girlfriend, Sara, for dinner.

Shae waited only a few minutes after he left to get on the phone and call Wallace—at home—and request a face-to-face meeting.

"I need closure," she said.

"Closure?"

"And to talk."

"Shae…"

"Please? I can come in early before anyone gets there. Or I could meet you at a coffee shop." She swallowed drily. Begging was so not her thing, but neither was feeling this desperate. She picked up a Macy's bill—the one she'd been afraid to open— then dropped it back down on the counter. "Ten minutes. I've gone the extra mile for you, Wallace. Please."

"You haven't gone the extra mile during the last year, but…" Shae bit her lip, held her breath. "Ten minutes. At the coffee shop across the street."

"Thank you."

Shae hung up, feeling as if she might have a toe-hold. Wallace had always had a soft spot for her. Maybe…just maybe…

"I'M NOT GIVING you your job back, Shae." At the last minute Wallace had called and asked her to meet him at the office after hours, which had made Shae hopeful that perhaps he was reconsidering. He was, after all, allowing her back on the premises, and he'd seemed more human than the last time she'd spoken to him.

Now that he'd made his proclamation, Shae wasn't feeling one bit hopeful, but she had him there and she wasn't giving up this easily.

"Not even in a probationary capacity?" Wallace picked up the pencil lying on top of a pile of spread-sheets, looked at it instead of at her. "It was Miranda who made the decision to let you go. I went over the performance evaluations with her, but it was obvious from the beginning that she'd already decided you were the one going."

That stung. "I don't understand. Why me? It isn't like I was slacking off while she was around, and you gave me a satisfactory evaluation."

"That," Wallace said pointedly, "was a gift. And—" he tapped the pencil again "—she didn't need to be at the office to see you."

"Meaning?"

"The cameras."

Shae's heart jumped. "She's using them?" The cameras had come with the building when the company had first moved in four years ago and as far as she—or anyone she worked with—knew, they'd never been turned on. *Well, guess again.*

"I did my job," she said stiffly.

"And a lot of other stuff."

"I didn't think a phone call here and there would matter."

"It did, and it was more than a *few* phone calls, Shae. Miranda's not happy, and she's making an example of you."

Shae let her head fall back. "A little warning would have been nice."

"I dropped some hints."

"When?" Shae asked, perplexed. Wallace pressed his fingers to his forehead as if staving off a headache and she abandoned the topic. "What about the good things I've done? Before the wedding plans," she added quickly. "What about the Tuscan Canyon Ranch? I put most of that purchase agreement together. I found the property, which wasn't even for sale, if you remember right, and matched it to the perfect client. We made a great commission and then we got the management contract on top of that!"

"You're good, Shae, when you focus."

"And I will focus. The wedding… I let it get out of hand." It was finally starting to sink in just how far out of hand she'd allowed it to go.

"But what if something else comes up?"

"I've learned my lesson."

Wallace gave her a doubtful look. "I'm not certain that would reassure Miranda."

Shae leaned forward, placing her palm flat on the desk. "I made a mistake. I can change. I need a job."

"Then you should have taken care with the one you had."

"And that's that?" she asked softly.

"Afraid so, Shae."

It can't end this way.

"Sorry," Wallace said.

"Yeah." Shae got to her feet, gave him a faint smile mustered from the need to hold on to a few shreds of her dignity, then turned to go, her stomach so tight she felt as if she was going to throw up. She was almost to the door when she glanced at the aerial map on the wall, then stopped. She slowly turned back, wondering if Wallace had indeed shrunk back in his seat as he met her speculative gaze or if she'd imagined it. "What about this?" she asked, pointing at the faded fluorescent-pink circle drawn around a mountain property.

"What about it?" Wallace asked slowly.

"Remember how Miranda was slated to sell it, but found out she couldn't?"

"Vividly," Wallace said. The sale had fallen through after she'd discovered she was not the sole heir to the place and apparently had been unable to hammer out a deal with her stepson, the other heir.

Shae was not surprised. Her own dealings with Jordan Bryan, brief as they'd been, had not gone well, either.

"But what if it made her some money while it was sitting there?"

"How so?" Wallace asked, his pale eyes narrowing, but Shae saw a spark of interest there.

"What if I could shape it into a guest ranch? Miranda has the operating rights." A fact she'd gleaned from office gossip and speculation after the sale fell through. "Why not use them?"

"Have you seen the place, Shae?"

"Mel and I went there once during college to collect a horse she'd bought from Miranda's husband. So yes, I've seen it."

"And how did it strike you?"

"Isolated. Run-down." Shae had excitement in her voice as she said, "But there were cabins there that the family had rented to miners during the gold strikes. Think how cool it would be if those could be refurbished. And there were quite a few other buildings, if I recall."

Wallace looked over his shoulder, as if checking for a camera or perhaps a recording device, before leaning across his desk to say in a low voice, "If it had any moneymaking potential, don't you think she would have thought about that?"

"Not if it's isolated and run-down." Shae pointed to the map. "Look—it's surrounded by Forest Service land. Perfect for riding. Fishing. But in a more—" she smiled slightly as a thought struck her "—*manly* environment than at Miranda's other two ranches." Both of which were sprawling properties with rich histories as working cattle ranches. Lots of little niceties included in the vacation package. Spas, babysitting, crafts classes for kids, riding lessons.

"Manly."

Shae walked back to his desk, plans already taking shape in her head. "Yes, manly. A more rugged experience. Not for sissies, that kind of marketing. Kind of a one-percenter ranch."

Wallace shook his head. She could see he was intrigued, but didn't want to admit it, so she gave one more small push.

"Come on…it's a great idea. Run it by Miranda."

"It's not bad," he agreed grudgingly. "She'll probably give the project to someone else if I pass it along—like, say, someone who works here?"

"I'll contract the job for eighty percent of my previous salary," Shae said, "for three months. I'll evaluate the property, make recommendations for renovations, handle any permitting nightmares. I'd hand her a finished product for less salary than she'd pay a regular employee."

"And if you succeed…?"

"It would put me in a position to discuss getting my old job back. I heard that Risa's not doing as well as hoped."

Wallace fiddled with the pencil he held, then exhaled slowly, his breath fluttering the spreadsheets in front of him. "I'll run it by her. No promises."

"None asked," Shae said feeling a faint welling of confidence. If she could get this second chance, it meant she could stay on her career path. And more than that, maybe she could prove she wasn't the loser that everyone apparently thought she was. Rebuild one or two of those bridges she'd obliviously burned.

WHEN JORDAN LEFT home to join the military, he'd told himself he wasn't coming back—at least not as long as Miranda was in the picture—and the Subaru was doing its best to help him keep his promise. He'd ended up staying three nights in Miles City just after crossing the Montana border, waiting for yet another repair part. And even though he was in

Montana and had a deep appreciation for the rolling hills in this part of the state, it wasn't his part of the state. In some ways he felt as foreign here as he had in Virginia.

Maybe that was why he spent all of his time in the motel, leaving only to walk Clyde or to get a cheap meal. Or maybe he'd hidden out because he was still raw when it came to people staring at him, studying the burns and what remained of the fingers of his left hand. He'd never liked being the center of attention and now people couldn't help but notice him.

He'd gone one night without taking a pill and had been slammed with another nightmare. After that he'd taken the pills every night. He had enough for three more weeks and he hoped that once he was at the High Camp, he'd be able to work his way past the dreams again…and past the cavernous emptiness that seemed to be enveloping him.

Was he ever going to get a grip?

Once upon a time he'd thought he was. The PTSD therapy had worked so well that Jordan had come to believe that his principal scars were the physical ones. Now he wasn't so sure…and it scared him.

He'd put all that time and effort into therapy, gone through the accompanying emotional trauma, and what had it gotten him? A six-month reprieve. No— make that four months. For the last two he'd been fighting against the insidious backslide.

The thing that scared him most was that he had

no idea what had triggered the backslide, the feelings of emptiness and uselessness. One day he was doing fine and the next…the next he felt overwhelmed. Trapped, yet at the same time drifting.

So now he was following his gut and doing therapy his way. He was going home.

DRIVING THE AUDI to the High Camp had been a mistake. It was a sturdy car, but parts of the road leading to the mountain ranch were rougher than Shae had anticipated. She carefully maneuvered her baby through a long stretch of six-inch-deep ruts, wincing at the sound of branches scraping the sides of the car, before easing back into the center of the track when the road once again smoothed out.

Shae let out a breath and loosened her death grip on the steering wheel. Scratches on the Audi were not the end of the world—she could afford to have them buffed out when she completed this contract.

A small smile played on her lips. *This contract.* She had a contract. Her impromptu proposal had worked. Almost as soon as Wallace ran her idea past Miranda, the ball had started rolling. Early Friday morning she'd been summoned back to the office to meet with Miranda herself.

Shae went into the meeting determined to prove herself and thirty minutes later the deal had been struck—a two-month contract at 70 percent of her former salary, instead of the 80 percent she'd suggested. At the end of that time, she was to have a complete proposal worked up, ready to put into place the next spring. If Miranda approved the proposal, then she'd oversee renovations and implement small-group beta test runs of all activities. After that…no promises.

Typical Miranda. But Shae had left feeling good—about the job ahead of her and about Miranda, who'd explained quite candidly why she'd let Shae go. Shae had to admit that given the same circumstances, she might have done the same thing. The job, whatever it might be, came first now, and, as Mel had pointed out when Shae called her with the good news, if she could get this project up and running, it would be gold on a résumé. She could see the presentation portfolio in her head—before and after pictures of the ranch she was about to rehabilitate on a shoestring budget. Smiling guests with big fish. A guy holding the horns of a trophy buck. A big campfire with manly men sitting around it laughing.

Good stuff.

But first she had to make it happen.

First she had to get there.

Shae rolled to a stop at the windfall tree across the road. Excellent. Getting out of the car, she walked to the tree, nudging it with the toe of her boot. Sturdy as a rock. There was no way she was going to move it.

She turned and looked at the road she'd just driven up. The trees had grown so close to the edge that it was going to be impossible to turn around, so she had two choices—drive the car in reverse down the road or walk on. It was the thought of backing around those ruts that convinced her. Not that backing around them would be any easier later in the day, but at least she would have completed the first step of her mission—to reconnoiter the abandoned ranch. As per Miranda's suggestion, she planned to eventually live there during the renovation. It was, after all, almost forty miles from Missoula, and five of those miles were on unpaved roads—not exactly an easy day trip. She definitely needed to know what was necessary to live there comfortably and since she'd come this far, there was no sense turning back now.

THE SUBARU RATTLED as it bumped over the cattle guard at the bottom of High Camp road, the familiar sound something Jordan had never thought about missing until now. Home. He was almost home, close to a place where he could hole up and let the world go about its business and forget about him. He would return the favor.

"Almost there," he said. Clyde bounced up to a sitting position, his tongue lolling out of his mouth as he watched the scenery roll slowly past. A rabbit darted across the road and the poodle practically hit the windshield in excitement.

Clyde was going to be a busy dog when they got to the ranch.

Jordan wondered what kind of shape the house was in. It'd been six years since he'd last seen the place; over a year since his father, who'd hayed the meadows and used the ranch as a hunting retreat for his buddies, had died. Jordan had no idea if his cousin Cole had done anything more than close the door.

Would it be full of mice?

Or just full of memories? He wasn't certain which one would be worse. He figured he could check the place out, sleep in the Subaru one more night if necessary, then head to Missoula to get what he needed to make the place livable.

Less than a quarter mile up the road, the gravel thinned to bare dirt in places and he could see fresh tire tracks. Narrow car tracks rather than truck tracks. Who, other than him, would drive a car up this road? There was only one set of tracks—going in—so apparently he would soon find out.

Company. Great.

It had to be someone sightseeing or berry picking. People tended to explore the woods during the summer months—and apparently ignore the Private Road sign next to the cattle guard—so that made sense. Ironic that he came here to escape people and it appeared that the first thing he was going to have to do was kick someone off his property.

"I'll be nice," he muttered to the dog, who had edged closer to him as the road grew more rutted and the trees closed in, pressing his firm, warm body against Jordan's side. Whoever had driven up the road hadn't been deterred by the ever-deepening ruts. He was actually glad to see the ruts, since it meant that no one had been traveling the road regularly. It was his property, but he didn't trust Miranda. He wasn't even certain he could trust his cousin, Cole, who'd thrown in with his stepmother when she'd coerced his dad, Jordan's uncle, to turn their ranch into a working dude ranch to make more money. Miranda did love money.

He rounded a sharp corner, then stopped. Ahead of him an expensive Audi was parked with its bumper practically touching the tree lying across the road. *What the hell? An Audi? Really?*

Jordan opened the car door and was instantly struck by the strong, familiar smell of pines and bracken and damp Montana earth. Something else he'd missed without even being aware of it.

"Stay here," he said to the dog, who jumped back over the console to his side of the car at the command, obediently plopping his butt down in the passenger seat. Jordan closed the door, wondering not for the first time if the poodle understood English.

The Audi was locked and empty except for a leather briefcase and two map tubes in the backseat. Odd, to say the least. Jordan stepped away from the car, his eyes narrowing as he slowly surveyed his surroundings, looking for signs of movement in the brush or on the road past the tree. Nothing except for Clyde bouncing up and down in the Subaru.

Cool. Well, until he got a chain saw, this tree was staying where it was and there was nothing he could do except to walk on to the ranch. He went back to the car, found Clyde's leash and settled his hat on his head, more than a little curious as to where the driver of the Audi was.

After crossing over the tree, Jordan put Clyde on the ground, where he raced around on the leash, sometimes getting jerked back if something particularly interesting caught his urban eye. And every now and again Jordan spotted footprints heading in the same direction as they were going—those of a smallish female wearing some kind of heeled boots. Not cowboy boots, but probably something along that line, which made him wonder if this person was part of Miranda's crew, up here doing a monthly check or something.

That would be nice…but unlikely. Miranda didn't like him enough to check on his property in his absence. Hell, she hadn't even contacted him once while he'd been recovering in the burn unit. She'd probably hoped he'd die and then she'd have everything, instead of almost everything.

One last turn in the road and first the ancient barn, then the almost-as-ancient house, came into view. Jordan slowed down and then stopped. Damn. It looked the same as when he'd left—from a distance, anyway—but he was not overwhelmed by any kind of sense of at long last being home. In fact the scene struck him as being very much like an old photograph—a place he'd once loved, but could never go back to because it was lost to time.

Physically the ranch was still there, but while surveying the familiar scene Jordan instinctively knew that it would never feel the same as it had before he'd left. His dad was dead. Miranda lived on. All this ranch could be to him now was a sanctuary, a way to escape from the world and heal. The old times were gone, never to be recovered.

And he could live with that.

Hell, he had to live with that. He hadn't exactly ingratiated himself to his superiors when he'd abruptly quit his job, so this was his future. Now all he had to do was figure out who was there horning in on his future.

As he got closer to the house, Clyde started pressing against his leg, as if sensing trouble ahead. The door to the house was wide-open and Jordan caught sight of movement inside.

Time for introductions and explanations.

He walked up onto the old porch, the thick boards echoing hollowly under his boots.

The woman he'd seen moving inside the house, oblivious to his approach, swung around at the sound of his footsteps, taking an immediate defensive stance as if she fully planned to take him out with a karate chop or something, her eyes wide.

Jordan stopped dead in his tracks at the sight of her.

No. Way.

The rodeo queen? Something else he'd held in his brain without realizing it: the memory of high-and-mighty Shae McArthur's face—living proof that beauty was only skin-deep. There'd never been one thing about her that he'd liked during the years they'd been on the rodeo team together…except for maybe that time she'd come onto him. He'd enjoyed her utterly shocked expression when he'd turned her down cold. She'd needed to be knocked off her high horse and he'd been glad to do the job. Literally, in fact.

"What are *you* doing here?" he demanded.

Shae blinked as he spoke, letting her hands drop a few inches. He could see when recognition kicked in, followed almost immediately by a look of horror. Of course. Beauty and the Beast. Face-to-face. As he recalled, Shae wasn't too fond of the imperfect. Nothing but the best for her.

"Good to see you, too, Jordan," she said huskily.

He walked into the musty-smelling living room, stopping to rest his good hand, the one holding Clyde's leash, on his hip. He purposely used his damaged left hand to rub his jaw, watching Shae's eyes as she took in the stubs of fingers he'd lost to shrapnel before the flash had burned his back and face. "You're working for Cedar Creek Ranch?"

She cleared her throat, but her voice was still husky when she said, "Yes."

"But you're here, not there."

"I am," she agreed. "Is Miranda expecting you?"

"Not unless she's a mind reader."

"You should have called her," she said.

"Why?"

"Because if you plan to stay here, it isn't going to work out."

CHAPTER THREE

"LIKE HELL IT WON'T work out," Jordan said through gritted teeth.

Shae tore her fascinated gaze away from his scars and met his eyes. This was bad in so many ways that she couldn't begin to count them. Jordan, the long-lost stepson—the reason Miranda couldn't sell the property in the first place as she'd wanted to—showed up now? Why? And where on earth had he been? Judging from his injuries, wherever it was, it hadn't exactly been pleasant.

"What happened to you?" she asked in a low voice, figuring there was no reason to pretend he hadn't changed since the last time she'd seen him.

She had a feeling he was going to say something smart-ass such as, "Cut myself shaving," but instead he said simply, "Explosion."

"Must have been bad." Her gaze drifted back to the scarred part of his face and then on to his damaged ear.

"Worse than *you* can imagine."

His emphasis led Shae to think she'd probably been insulted, but she didn't much care. Scars aside, Shae had forgotten how fierce Jordan Bryan could look when crossed. She'd only crossed him once back when they'd been in rodeo, and that once had been enough. Flirtation had been wasted on the man. The one time she'd tried...well, she'd never bothered trying again.

"What are you doing here?" he repeated.

"I have a contract to work on the place."

"Why would you be working on my place?"

"Your place?"

"Shit." He rubbed his injured hand over his face again and Shae couldn't help staring at it, her insides clenching at the sight of the twisted, shiny skin. She hoped no signs of disgust crossed her face, but she couldn't be certain. At the moment she was having a difficult time processing everything—the man, the injuries, the possible consequences to her employment contract.

"She's at the ranch?" he asked abruptly.

Shae swallowed and met his eyes. Deep blue eyes, filled with cold, cold anger. "Miranda? I don't know."

He turned without another word and walked out the door, the curly white dog trotting daintily behind him. An odd picture, but Shae was in no mood to reflect on why a guy like Jordan Bryan would be here with a poodle. She stayed where she was, next to the map tubes she'd placed on the dusty oak table, watching through the open door until she saw Jordan disappear down the road.

Once she was certain he was gone, Shae stepped

out onto the porch, squeezing her forehead with one hand to stave off the headache that was starting to build. The prodigal had returned at the most inopportune moment and it appeared that Miranda was in for one hell of a rude awakening.

She couldn't let that happen. Not if she wanted to keep her job.

Shae went back into the house and picked up her backpack, leaving the map tubes where they lay. There was no way she'd be able to reach her car before Jordan reached his, but she could follow a few miles behind him to the highway and call Miranda once she got into cell-phone range. She needed to warn her boss that trouble was coming.

BLOOD POUNDED IN Jordan's temples as he stalked down the rutted road, barely aware of Clyde struggling to keep up with his long strides. The Subaru keys were in his hand, held so tightly that he was pretty damned certain there'd be a permanent imprint in his palm, but he didn't relax his grip.

Miranda Bryan had just officially screwed with his life once too often and she was going to be one sorry woman when he caught up with her. He swallowed drily as he rounded the last corner before the windfall. Just a few more minutes to the car, then forty-five minutes to the ranch. Once there he knew exactly what he was going to do. He was going to throttle her.

Oh, damn, yeah. He was going to put his hands

around her neck and— Jordan exhaled sharply, feeling his short nails dig even deeper into his palm —go to jail for assault, no doubt, once her henchmen pulled him off her.

That would solve everything—for her.

Shit. What was he doing, heading off half-cocked like this, blinded by rage? More than that, what was he thinking? Throttling Miranda wasn't the answer. Nor was having a shouting match with her at the ranch, where she could have him arrested for trespassing.

Jordan forced himself to stop in the middle of the narrow road and release the death grip on the keys. Slowly his cramped fingers obeyed. And then he drew in a long breath and exhaled again as his head bent forward and he pressed his injured hand against his forehead.

Think. Think hard. Don't let her gain control.

The ranch was his. Miranda hadn't inherited her husband's share of the common tenancy Jordan had shared with his father and he had the papers to prove it. He'd been the sole heir of the High Camp. So what the hell? Something was very wrong here.

Was she actively working on his ranch because she was so certain he was never coming back?

Was she that ballsy?

A definite *yes* to the latter, as he knew from personal experience, but Miranda was also careful, which concerned him.

No, it chilled him. Miranda did not leave *i*'s undotted and *t*'s uncrossed. If she was working on the High Camp, she felt safe doing so, and Jordan needed to find out why. And he had to be careful as to how he did it.

He crouched down and stroked the dog's curly head, the corners of his mouth lifting in spite of himself as the poodle laid his chin on Jordan's knee and stared up at him, his expression clearly indicating that he didn't know what was going on, but whatever it was, he had Jordan's back.

Jordan scooped the dog up and stood, holding the sturdy little animal to his chest, feeling better knowing he was not alone. Miranda was not taking over his property as she'd taken over everything else Jordan held dear. But before he did anything, he needed to find out what in the hell was going on. He could think of only one person who could help him—if the guy was still alive.

"Is Miranda at the ranch?" Shae demanded the second time the guest-ranch receptionist, who'd identified herself as Ashley, tried to put her off. "Because this is an emergency and I need to talk to her."

"What kind of emergency?" Ashley asked in an ultraefficient tone that made Shae want to shake her.

"The kind where you'll get fired if you don't let Miranda know I'm on the phone. *Now!*"

"I don't know where she is," the girl snapped. She abruptly stopped, as if hearing the tone she'd been taking, and when she spoke again, she was once more the picture of überefficiency. Miranda, unfortunately, trained her help well. "Her car is here," Ashley said, "but she's not in the house. Sometimes she goes riding with the guests."

"Call her cell."

"The trails are no-cell zones," the girl said primly.

"Is there a manager? Someone I can talk to?"

"The housekeeper. Everyone else is out working."

Shae glanced at her watch. She'd be there in half an hour. She figured Jordan was at least fifteen minutes ahead of her.

"Look. There's a guy who might show up. Her stepson. And he's not in a good mood. If I were you, I'd tell him that Miranda isn't there. You got that? Miranda isn't there."

"But if he's her stepson—"

"They don't get along," Shae said from between gritted teeth. "If you see Miranda before I get there, have her call me. Shae. And you might tell the manager or any other burly guys hanging around that there could be trouble. Understand?"

"Y-yes."

Finally she'd gotten through. "Thank you." Shae punched the end button and dropped the phone onto the console, pressing down on the accelerator, hoping she'd done the right thing. If Jordan showed up and was the picture of politeness, she was going to look stupid, but somehow she didn't see that happening. Not if he was in the same temper he'd been in when he'd abruptly left the ranch house.

So what was she going to do once she arrived at the ranch?

As if she had a clear idea. It wasn't that she particularly liked Miranda, but she didn't want to see her ambushed.

And you don't want the chance to get back your job screwed up.

Yeah. That, too.

So whatever was going down, she wanted to do what she could to salvage the situation. She just hoped she somehow got there before Jordan and didn't walk in on a battle royal.

THE WEATHERED SHINGLE identifying Emery Anderson as an attorney-at-law still hung beneath the beat-up mailbox on Pole Line Road, five miles from the Cedar Creek Ranch. Jordan parked next to a late-model pickup truck and cracked the windows open so that Clyde could get some air while he talked with his father's lawyer and friend.

Or at least he'd been a friend until Miranda entered the scene.

Miranda hadn't liked Hank to spend too much time with people other than herself. Jordan's mouth thinned as he opened the rear door and pulled out the small lockbox. He slammed the door shut and was heading toward the walk when the door opened and an older man stepped out onto the porch. Emery wasn't dead, but his deeply lined face indicated that he'd lived every one of his seventy-nine years. His hair had thinned to practically nothing and he'd lost at least fifteen pounds since the last time Jordan had seen him, but his white handlebar mustache was as gloriously full and carefully groomed as always.

For a moment the two men simply stared at one another, and then Emery, his face screwed up into an expression of concern, said in his raspy voice, "You look like hell, Jordan."

"Time has not been kind to you, either."

A slow smile spread over the man's face, almost but not quite masking the deep concern in his eyes. "Well, why are you standing there? Come on the hell into the house. I have cold beer."

"I don't drink anymore," Jordan said as he tucked the lockbox under his arm and started for the gate. "Alcohol interacts with pain drugs, so I just quit."

"Tea, then."

Five minutes later Jordan had a jar of iced tea in front of him and was stirring sugar into the bitter brew. "Iced tea's not supposed to be this strong," he muttered as Emery read over the inheritance documents Jordan had given him, letting out an occasional snort.

"Don't be a sissy," Emery replied absently. He hadn't asked about the accident, had barely acknowledged Jordan's injuries other than telling him he looked like hell. And Jordan was thankful. He was tired of having the accident define him, tired of living the aftermath.

Emery gave one final snort and when he raised his eyes, Jordan instantly knew he'd been hosed. "How'd she do it and how bad is it?"

"It's just a guess," Emery said, scooting closer to Jordan so that he could point to a clause in the document. "But you see here where it says that while you've inherited Hank's share of the common tenancy, all the leases will be honored?"

"That's what it says?" He wasn't stupid, but legalese was damned hard to follow, using twenty-five words to say what five could.

"Yeah. And my guess is that Miranda must have inherited Hank's farm lease on the place."

"Great," Jordan said flatly. The lease had been made to protect Hank's farming operations on the land they shared, and it'd only been made in case something happened to Jordan and Becky inherited.

"That makes no sense," Jordan said, looking up from his drink. "What does she want with a farm lease? She encouraged Dad to stop farming our place when the guest ranch took off. I think they only raise enough hay to feed the livestock now."

Emery shrugged. "Probably to keep you away from the place. It isn't like you two got along."

"No. She hates me." And he returned the sentiment with enthusiasm.

"So you come back from the service—" Emery's gaze lingered on Jordan's injured hand for a moment "—plan to take up residency and, surprise, even if Hank were still alive, Miranda controls the operations on the land. Just another way to stick it to you."

"Dad wouldn't have let her do anything to me."

"Not while he was alive." Emery's voice softened. "But he was sick off and on, you know."

"I know. But why have her inherit the lease? Why screw me over?"

"He may not have known. It could have been one small clause in a new will he signed. Or it may not have happened at all."

"No. Miranda wouldn't do something without covering her butt legally—especially if I'm involved." Jordan pushed the tea aside and pulled the box toward him. Pulling out another paper, he handed it to Emery. "The tenancy agreement."

"I know this conveyance," Emery said, unfolding the document. "I wrote it." He skimmed it anyway before saying, "Standard tenancy in common. You and your dad owned the property equally. You both have—or, rather, had—the right to lease, rent or sell your half. Upon sale of the entire property, the proceeds are to be split evenly, which no longer matters since you inherited Hank's part of the land." Emery twisted one corner of his thick white mustache. "Do have a copy of the lease in that magic box of yours?"

"Yeah."

"I didn't write this agreement," Emery said as

he took the folded paper from Jordan. "Lucy was sick then."

"I remember," Jordan said. Emery's wife had died not too long afterward, sending Emery into a tailspin. "That paralegal that hooked up with Lucy's nurse wrote it."

"Wonderful fellow, young Jasper."

"Lucy's nurse seemed to think so."

"But her husband didn't." Emery scanned the paper. "Fairly straightforward. Hank leased the meadows and fields for operations. He had rights to the barn, the tool and equipment sheds, the equipment itself…everything south of the east-west fence line." Emery waved his hand and read on silently. "He had rights to seasonal recreational use." The old man cracked a smile and met Jordan's eyes. "Damn, but I loved those hunting trips. Remember how fast Dr. Hartley could butcher a deer? And how Milton Dexter wore those damned electric socks that kept shorting out?"

"Oh, yeah," Jordan said, even though he'd probably only been ten or eleven at the time. "Anything else in there?"

"You had to maintain fences to keep livestock out of the fields. Money would exchange hands yearly." He looked up. "Have you gotten money?"

"A check went into the bank January first. I never got around to returning it."

"That check may well be yours."

"I don't want it."

"You may not have a choice."

Jordan's gut twisted. "I don't get this. If Miranda has the farm lease, then why was Shae McArthur there? It isn't like she's going to jump on a tractor or anything."

"I do remember Shae as being a bit too prim for farm work. Her sister, on the other hand…"

"Yeah. Liv was okay," Jordan agreed absently. "Am I jumping the gun, Em? Any chance that she didn't inherit and we're reading a whole lot into this?"

"There's a chance." Emery's frown deepened as he again studied Jordan's face. Jordan knew he honestly did look like hell and it wasn't because of the scars. The quick look he'd taken in the rearview mirror had startled him. Heavy stubble covered the unscarred part of his face and the lines around his eyes and mouth were deeper than before, his cheeks gaunter. He looked skeletal. He felt skeletal—as if everything that mattered had been stripped away, leaving him nothing but a shell of what had been and would probably never be again.

Jordan took a sip of the overly sweetened tea. "I'm going to have to talk to her."

"Let me do it. As your lawyer."

Whom he couldn't pay. "No. I can handle this."

"You don't have to," Emery repeated.

Jordan shot him a speaking look. "I know I look like I just stepped out of the asylum, but that's what a cross-country trip and three breakdowns will do to a guy. I'm fine." He somehow got the lie out while staring Emery down. It even sounded convincing. "All I want is the truth so that I know how to proceed."

"Proceed with what?"

"Making Miranda miserable."

"And yourself?"

Jordan scowled at the lawyer, not comprehending.

"Making Miranda miserable is going to come at a cost," Emery explained.

"Believe it or not, I'm quite familiar with misery."

"Yeah, boy, I bet you are," the old man said softly, folding the documents and sliding them across the table. "Sorry I wasn't in contact after the accident."

Jordan dropped his gaze, studying the pit marks in the ancient mahogany table. "I...didn't want contact." He'd sent his cousin Cole away when he'd come to visit.

"And now?"

Jordan just shook his head, still focused on the tabletop. "I don't know what I want other than some solitude. That's why I came here." He placed both palms on the table and looked up at the ceiling. Looked anywhere but at Emery, who he was afraid was going to suggest the obvious. "I hadn't expected this."

Emery then did exactly what Jordan had dreaded, yet expected. "There are some resources here, you know. The VA—"

"No."

"But—"

"No." Jordan's voice held an edge of steel that he hoped hid the anxiety he felt at the mention of help. He'd been helped the conventional way and it hadn't taken. He wasn't beyond trying again, just not yet. Not…yet.

Emery was staring at him now, his lips pressed tightly together beneath his white mustache as if he was trying very hard to keep from speaking.

"Sorry," Jordan muttered.

"Nothing to be sorry for. I imagine you've been to hell and back."

"A couple times."

"Pain still bad?"

"Getting better."

"What're you going to do now?"

Jordan started putting his papers back in the metal box. "I guess I'm going to start moving onto my ranch."

"I mean for a living. You were never good with free time."

Jordan almost said that he'd changed, but after the VA discussion he decided against it, saying instead, "Maybe I'll drive by Claiborne's place and see if he has any rank colts." Which was how Jordan had made spending money during high school and college—starting those ornery animals.

Emery gave a short laugh. "When doesn't he have rank colts?" he asked, seeming relieved to have a safe subject to talk about after delving into matters that edged into personal territory. "I've never seen a guy with so many wild two-, three- and four-year-olds. And every year he produces more foals. The guy's got more money than brains."

"He promised he was going to stop breeding when I left."

"He lied." Emery got to his feet and, once Jordan had the box locked, walked with him to the car, stopping in his tracks when he saw Clyde's nose pressed up against the driver's-side window. "You're a poodle man now?"

"Stray," Jordan said. "He's been good company—seen me through a few rough spots on the trip. Subaru broke down a couple times."

"I'm not surprised," Emery said, cocking a thick white eyebrow as he studied the rusty little car. Then he looked back up at Jordan. "Speaking of rough spots…if you should get into any kind of trouble and you don't call me, I'll kick your ass to Missoula and back."

"How would I get into trouble?" Jordan asked, straight-faced.

"I'm serious."

"I'm just going to take care of what's mine." He got in the car and Clyde instantly jumped onto his lap, balancing his front paws on the door while his hind feet dug into Jordan's thighs. Jordan rolled down the window a few more inches. "I appreciate the help and I won't get myself into trouble."

Much. He hoped.

Emery dug in his pocket and pulled out his wallet. He removed a worn card and handed it to Jordan. "That's my number. Call."

Jordan took the card and put it in his own wallet, then Emery stepped back, looking, if anything, even more concerned than when Jordan had first stepped out of the car. Jordan wanted to tell him not to worry, but it wouldn't have done a hell of a lot of good. So instead he nodded at the old man and put the car in reverse.

After driving a few miles, out of sight of the house, he pulled to the side of the gravel road and counted the bills left in his wallet. The Subaru repairs had made a deep dent and his disability check wouldn't go into the bank for another seven days, but if he was careful and not too concerned about the quality of his purchases, he had enough to make do.

Pocketing his wallet, he smiled grimly at the poodle. "We have work to do."

SHAE PULLED THE Audi to a stop behind the main guest-ranch house at Cedar Creek, pulling the keys out of the ignition and pocketing them. It was impossible to tell if Jordan had gotten there ahead of her, but all seemed quiet when she walked into the reception area, brushing off the powdered road dust that had filtered onto her jeans when she'd opened the car door. A young woman dressed in dark jeans and a crisp white Western shirt with a bolo tie at the neck came around the reception desk to meet her.

"Hi," she said cheerfully. "Welcome to the Cedar Creek Ranch. I'm Ashley."

"I'm Shae McArthur," Shae replied, wondering whether she'd actually beaten Jordan to the ranch—and if so, how?—or if he was simply somewhere else, having it out with Miranda. "I'd like to see Miranda."

Ashley's instant change of expression was almost comical as she realized who was standing in front of her. "She's not back yet, but the trail riders should be arriving any minute now."

"Where?"

"The far barn."

"Has anyone showed up looking for her?"

Something that looked very much like a smirk twisted Ashley's lips. "No. No one at all."

"Thank you." Shae reversed course and headed for the far barn, relieved to see a group of people dismounting as she approached. Miranda was easy to spot in the small crowd, with her pale auburn hair and megawatt smile. The smile that faltered slightly when their eyes met. Miranda handed her reins off to the wrangler closest to her, murmuring something to him before heading to meet Shae.

"Shae. What are you doing here?" she said in the falsely bright tone she used in front of the guests.

"Jordan showed up at the High Camp today. He seems to think he owns the property."

Miranda took hold of Shae's upper arm, gripping tightly. "Jordan?" she asked. "Here?"

"He left and I thought he was coming to Cedar Creek. Apparently he hasn't arrived yet."

Miranda let go of Shae's arm. "Well, this is a surprise," she said sardonically, more to herself than Shae. A young couple dressed in obviously new Western clothing walked by and Miranda smiled at them. "Megan. John. I hope you enjoyed the ride."

"Gorgeous," the woman replied. "Absolutely gorgeous."

"Can't wait to wet my line tomorrow." The man put a hand on his wife's shoulder. "We're having a great time."

"Glad to hear it." Miranda beamed at the couple, then turned back to Shae. "Let's go to my office," she said in an undertone, starting to walk without waiting for a reply. Shae fell into step, smiling and nodding at the guests Miranda greeted by name on her way to main house. The woman was so damned good at making people feel special, both guests and employees. Quite the chameleon at times.

"Good afternoon, Ashley," Miranda said as she passed by the desk. "Any messages?"

"Only the one from Ms. McArthur," the girl replied with a tight-lipped smile.

"Thank you." Miranda led the way up the stairs across the room from the reception area, unlatching the small chain that barred access, and then relatching it after Shae had passed through. Shae hadn't spent much time at the guest ranch, except for company picnics and the Christmas parties, but she knew that the second floor was the family's—and now Miranda's—private sanctuary.

The stairs led to a large, comfortable room with a fireplace and several sofas upholstered in Indian prints. A large fur rug covered the hardwood floor in front of the fire and original oils of cowboys and Native American scenes hung on the walls. Miranda walked through the room, down a short hall, and opened the frosted glass door leading to her office.

"Tell me exactly what happened," Miranda said, taking a seat on the opposite side of the sleek oak desk, letting Shae know, even under these circumstances, exactly what their positions were—that of employer and temporary employee.

"I'd only been at the ranch for about half an hour. I had to walk in because there was a tree down across the road, so I was later getting there than planned. I was in the house and a man—Jordan—walked in. Scared the hell out of me."

"No doubt. What does he look like?"

Shae gestured helplessly as she tried to come up with an adequate description—as if it mattered. "One side of his face is scarred and his left hand is…really damaged. Burned and missing some fingers."

Miranda grimaced, but didn't appear particularly sympathetic. "Was he agitated?"

"He thinks he owns the land. All of it."

"I understand that," she said coolly, making Shae wonder just who did own the land.

"Yes, he was agitated. And tired and edgy and he'd looked as if he'd been sleeping in his clothes." *And I'm worried as hell that he's going to screw up this job for me.*

Miranda tapped a short manicured nail on the desktop, her lips pressed together as she thought. "All right," she finally said, meeting Shae's eyes. "I appreciate you driving all the way over here to warn me."

"Well, he did seem…agitated," she said.

Miranda rose to her feet. "I'll take care of matters," she said reassuringly. "Would you mind giving me your cell number so I can get hold of you later?"

Shae's stomach clenched. Was she going to get fired again? Twice in one month? "Sure," she said, taking up a pen off the desk and writing her number on the small notepad in the gold holder.

"I'll be in contact," Miranda said. "Soon." Shae forced a smile before she headed for the stairs. "Shae?"

Shae turned back.

"Don't worry. Okay?"

"I won't," she lied, then disappeared down the stairs.

CHAPTER FOUR

JORDAN STOPPED AT a highway service station just before the ranch turnoff and quickly washed up and changed his clothes. There wasn't much he could do about the dark circles under his eyes, but he would at least be semipresentable when he confronted Miranda.

And then what?

Miranda was probably banking on him losing his temper so that she could use the incident to her advantage. A restraining order, perhaps? Jordan wouldn't be one bit surprised. She was so damned good at whatever role she chose to play and the brave victim was one of her favorites. How many times had she played it with his father and how many times had the old man fallen for it?

Jordan's fingers tightened on the steering wheel. Hank had fallen for just about everything about his young wife. She was attractive, intelligent and devoted to him, but there was something about her that had kept Jordan from warming up to her. In the beginning he'd been candid about his feelings with his father, until he saw just how much the woman meant to Hank. After that he'd kept his opinions to himself. If Miranda made Hank happy, then he had nothing more to say…until his stepmother had slipped into his bed late one night half a year after the wedding.

Being turned down by a shocked eighteen-year-old had been an unpleasant surprise to Miranda and before she'd left his room, she'd made it very clear that Jordan had two choices—he could destroy his father's happiness or he could keep his mouth shut. And regardless of what he said, she would deny it to the death.

In the end, Jordan had decided to keep his mouth shut and leave the ranch. He couldn't stay and watch the woman manipulate his father, especially when Miranda was so damned good at subtly twisting things so that it appeared as if Jordan harbored an unfounded dislike of her. Even when he and Hank were alone, it was as if she were there, coloring their conversations and interactions. So much had gone unsaid between Jordan and his father during the Miranda years.

So much that would now never be said.

Given the circumstances, was it possible for him to go face-to-face with Miranda without losing it? He'd changed since the accident; his patience level didn't rise far above the zero mark a lot of the time and his former stepmother knew exactly which buttons to punch.

He had to hold on to his anger. She wouldn't lose control, so neither would he.

An hour after driving away from the truck plaza, he pulled into what used to be his home and parked next to the house. Then, for a moment, he sat, staring straight ahead. He could do this. If he started to lose it, he'd just leave, as he'd left the rodeo queen at the High Camp. No harm, no foul.

Clyde put a paw on Jordan's thigh and he absently patted the dog's head before he pushed open the door and headed for the front of the house, even though he'd always gone in through the back before. No longer his place. He rounded the corner to the front walk, then abruptly stopped as Shae McArthur came barreling around the same corner. They stopped just short of one another, Shae's head jerking up as she met his eyes and he was struck by how guilty she looked. Because he'd caught her warning Miranda that he was back?

"Jordan," she murmured in acknowledgment, her gaze stalling out on the scarred side of his face, making Jordan wonder if she was even aware she'd spoken.

He gave her a cool nod and walked around her. He was almost to the porch when he noticed a broad-shouldered cowboy heading his way, pocketing a cell phone as he walked. Jordan ignored him and headed up the porch steps.

Once inside the house, he stopped dead. Miranda had made changes to the place before he'd left home, but now the house was barely recognizable. She'd knocked down walls, put in a large stone fireplace and replaced the old floors with new hardwood. Large oil paintings and blankets hung on the walls and the room smelled of pine and flowers. Had he woken up in this place, he never would have recognized it as the house where he'd grown up.

"May I help you?" A brisk feminine voice sounded from behind him just as the cowboy entered the room, his heavy boots echoing on the hardwood floor.

Jordan turned and for a moment simply stared at the two of them—the slender girl with the white shirt and bolo tie and the oversize guy in classic dude-ranch cowboy wear—then he cleared his dry throat and said, "Would you please tell Miranda that Jordan is here? She'll know who I am."

"Uh, sure," the girl said, stepping around the desk and picking up the phone. Miranda already knew he was there. Shae had warned her he was coming and she'd summoned a bodyguard. He wondered if King Cowboy Kong was going to be in the meeting with them.

His body thrummed with adrenaline as he waited for the girl to speak to his ex-stepmother, and if he unclenched his good fist, he was pretty sure his hands would be shaking from the effort of putting on a good face, but he was doing okay. The big cowboy wasn't wrestling him to the ground or anything and the girl was politely trying not to stare at his burns while she waited for Miranda to pick up—

unlike Shae, who'd once again given his injuries the full once-over.

"Jordan's here," the girl said into the phone. "All right." She put the phone down, missing the cradle on the first attempt and then settling the receiver in place on her second. "She'll be right down."

"Thanks," Jordan murmured, feigning interest in the painting closest to him. It screamed big money, with its thick slashes of oil that somehow formed a desert landscape if one stepped back far enough. Still the big cowboy lingered. Jordan ignored him.

The sound of heeled boots on the stairs drew everyone's attention as Miranda descended the steps. "Jordan," she said after unhooking a small chain across the entryway. "You didn't tell me you were coming home."

He felt every muscle in his body go tense as she said *home.* The woman who'd done and was doing everything she could to make sure this wasn't his home. *Well played, Miranda.* And he realized then that he could fantasize as much as he liked, but he would never put his hands around her throat, because he couldn't stand the thought of touching her and he cringed when he recalled how she'd touched him.

"It was a spur-of-the-moment thing." The words came out huskily, but he did manage to get them out. He couldn't smile, though—couldn't fake it that much.

Miranda could. Her smile seemed to light her

face and she gave no sign of even noticing he looked much, much different than the last time she'd seen him. She must have practiced. "Come upstairs and we'll talk."

Jordan nodded and as he started toward the stairs, he caught the quick look Miranda sent the big cowboy. "Stay here and listen for trouble," it clearly said. He felt like saying there wouldn't be trouble, but refrained, playing the game. If Miranda could do it, so could he. He hoped.

The upstairs was no more recognizable than the first floor. There was another stone fireplace, more hardwood and tile. Expensive furniture.

"Let's talk here," she said, taking a seat on one of the sofas.

"Fine." He sat on the sofa opposite of hers, his eyes never leaving her face.

"I'm glad to see you're recovering from your accident," she said, tilting her head to better see his injured face. "I wish you would have accepted our offer to come home and recuperate."

Made just before his father had passed away, when he'd still had months of hospital therapy ahead of him. He hadn't heard one word from her after his father had passed.

"What's going on with the High Camp, Miranda?" His voice was low, but steady, which was nothing short of a miracle considering the amount of adrenaline coursing through his body.

"You mean why is Shae McArthur there?" Miranda leaned back against her cushion, stretching an arm along the back of the sofa. "Because she's working on a proposal for the property and I'm eager to see what she comes up with."

At which point in the conversation, he was probably supposed to explode.

Surprise, Miranda...I'm not going to give you the satisfaction.

Flicking a piece of lint off his sleeve, he said, "I mean, why on my property without consulting me?"

A tiny smile began to play at the edges of Miranda's mouth as she seemed to realize that her opponent was of a higher caliber than she'd anticipated. "I inherited the operations lease from your father."

Jordan kept his expression as blank as possible, watching for Miranda's reaction to his *lack* of reaction. Nothing. "Will you be farming?"

"No. I'm looking at creating a satellite guest ranch there."

Jordan's pulse spiked and he knew from Miranda's expression that she'd observed and noted his reaction. One point for her.

"What makes you think you have a right to do anything but farm the place?"

Miranda gave an exaggerated shrug. "Because upon reading the lease, I noticed that it said, 'operations.' It didn't say, 'farm operations.' Simply 'operations.'"

"The lease was written for farming."

"Then it was written poorly, because it is not exclusive to farming," Miranda said. "And there's also that recreational-use clause. I'll have my lawyer send a copy if you don't believe me. Should it go to you or…?"

"Emery Anderson." Who would no doubt confirm what she'd just said, but maybe he could also find a loophole.

"As you wish. And, as you no doubt recall," she said smoothly, "the lease is for twenty years. There are twelve years left on the contract."

Jordan focused on the spotless glass coffee table in front of him, the muscles in his jaw tightening as he considered twelve years of battling Miranda. Which was exactly what she was counting on. That and his losing control. If he did, then Miranda would win the first battle—and the big cowboy waiting downstairs would probably feed him the floor. Slowly he raised a steely gaze back up to his former stepmother.

"You understand that you can't interfere with my operations on the place," she said.

"And you can't interfere with my occupancy," he replied. "You have right to some of the buildings—"

"All of the buildings."

"Only those south of the east-west fence line. Not the house."

Miranda's pale red eyebrows drew together. "Have you been reading the lease contract?" she asked curiously.

"I'm not that out of it or damaged or whatever the hell you think I am. When I found Shae there, I decided to check into things."

"You were fast."

"I've learned from experience it doesn't pay to be slow when you're involved."

"Would you be interested in selling?" she asked, as if he hadn't spoken. Jordan had fully expected a buyout offer, but he hadn't expected it today. He'd figured she'd attempt to drive him out first. "I'll pay you market value, which might not be as high as you like, but would easily give you enough to buy elsewhere." She cocked her head, her red hair sliding over her shoulder. "Away from the memories. I recall that you don't much care for this ranch in its present incarnation and you probably won't like the High Camp after I get done with it."

"No."

"You don't like the ranch?"

"I'm not selling."

"Don't be hasty, Jordan. Think about your future. Don't let stubbornness cause you to make the wrong decision. It won't be easy to sell the place, encumbered as it is, if at some point in the future you find you don't like living there. And if it comes to that—" she gave an elegant shrug "—my offer may not be so generous."

Jordan got to his feet, glanced around the room, which had at one time held exactly one worn sofa, reloading and fly-tying equipment, and leather tools. There'd been a time he'd associated this room with his dad. No more. The woman had wiped all signs of Hank Bryan out of this house.

Miranda stood and calmly met his eyes. "Think about my offer, Jordan. It makes sense. Staying at the High Camp will only continue to remind you of everything you've been so open about despising. You know…the things that have made this ranch a viable operation." She took a step forward, as if she were going to touch him, and Jordan automatically stepped back. "I can help you find another place. I have the resources."

His anger began to rise, but he choked it back down. "Thanks," he said flatly as he turned to go.

"If you change your mind, the offer stands." He didn't slow down, gave no indication of having heard her, taking the stairs two at a time and then walking past the bodyguard and receptionist without looking at either one of them.

Oh, yeah. He was certain the offer would stand. And just as certain that he wasn't taking it. Miranda had won every throwdown between them. She wasn't winning this one.

"Jordan!"

He stopped on the porch and turned to see Miranda behind him. She must have taken the steps two at a time herself. "What?"

"My lawyer and I will be in contact. Soon. Just

so we understand one another. And in the meantime…cooperate with Shae."

THE ONLY THING Jordan didn't buy on his supply list was a chain saw to take care of the tree in the road. He recalled an ancient McCulloch at the ranch—if he could find it, he'd try to get it running. If not, he was fairly certain that Miranda would see to it that the log was removed. After all, she was the operator of this ranch…for now.

When he reached the log, he parked the Subaru a few feet away from it in the middle of the road and then started unloading his purchases, wondering if Shae was going to risk her Audi again tomorrow. She'd obviously reversed all the way back down the road earlier today. He'd seen where she had finally found a spot wide enough to turn around, and he'd also seen the numerous places where the car had slid into the deep ruts. Seeing the marks in the dirt had given him a sense of satisfaction. No one should drive an Audi on a road like this and if they did, they deserved what they got.

So what was he going to do when Shae showed up again?

He figured the first thing he should do was to take off his shirt. She'd been openly shocked when she'd seen the fingers that had been amputated by shrapnel and then burned by the flash of the explosion. The burns continued up his forearm, around his side and onto his back, where the worst scars lay, and the deep-tissue skin grafts were still healing. Remarkably, the majority of his shoulder had been spared, so he had mobility there, and the burns up his face were for the most part superficial. If you could count losing part of his ear as superficial. No grafts had been necessary there, but the damaged skin was red and shiny in places. Ugly.

Shae McArthur didn't appear to do well with ugly, and he was going to use that to his advantage. He had to concede, though, that she'd made no attempt to hide the fact that she had been staring at his injuries. There were none of the darting glances that he'd come to expect as people attempted to wrap their minds around the extent of his injuries without appearing rude—and a part of Jordan kind of appreciated her openness. At least she was honest. The scars were there and she didn't pretend they weren't.

And she didn't pretend they didn't bother her, either.

Okay. One point for Shae for honesty.

But he was still taking his shirt off whenever he could.

Jordan unloaded his brand-new cheap tent, the sleeping bag he'd used on his cross-country trek, a box of groceries and his duffel bag of clothes, then proceeded to carry them around the windfall and load them onto the sturdy rubber-wheeled gardening wagon he'd bought. At almost two hundred dollars, it had all but wiped out his cash supply, but there was no way he'd be carrying much weight on his back and he figured the wagon would come in handy around the ranch.

Clyde instantly got the hang of what was going on and jumped up on top of the gear Jordan had piled into the wagon, his small body lurching and swaying when Jordan started pulling. Only a mile. No sweat.

Except that the wagon was heavy. He wasn't used to the altitude and despite working out as much as his body would allow, he was gasping for air by the time the ranch came into view. The sun was starting to set and he still had a lot to do.

But at least he was alone.

It wasn't until he'd unloaded everything into a pile that Jordan realized he'd left his pills in the car. He was not going back—it would be a pill-free night. If he didn't sleep, tough. He wasn't exactly a stranger to sleepless nights. And if he had a nightmare, the only one he'd disturb was Clyde—who was sticking to him like glue now that it was getting dark. Jordan didn't know what kind of shape the house was in, and since he didn't want to share with rodents, he started setting up his tent. If the fabric had been any thinner, it would have qualified as disposable, but it was all he'd been able to afford after the wagon purchase, and if the zipper worked, he could keep the rain off and the mosquitoes at bay.

He and Clyde had shared a couple of hamburgers

prior to driving back to the camp, but now he was hungry again. Apparently Montana air was good for him, because food hadn't been any kind of priority over the past year—just something he needed for survival. Until recently chewing had felt awkward and uncomfortable as the skin on his face healed, so he hadn't taken much pleasure in food. Now he wished he had another burger. Instead he made do with a peanut-butter-and-jelly sandwich made by the light of a battery-operated lantern.

Feeling ridiculously exhausted after dragging the wagon to the ranch, he laid out his sleeping bag and settled on top of it, letting the sounds of the wilderness lull him. He didn't expect to sleep that night—not easily, anyway—because sleep was never easy without the meds, but at least he could listen to the sounds of his childhood instead of the traffic on the thoroughfare near his Virginia apartment.

Clyde appeared to prefer the traffic noises. After nervously pacing the tent for at least ten minutes, snuffling the air and trying to see through the nylon at what was causing the fascinating noises outside, the poodle finally turned a few circles and collapsed in a curly heap against Jordan's side. His eyes remained stubbornly open, though, fixed on the tent door. Jordan reached down to idly ruffle the hair on the poodle's head, then a few seconds later his hand relaxed on the dog's warm body.

That was the last thing Jordan remembered.

CHAPTER FIVE

SHAE SPREAD THE packet of eight-by-ten aerial photos on the dining room table, determined to get the general overview she hadn't gotten that afternoon due to Jordan's arrival. Each day was precious and she'd lost one, but Miranda had said not to worry. Shae was going to do her best not to.

Except that was impossible.

Finally she picked up her phone and called Mel, who, despite her invitation to Shae to call anytime, did not answer. Study time. Mel was going to make a great lawyer because she had laserlike focus. Well, so did Shae, but somehow organizing marketing events, rodeo-queen competitions and weddings—all of which took an incredible amount of planning and effort—just didn't generate the same respect as pursuing a law degree did. Shae smirked at herself, lifted her wineglass and took a healthy swallow. Nope. No respect for the wedding planner.

Not even from the groom, who'd said he'd felt secondary to the process more than once. And she had not listened. That had been a mistake.

The phone rang and Shae scooped it up, thinking Mel had taken a break.

"Shae." Not Mel.

"Miranda?" Shae took a fortifying swig of chardonnay.

"Yes. Would it be possible for us to meet informally? Tonight or tomorrow morning?"

Shae almost choked on the wine. She was being fired. "Tonight?" It was close to ten o'clock.

"I've driven in from the ranch to attend to some business, so I'm in town right now."

"Then why not tonight?" Shae said. Because she wasn't going to sleep until she knew what the deal was…although she probably wasn't going to sleep afterward, either. "Would you like to come here?" Home territory. That way she wouldn't have to drive home while upset. She'd done enough of that recently.

"That would be fine."

Shae gave Miranda the address, hung up and then collapsed on her sofa, letting her head fall back against the cushions. The phone rang in her hand and Shae raised it to see the caller. Mel.

"How was your first day on the job?" Mel asked cheerfully.

"Not what I expected," Shae said flatly. "Jordan Bryan showed up."

"Jordan!"

"Funny thing. Miranda had the same reaction."

"The last I heard from the grapevine—" meaning her sister, Dani, who kept close tabs on everyone they went to high school with "—he was recover-

ing from his accident in some kind of special care
facility."

"He's out. He's back. And he thinks he owns the
property I'm working on." Shae took a couple agitated paces toward the darkened window. "Why
didn't you tell me how seriously he'd been hurt?"
She vaguely recalled hearing that Jordan Bryan had
been injured in a military accident. *Injured.* That
had been the description, which in her mind had
meant broken bones or injuries one healed from.
No one had said, "seriously injured" or "heinously
injured." In fact, no one had ever brought the matter up again, that she could recall.

"Honestly, Shae, I thought I had. But you were
pretty immersed in other things when it happened,
so maybe I didn't."

Other things. The wedding, of course.

"How bad is it?" Mel asked softly. "I know that
Cole flew back east to see him, but the visit didn't
go well."

"It's bad." She described what she'd seen—his
hand, his face. "I don't know what the rest of him
looks like and I don't know that he's all there, Mel.
Mentally, I mean. He looked pretty out of it." Which
concerned her if she was returning to the property.

"So what happens now?"

"It's complicated. Miranda's on her way over to
explain it to me now." *And probably to fire me.* But
if she did, Shae was going to do her best to finagle
another shot at her old job.

"Miranda's coming to your place at this time of night?"

"Yeah. I know. Doesn't sound good, does it?"

She heard Mel blow out a breath. Answer enough. "Let me know what happens," Mel said.

"Will you pick up?"

"Yeah. I'll pick up."

A soft knock on the door made Shae jump. "Miranda's here. I'll talk to you later." She set the phone on the glass coffee table and crossed the room, heart pounding.

She pasted a smile on her face as she swung the door open. "Miranda. Hi."

"Shae. Thanks for allowing me to come over."

Oh, yeah. As if she wouldn't.

Miranda walked inside, glanced around and gave an approving nod before moving over to the table where Shae had spread the aerial photos.

"Will I need those?" Shae asked, deciding they might as well get to the crux of the matter.

Miranda traced her finger over the photo with the ranch buildings before looking up. "I certainly hope so," she said and Shae felt a swell of optimism. "But there are issues. That's why I need to make certain you know exactly what's going on, so that you can tell me whether or not you want to continue."

"I signed a contract."

"And I'll release you. If you want, that is."

"Does Jordan own the property?" Shae asked.

"He does." Miranda met her gaze square on, a

touch of challenge in her pale green eyes. "Hank held the land in common tenancy with Jordan, who inherited Hank's part of the tenancy, meaning the actual land, upon his death. However—" Shae found herself holding her breath, sensing this was a big *however* "—I inherited Hank's lease on the property, which allows me to conduct business operations. The guest ranch is a business operation and I plan to proceed with the proposal."

"Does Jordan know this?"

"He does now."

"And he's okay with it?" Which she was going to have one hell of a time believing.

"He doesn't have much choice."

Shae exhaled, focusing on the photos. Nothing was ever easy. "Is he leaving, then?"

Miranda slowly shook her head. "Probably not until he understands that I'm serious about developing this property."

"He can live there."

"Yes."

Shae set down the photo, wanting more than anything to reach for her wine and empty the glass.

"Would you like some wine?" she asked, realizing she hadn't been at the top of her hostess game.

"Please," Miranda replied, sounding as though she needed it as much as Shae. "Then let's sit and talk about this…situation."

"Yes," Shae said on a drier note than she'd intended as she walked the few feet to the kitchen to pull the chardonnay from the fridge. "Let's."

Miranda leveled a candid look at Shae when she returned to the living room. "I know at first glance this situation doesn't cast me in a positive light, what with Jordan having suffered his accident and all, but trust me—there's more to this than meets the eye. He would have done this regardless. It isn't like he's here to recuperate."

"I see," Shae said as she handed off the glass of wine.

Miranda took a quick sip. "I know what I'm about to say will not go farther than this room."

"Of course not."

"If Jordan stays it's for one reason only—to cause me trouble. It's always been like that between us." Miranda gestured with the glass. "There was a reason Hank wanted me to have the rights of operation on all of his property. Even he saw that Jordan's hatred of me was way out of proportion. We thought he'd outgrow it, but he never did.

"The years while he was home were hell on Hank." Miranda bit her lip, studying her glass. "More painful than you can imagine. Finally they had it out and Jordan made it very clear when he left this ranch that he was never coming back. Now he's returned and it's not because he wants to live at the High Camp. This is the only way he has now to get back at me for what he perceives as the many wrongs I did him." Miranda let out a small huff of air. "He thinks I stole his father from him. If I walk away now, who knows what his next step will be? He won't leave me alone. I promise you that. He never has."

Shae didn't know what to say. What did one say when her boss poured out family secrets? Nothing.

Miranda gave her head a disgusted shake. "I wish I hadn't backed down so many times in the past. Let him have his way in the name of peace. Because it was never enough. It only encouraged him to push harder. Maybe this time, when he sees that I'm not backing down, he'll move on."

"So…he's going to be there and we're going to work around him." It sounded as if she definitely had a job—if she was willing to become embroiled in a family drama.

"Essentially, yes."

Shae felt compelled to say, "I don't think he's going to cooperate."

"Then there will be consequences."

This wasn't what Shae had signed on for. Not even close.

"Shae." She looked up to see Miranda studying her intently. "If you see this through, I'll make it worth your while."

"How?"

"First of all, let's address what I want. I want a satisfactory proposal for a unique guest property that I can have up and running by early summer next year. The emphasis is on unique. Something my other two ranches don't offer. I want to use the existing structures—the cabins, the bunkhouse, the bathhouse."

A reiteration of what they'd agreed upon less than a week ago, so Shae simply nodded.

"It's more important than *ever* that this proposal be viable." There was a steely note in Miranda's voice, very much like the one in Jordan's earlier that day when he'd asked if Miranda was at the ranch.

"I understand," Shae said. Miranda's initial I'll-see-what-you-can-do-before-I-commit attitude had changed radically now that Jordan had become involved.

"Jordan must know that I'm not backing down. I will use the High Camp as I see fit. Hank wanted me to have the rights and I'll exercise them."

Shae's stomach was starting to knot at Miranda's adamancy, but if anyone could go face-to-face with Jordan, it was her. She'd already done it once and survived.

"If he can live with the changes, he can stay. I don't care," Miranda said matter-of-factly.

But it was pretty obvious she did care, and after hearing what she had to say, and seeing Jordan's reaction to her, Shae understood. Jordan's hatred had been palpable and it had to be unnerving for Miranda to have him nearby.

"Do I need to be concerned about being at the High Camp alone with him?" Shae asked.

"Not after I get done. I plan on meeting with my

stepson. Straightening out a few legal issues. After that, you'll be fine. Now…let's talk compensation."

"Yes," Shae said, meeting Miranda's gaze full-on, figuring if she didn't go for the brass ring now, she might never get another chance. "If I see this through successfully and Jordan…comes to accept the situation…I'd like my old job back."

"That can be done."

"And I'd like to have a contract of employment instead of working at will."

Miranda tilted her head, a small smile forming on her thin lips as she studied Shae. "That's a possibility, as long as everything at the High Camp works out in a satisfactory manner."

"You want Jordan gone," Shae said, finally addressing the elephant in the room.

Miranda smiled, setting down her still half-full glass and standing. "If you can do that, you can have a job for life. However, I will not put that burden on you. All I want is a viable proposal in which Jordan's occupancy of the ranch does not interfere."

"You'll get that."

At the door, Miranda hesitated before reaching for the knob, then turned back to Shae. "I'm going to set up a meeting with my attorney and Jordan, just to make certain he understands the parameters of the agreement. I'd like you to be present."

"Of course. Just let me know when."

"I'll call you as soon I know."

The call came less than a half hour after Miranda had left. There was no cell service at the High Camp, so the only sure way to contact Jordan was to physically meet with him, which was exactly what Miranda proposed. Tomorrow Shae was to meet Miranda and her attorney at the windfall and they would walk in from there. Not exactly the customary way to do business, but if it got Shae on the property and working, she was good with the strategy.

She went to bed immediately after the call, but couldn't sleep. Oddly, it wasn't thoughts of Jordan that kept her awake—it was wondering what was going to happen if she couldn't work around him. How was she going to get another job in her field? After her fruitless job search, she was certain that Miranda had already let it be known among her colleagues that Shae had failed her. What would happen if she failed twice?

Not an option.

So it was with an air of grim determination that Shae drove the Audi up the rough road early the next morning and parked behind a shiny new Ford truck with a Cedar Creek Ranch emblem on the front doors that was, in turn, parked behind the Subaru nosed up against the tree. Miranda and her attorney got out of the truck as Shae turned off the ignition.

"I'll have someone from the ranch take care of this," Miranda said, gesturing at the tree. "In the meantime, let me fill you in on a few things as we walk. If all goes well, you'll start work today."

Shae slung her backpack onto one shoulder and gave Miranda a confident smile. "I'm ready." Jordan Bryan was not going to stop her from getting her job back.

Miranda gave a soft sniff. "So am I."

THE FACT THAT there was no cellular service at the ranch had never been more satisfying than when Jordan saw Miranda and Shae hiking up the road with some guy he didn't know. *If only she could have called and saved herself the trip...*

Jordan had walked out of the house when Clyde alerted him to the visitors. Running his hand over his jaw, Jordan debated strategy before descending the steps to meet them. He knew he looked scruffy and unkempt. The electricity had yet to be turned on and he'd been unable to shower. Later in the day he planned to take a dip in the ponds a quarter mile or so from the house, clean up. He'd never dreamed he'd have visitors of such import before then.

"Jordan," Miranda said, stopping several feet away from him as if afraid that he might suddenly lunge for her throat.

There'd been times that had seemed like a viable course of action—like yesterday. But not now. Not even if Mr. Beaver Hat hadn't been there by her side, looking stern and official and as if he was about to take Jordan into a hammerlock if he made a wrong move. And Shae…Shae stood a few feet away from Miranda, looking poised and confident, ready to march in and do whatever Miranda ordered. She met his gaze, lifted her chin slightly as if challenging him…or waiting for him to challenge her.

"Miranda," he said, swinging his attention back to his equally poised ex-stepmother.

"Jordan. This is Noel McCord. My attorney."

Jordan crossed his arms, watched the guy's expression shift as he caught sight of Jordan's left hand. "Nice to meet you," he said without offering his hand. "Out for a hike?"

Miranda smirked at him. "We're here to make certain you understand the legalities of the situation here at High Camp before Shae starts work."

"You made them clear yesterday. I don't interfere with your operations and you don't interfere with my occupancy." He sneered right back at her, even though it cost him. He'd slept last night, despite not having the pills, but he was still exhausted. Freaking stress.

"So you understand," Beaver Hat said in a deep voice, "Miranda has full rights to all structures—"

"Except the house."

"Except the house. Equipment and tool sheds…" Jordan swallowed his impatience and let the lawyer drone on. When the guy had finally finished reciting the contract he must have memorized, Jordan pushed back his hat.

"Understood," he said.

Miranda blinked at him and then he shifted his attention to Shae, who was frowning slightly. No one, apparently, had expected him to be agreeable. He didn't want to be, but it had occurred to him early this morning that he needed to pick his battles. He couldn't come up with a way to keep Shae off the property, but he was hoping against hope that, given time, Emery might be able to find him some kind of loophole that would limit Miranda's activities to farming. The problem was that stupid recreational clause Hank had put in so that his buddies could continue to hunt from the property, regardless of who owned it.

"Questions? Comments?" the lawyer asked.

Jordan shook his head.

"It would be much easier if we come to a working agreement now," the lawyer said. "So if anything at all occurs to you—"

"Shae and I will work things out if I come up with questions." He nodded at Shae, who narrowed her eyes at him.

"You'll work it out with me," Miranda said.

Jordan hooked his thumb in his belt loop, said nothing.

The lawyer inclined his head slightly. "If you want to travel the hard road—"

Jordan turned the scarred part of his face toward the man. "I'm no stranger to the hard road. Now, if you two are done, I have some unpacking to do."

"You will cooperate, then, with Shae?" Miranda asked, as if determined to get in the last word.

Jordan walked away without replying, heading for the house, where Clyde's little nose was pressed against the inside of one of the windows. The poodle greeted him joyously as he walked into the house and shut the door behind him, so damned pissed he could barely see straight.

He pushed the ragged muslin curtain aside and watched as Miranda, Shae and the lawyer had a brief meeting. They glanced at the house a couple times. The lawyer waved his hands, Miranda scowled and Shae looked impatient.

Jordan turned away from the window, rubbing his hands over his face.

It was killing him that he didn't know how to play this. Emery had to come up with something. There was no way he was going to get better if he had to deal with Miranda, but what choice did he have? He couldn't afford to walk away and there was no way he was going to sell the one thing he had left from his father.

More than that, there was no way he was going to let her win again.

A knock on the door startled him and he muttered a low curse as Clyde started yapping. This was his reality now and he needed to start dealing with it.

As far as Shae could tell, all Miranda and her attorney had managed to do with their official lay-the-ground-rules visit was to piss off Jordan, and since she was the one left there—alone—trying to get something accomplished, she figured it was to her advantage to hash things out now, before she started work. And she had to do it while looking at him square in the eye, as if his injuries didn't bother her.

They did.

Jordan scowled fiercely at her from the other side of the doorway and for a moment she, who was never at a loss, fought for words. Finally she settled on, "Look, I know this isn't what you expected when you came back home."

The poodle sat down next to Jordan and when Shae glanced down at the animal, he silently raised his upper lip to show his teeth.

Really?

Shae looked back at Jordan. "I'm here to do a job," she said, "and if I don't do it, Miranda will find someone else who will."

"Is that supposed to make the situation more acceptable to me?" he asked.

"No. But it's a fact."

"And if I tell you to take your facts and stick them up your ass?"

"It won't change a thing," she said.

"Anything else?" he asked in a stony voice.

"Things will be a lot more pleasant if we can be civil to one another."

One corner of his mouth lifted. "Civil."

"Yes," she said. "Civil."

"I don't remember that being your strong suit, Shae."

Her eyebrows arched up and she wondered if he was going to bring up that time in the bar. If so, she had a few words to say on the matter. "What do you remember as being my strong suit?"

"Manipulation," he said without missing a beat. "Getting whatever you want regardless of what other people want." He leaned forward as he spoke, pointing his finger at her chest, and Shae automatically took a step back before she could stop herself. Jordan stepped forward again and Shae jammed her hand into her pocket.

"I have pepper spray," she said conversationally.

Jordan abruptly stopped moving and she realized that any kind of burning substance would be devastating to him in his condition. But she didn't back down. Not one bit.

"You don't need pepper spray," he said roughly, folding his arms over his chest.

"This isn't personal. I have a job to do." She mirrored his stance, crossing her arms, glancing down at the poodle again. The dog stared balefully back at her. "Don't get in my way, Jordan."

"Kind of your motto, right? 'Don't get in my way'?"

"Best pay heed," she said. It sounded like something Liv would say, but she was satisfied with the effect. Jordan's eyes narrowed as he studied her, as if looking for signs of weakness, but he didn't have a comeback. Or maybe he was done with the name-calling and was going to resort to other tactics. She drew herself up straighter. "I have to get to work," she said.

He inclined his head solemnly, as if giving permission, then stepped back and closed the door in her face. Shae stood for a shocked moment, staring at the weathered oak a few inches too close to her nose for comfort, the muscles in her jaw tightening as she clenched her teeth. She turned and stalked off the porch, crossing the wild yard to where she'd left her backpack. So much for making peace with the jerk.

Shae headed across the hard-packed ground toward the bunkhouse. What had she expected? A kiss and a hug? No, but she hadn't expected a personal attack.

Cut him a break. He's been through hell.

Right—but it wasn't as though he had a history of being pleasant to her, or anyone else she hung with. He had been quiet and intense; the buckle bunnies had been all over him back in their rodeo days, but he hadn't taken much stock in being a babe magnet. He'd dated, but never the flashy girls who openly chased him, preferring quiet girls who reflected his own personality…which had led to the bet that Shae couldn't get lucky with him, which in turn had led to a rather public humiliation.

He could have said, "Not interested," after she

had settled herself on his lap instead of dumping her on her ass and walking away.

He warned you. Twice.

Yeah, well, she hadn't thought he was serious.

Massive fail, that, but Shae had walked away telling herself that life was too short to waste on a guy who didn't appreciate her. Now here he was back in her life, scarred and wounded, and right where she didn't need him.

PEPPER SPRAY.

Jordan wondered if Shae had been lying, but from the very serious look on her face when she'd made her claim, he doubted it. He'd been sprayed as part of his duty training and wasn't about to take the chance of getting that shit on his healed wounds and skin grafts. And he wondered, too, if Shae had any idea what pepper spray would do to damaged skin. Would she even care? Shae wasn't exactly known for thinking of others.

He went to stand at the window, staring down at the open door of the bunkhouse. What had prompted her to bring pepper spray in the first place? Had he really come off as that threatening? Did he look demented and dangerous? He ran a hand over his bristled chin.

If so, good. It'd keep her at bay.

And that would get him…nothing. But it would give her the ability to go about her job without interruption.

Jordan paced through the house, feeling trapped. If he felt like this now, with only Shae on the property, what was he going to feel like when there were greenhorns walking around, "experiencing" all Montana had to offer?

Like hell.

It hasn't happened yet. He was counting on Emery to come up with that loophole, but until he did, he couldn't just stand by and let Shae work. That would feel too much like conceding to Miranda's will while he waited for his lawyer's answer.

HEAVY FOOTSTEPS SOUNDED on the steps outside the bunkhouse and Shae looked up to see Jordan standing in the doorway.

What would he do if she crossed the room and closed the door in his face?

Nice fantasy, but it didn't jibe with her intention of keeping a professional demeanor. Fighting with Jordan wasn't going to accomplish anything, no matter how tempting it might be.

"Hello," she said pleasantly before backing up a few paces to photograph the interior of one of the twelve cell-like rooms that lined one side of the bunkhouse.

She'd done some research over the past few days and had discovered that the building, like the four cabins that sat near it, had been used to house miners working placer claims nearby during the early part of the last century—a way for Jordan's great-grandparents to help keep the ranch afloat during lean times. After the gold had petered out, the building had then been used for storage and for the most part neglected. But the roof was good and it was free of rodents—two of the most important considerations when it came to renovating an old building. Shae was excited by its unique potential, but damned if she was going to let Jordan know what. The way he was taking this invasion, he might just torch the place to keep Miranda from using it.

"I hear this was your idea," he finally said. "Turning my place into a dude ranch."

"I proposed it," Shae said slowly.

"Why?"

Shae shrugged a shoulder. "It seemed like a good idea. It's close to the Cedar Creek Ranch, but can offer a more rugged experience."

Jordan looked around the bunkhouse. "Rugged?"

"Compared to Miranda's other ranches," Shae explained patiently.

"The guests will have to walk to the spa instead of having one in their room?"

Shae dropped the camera into her pocket and walked by him on her way to the door. "Excuse me," she murmured.

"Done?" Jordan said softly.

She ignored him, walking out the door. She heard him follow and stopped abruptly, swinging around on him. "Please don't follow me."

He simply raised a dark eyebrow. Shae's lips

parted and then she clamped her mouth shut and walked toward the barn. After she took photos of the barn and the bathhouse, inside and out, she'd get the hell out of there, work at home for the rest of the day.

That was exactly what he wanted. Okay. She wouldn't get the hell out of there.

And he wasn't going to stop following her. She heard the sound of his footsteps in the dry grass and turned again.

"I'm interested in what you're doing," he said in answer to her silent question.

"I bet."

"Who would be more interested?"

Ignore him and he'll stop. Vivian's advice to Shae's introverted stepsister, Liv, when a kid had been bothering her at school. Shae had listened as she'd worked on a school project, thinking that ignoring someone was an odd way to change their behavior. Shae generally confronted anyone who was bothering her and let them know what the problem was and how they could fix it. And then they pretty much left her alone.

She had a feeling, though, that that approach wasn't going to work with Jordan, though it was just that—a feeling. She didn't know the man or how he would react. As much as Shae hated backing down—from anything—there was something about the way he held himself and his expression of mixed desperation and determination that gave Shae the strong feeling that she didn't want to stand between him and his goal without some kind of reinforcements. Shae was stubborn, but she wasn't stupid.

She gave a nod, somehow tore her gaze away from his fierce blue eyes and opened the barn door, stepping into the dim interior.

"What exactly are you doing?"

"I'm analyzing the existing structures."

"And then?"

"It depends on what kind of shape they're in."

"Let's say they're in the shape these buildings are in?"

"I'll work up some costs," she said. She'd also determine how many guests could be accommodated, how to best address shower and cooking facilities. Mark out riding trails, meet with the Cedar Creek Ranch wildlife and fishing specialist to determine what kind of day trips they could plan from the High Camp. Handle permitting. Put together sample packages with pricing that was realistic for what they had to offer. If everything went smoothly, she might even start talking to contractors about restoration and renovation before the end of her contract.

"So this plan of yours isn't necessarily a go."

"Oh, it will be a go."

He shifted his weight, slipping the thumb of his good hand into a belt loop. Her gaze drifted to the other hand, her stomach tightening involuntarily as she studied the gnarled flesh. Did it still hurt? It looked like hell, the skin twisted and discolored.

Jordan pointedly glanced down at his hand, then back up at her. Shae said nothing but she couldn't keep herself from swallowing uncomfortably.

"How long have you worked for Miranda?"

"Technically I worked for Cedar Creek Enterprises."

"Miranda," he corrected and she had to admit he was right. Miranda was Cedar Creek Enterprises. She might have managers, and she might not have an office or be on-site, but nothing happened without her ultimate okay.

"Five years. I started right out of college." Which had lasted a few years longer than it should have. She'd frittered away her first two years partying and then managed to get a business degree by the skin of her teeth. Mel had arranged for her to get an internship at Cedar Creek and to Shae's surprise, she'd liked the work. Loved dreaming about possibilities and then putting her plans into action. Matching properties to people. Analyzing potential. She'd been good at it, and she could see, now that she'd lost her job, that she'd appreciated being good at something.

"Worked?" he suddenly said as if picking up on her thoughts.

"What?"

"You said, 'I *worked* for Cedar Creek Enterprises.'"

Shae pulled out a notebook and a tape measure

from her backpack. "Slip of the tongue." Because damned if she was going to explain it.

Miranda had said to work around Jordan and that was exactly what Shae ended up doing. He stood silently, making her more aware of his presence by saying nothing than if he'd been talking. And he was doing it on purpose.

Work around him.

Oh, yeah. She was trying to do that, even though having him there made her feel ridiculously self-conscious, which was strange.

When was the last time she'd felt self-conscious? Maybe when Vera had walked her out of the Cedar Creek offices. No, that had been embarrassment. Self-consciousness? Not in her repertoire. She was sure of herself, confident in her abilities. So what was going on?

She'd been dumped and fired. Her world was not as it once was—or as it should be—and she was… shaken. She'd be all right in time, but right now, she just wanted to be left alone to do her job.

"Are you going to follow me the entire time I'm here?" she finally asked as he walked with her to the bathhouse.

"I don't have much else to do."

"Then why are you here?" she said, suddenly stopping. "Why not go somewhere where you do have something to do?"

Jordan considered for a moment before saying, "Not everyone has your resources, Shae. Maybe some of us can't waltz through life getting everything we want."

"I don't get everything I want," she said with a faint sneer, determined not to let him see that he'd just touched a sore spot. "Never have."

"Could have fooled me," he said. "If I recall, you were the member of the rodeo team with the best horses, nicest truck, no curfew, no rules…"

"And a boatload of people who disliked me because of it." The sneer intensified.

"Maybe they didn't dislike you because of that, Shae. Maybe they had other reasons."

Shae blinked at him and it took her a moment to say, "Like what?"

"Maybe it had something to do with you being so self-centered that you were only concerned with how things affected you. Kind of like right now."

"And maybe you can just go to hell, Jordan Bryan."

"Been there," he replied quietly.

CHAPTER SIX

JORDAN BRYAN DIDN'T know her at all, but he'd certainly formed one hell of an opinion of her. Shae relaxed her grip on the steering wheel as she approached the Missoula city limits. Why did that bother her so much? She'd always known people were jealous of her and had simply shrugged it off. Why did his assessment bother her?

Maybe because it was so damned direct.

Or maybe because it brought up ghosts of the way he'd humiliated her years ago.

One moment in time. Get over it.

She was over it. It'd been shocking when it'd happened. People didn't treat her that way, at least not to her face, but she was well beyond it.

She pulled into her parking space at the apartment complex, gathered up her backpack and travel mug, then got out of her dusty car.

"You deserve better," she muttered to the car as she closed the door. It was obvious she couldn't keep driving the Audi to the High Camp and she could only think of one solution. Pulling her cell phone out of her pocket, she dialed her brother's number as she walked to her ground-floor apartment. She hadn't taken money from either him or her parents. There was no way she was taking money after their last discussion, but maybe she could trade him the Audi for a truck until she got done at the High Camp. Surely there was nothing wrong with that? A trade?

"Hey, Shae." The connection cut in and out briefly, telling her he was still on the road, returning from a team roping event.

"How'd it go?" she asked, digging her keys out.

"I caught, Steve missed. Twice. Burned that entry fee."

"Sorry to hear that. Maybe Dillon will go better next week."

"One can only hope. What do you need?"

Shae frowned as she juggled the keys. Did she *only* call when she needed something? "I want to trade the Audi for one of your trucks to drive to the High Camp Ranch."

"How'd you get there today?"

"The Audi."

"Really?"

"I didn't exactly have a choice."

Brant sighed. "I'll have Sara drop off a truck and I'll pick her up at your place. I'm only an hour away. Does that work?"

"What about the Audi?"

"If you take Killer, you can keep it."

Shae bit her lip. Killer was a 1987 Chevy with a puttied door that got about eight miles to the gallon. Could she afford Killer? Did she have a lot of options here?

"I owe you."

"I'll add it to your tab," her brother said with a laugh, but Shae heard a note in his voice she'd never noticed before…long-suffering patience. Had it always been there? Or was she just hypersensitive at the moment because of the crap Jordan had thrown at her?

"Hey," Shae said before he could hang up. "You remember Jordan Bryan?"

"Of course."

"*What* do you remember about him?"

"He was the best bronc rider I ever saw."

"Anything else?"

"What exactly are you looking for?"

Shae dumped her pack and shrugged out of her jacket. She didn't know what she was looking for. Vindication, maybe. "Was he friendly, unfriendly, mean, judgmental…? What was he like?"

"Quiet. Why?"

"I'm sharing the High Camp with him."

"No kidding." The phone cut out briefly, then Brant said, "He's back? How's he doing?"

"He has some nasty injuries." Shae went back outside to unlock her mailbox and pull out a handful of envelopes and catalogs. "I think he's still suffering from the aftermath."

"And you two are working together now."

"It's a long story," Shae said as the phone sputtered again. "I'm losing the connection. I'll tell you when you get here."

"See you in an hour or so."

Shae dumped the mail on the table after ending the call and shuffled through it. Bills. Lots of them. Beyond the deposits she'd lost, she was paying for a lot of extras she'd thought she'd need for the wedding. Orders that couldn't be canceled. Invitations. Matchbooks. Clothing for her honeymoon. Clothing she didn't think she'd be able to wear.

She opened the fridge and pulled out the wine as the phone rang again. Miranda.

"Hello," she said in her professional voice.

"Shae. Miranda. How'd it go today?"

"No problems," Shae said. "I got a good start evaluating the existing infrastructure."

"And my stepson?"

"Not a problem." Not one she was going to talk about, anyway. She sensed that the more capable she was dealing with Jordan, the more satisfied Miranda would be with her job performance and the closer she would be to a contract.

"Good to hear. Hope you have the same experience tomorrow, but if not, let me know and I'll handle things on my end."

"I think it'll be fine," Shae said. She hoped it would be. Shae poured her wine as she filled in Miranda on her plan of action for the next several days. Miranda appeared cautiously satisfied, again admonished Shae to let her know the instant her stepson ceased to cooperate and hung up. It sounded as if Miranda wanted him to interfere. Jordan was probably going to get his ass sued before this was all said and done.

Shae sat back on the sofa and picked up her wineglass from the end table. Tomorrow was going to be a long day if the guy insisted on shadowing her as she worked, making it damned difficult to concentrate—which was obviously why he was hanging around so persistently. He realized the effect he had on her...and Shae had a feeling that he thought it was his injuries alone that were getting to her. No. It was him. The whole package. Something about those eyes, cold one minute, haunted and vulnerable the next. What had he been through and why had he come back? And why wouldn't he simply take Miranda's offer if he hated her so much?

He wanted payback, just as Miranda had said. Revenge for taking his father away from him. And she was smack in the middle.

Shae took a sip and closed her eyes as she swallowed. Tomorrow was going to be different. Tomorrow she was going to take control. She was not going to lose it again, not going to tell him to go to hell.

Because apparently he'd already been there... and the expression on his face when he'd said that troubled her.

WHAT WAS HE going to do while he lived on the ranch?

Good question. One that had nagged at him during the drive cross-country, but when no easy answer had popped into his head, he'd ignored it. All he'd wanted to do was get back to a place where he felt at peace and build a plan once he got there.

Well, that was out the window, thanks to Miranda. And to his father.

Had his dad knowingly bequeathed the lease to Miranda? If so, had she couched things in such a way that it'd seemed reasonable to leave his rights to her? Or had her lawyer slipped the clause in, as Emery had speculated? Perhaps his dad simply hadn't cared.

Jordan pressed the cold can of iced tea, fresh from the creek, which served as his impromptu fridge, against his forehead. Was that possible? His father had been so enamored of Miranda, so thrilled that such a woman would marry him. Things had changed between him and his father once she'd come into their lives and, despite Jordan's best efforts, had stayed changed. His father had become… less available. Mentally. Emotionally. It had killed Jordan at the time.

Still killed him a little.

And then there was the stunt Miranda had tried to pull with him. That hadn't helped matters one bit.

He shoved the thought aside, refusing to go there again. He unzipped the tent flap and Clyde sailed inside, curling up on the sleeping bag as if claiming the good spot. Jordan pried off his boots and set them neatly in the corner of the tent, gently pulled off his T-shirt and reached for the cream that he rubbed into his damaged skin. Idly he started to rub, the movements now second nature and soothing, as he tried to focus on positives.

He had his life. It was shit at the moment, but he could work on that—even though he was sorely tempted to crawl off into a corner somewhere. His movements slowed for a moment as it struck him that coming to Montana to hole up on his ranch had been akin to crawling off into a corner. That option was out now. There would be no quiet corners, just a fight for what was his.

He slipped on a long-sleeved T-shirt to keep the cream from staining his sleeping bag and then lay down next to Clyde. Too hot to get inside yet. So what the hell was he going to do? Continue to follow Shae McArthur around just to annoy her?

Yes. For the time being. At best it was a lame tactic, but he saw no reason why she should be comfortable as she made plans to make his life uncomfortable.

He gave a soft snort. Good for the short term. What about the long term?

He didn't seem to be able to think past the next few days. He reached for the pills he kept in the plastic box that held his toiletries, shook one out of the bottle and held it in his palm.

He'd slept okay without it last night, despite the

Miranda-induced trauma. What did he have to lose by trying again? It wasn't as if he was going to disturb the neighbors. He'd only disturb himself…

He wanted to be fresh tomorrow when he took care of that felled tree in the road and fought the next round with Shae. The nightmares left him ruined.

He popped the pill into his mouth and washed it down with the last swallow of tea.

THE LOG WAS GONE—sawed into rounds that had been pushed to the side of the road. Had it been removed by Miranda's man or Jordan? Could Jordan handle a chain saw with his damaged hand? It was ugly, the kind of ugly that made her fight not to look away, but was it at all functional?

When the house came into view, Shae slowed, surveying the scene before her. It looked the same as when she'd arrived that first day: deserted. No man. No dog. She parked Killer next to the Subaru and got out of the truck, closing the door quietly. The place was still, but she wasn't alone. No—she wasn't that lucky. Not lately, anyway.

He was probably in the house. A chain saw sat on the porch step, answering her question as to who had sawed the log. Shae started walking toward the building and as she got closer, she could see the edge of something blue behind a thick hedge of lilac bushes in the backyard. A tent. The guy had bivouacked. She'd been wondering how he was dealing with the mountains of dust and debris in the house. Now she knew. He wasn't. Yet.

A wildly yapping ball of dirty white curls suddenly charged around the house and barreled toward her. Shae stopped dead in her tracks. The poodle slid to a stop in front of her and snarled.

"Hi…little dog," Shae said soothingly, taking a slow step forward. The poodle did an aggressive jump toward her with his lips curled to show his teeth and then sprang back again. Shae stopped, having no desire to end up with a dog attached firmly to her ankle.

Jordan came out from behind the house, attracted, no doubt, by the sound of his lethal poodle. He stopped when he saw her, their gazes connecting over the guard dog, and the reality of his scars hit her hard. Again. Damaged, damaged man. Finally Shae drew in a long breath.

"Would you mind calling off your animal?" she asked.

"Clyde."

The dog stopped yapping at the sound of Jordan's voice, but stayed where he was, keeping Shae at bay, small teeth still bared. Shae tossed Jordan a look. She didn't have time for this.

"Clyde," he repeated softly. The dog glanced over his shoulder as if ascertaining that Jordan truly wanted him to back down from the threat that was Shae, then slowly turned and went to sit protectively on his owner's boot.

If anything, Jordan looked worse than yesterday. The dark stubble that had covered the unscarred parts of his face yesterday was developing into a rough beard. His shirt hung on him, as if he'd lost weight since buying it—which he probably had during his recovery—but as before, it was his eyes that caught and held her attention. Today there was no sign of vulnerability. His gaze was cold, impersonal, determined.

Determined to do what? Make trouble for Miranda, thereby making trouble for her?

Wasn't going to happen.

"I'm working in the bunkhouse today," she said, having decided on the drive that she'd do the job in a professional manner, which meant doing him the courtesy of letting him know where she would be while on his property. If he wanted to take the low road, follow her around, insult her, fine. She'd spent a lifetime with people sniping behind her back because of the perception that she was spoiled. Jordan had done one better and sniped to her face, but she could take it. "You're free to join me," she said. "If you have nothing better to do."

Jordan's eyes narrowed slightly. "This is my ranch, my property, regardless of who holds the lease. I want to know what's going on."

"I'll keep you informed," she said.

"I bet."

"Look," she said. "You're the one that signed the lease. Not me."

"I signed with my father," he said in a gritty voice.

"Who left it to Miranda. Again, not me. I'm just doing the job I was hired to do."

"The job you initiated."

She put her hands on her hips. "All I knew when I made that proposal was that Miranda controlled the property and couldn't sell it. I figured you co-owned it. *No one* knew the particulars."

"Doesn't that tell you something?"

"Miranda's a brilliant businesswoman—"

"And you admire her," he finished mockingly.

"I can think of worse role models," Shae said. "She's very good at what she does. Dedicated to excellence." And demanded the same of others, as Shae had found out. No slacking allowed on Miranda's turf. "When I made the proposal, I had no idea that you'd show up again. No one did."

"Because the only person who cared about where I was is dead."

"I hear your cousin Cole cared."

"Point taken," he said coldly. "And after you spend months in and out of the hospital while dealing with the death of your father, you'll be qualified to judge me on that count."

Shae stilled, staring him down as she told herself to shut her mouth and walk away. This wasn't a battle she was going to win.

She couldn't do it.

She wanted to establish a middle ground so she wouldn't have to go through this on a daily basis.

"What is it you want, Jordan? How do you want to handle this?"

"I want you gone."

"That isn't going to happen." She sauntered a step closer as she spoke, realizing that despite his scruffy appearance, he smelled like soap. Soap and man. She was pretty certain the electricity and water had yet to be turned back on, but he'd bathed somewhere. The water trough? The ponds?

"What *is* going to happen, Shae?" he asked in a low voice, his gaze intense, laserlike, as he waited for her to reply.

"What's going to happen is that I'm going to be here," she said, pointing a finger at the ground, "every day for at least eight weeks. I'm going to put together a proposal package. I'm going to sell Miranda on my ideas and I'm going to have this place up and running by hunting season." Which was an exaggeration, since she wouldn't be able to get the permits that quickly, but she wanted him to know just how serious she was. "And we can work together or you can shadow me and try to unnerve me." Her eyes cut to his arm and back to his face. "Your choice. If you want to continue harassing me, I'll be in the bunkhouse."

Shae stalked away. She had no idea if he was watching her leave, but she felt as if his gaze was burning a hole in her back. Tough. He was going to have to accept reality or leave. Could she change things? No. Miranda was going to build a guest ranch here come hell or high water now that Jordan was back. That had become more than apparent during their last discussion. The entire flavor of the project had changed, which was good for Shae in that she would have the project development on her résumé. Not so good for Jordan and whatever game it was he was playing.

JORDAN CONSIDERED HIS options as he watched Shae march to the bunkhouse, her backpack bumping on her ass. Yesterday had exhausted him. The last thing he'd wanted to do was to dog Shae again, but he needed to make the point that he wasn't going to stand back while she and Miranda ran roughshod over his ranch.

He ran a hand over the back of his scarred-up neck and glanced down at Clyde, who was also focused on Shae, his bright eyes intent. As Jordan saw it, he only had a handful of choices—hang around and make his presence felt, visit Emery and see what he could do legally, or take himself off somewhere and accept the inevitable. Miranda was going to transform his ranch into a dude ranch. Had he ever once known Miranda to fail at something she put her mind to?

Him. But other than that…

There was always a first time. He just needed a break.

He busied himself cleaning and oiling the chain saw again even though it didn't need it. He'd woken up at a ridiculously early hour despite the pills and decided he might as well tackle the road. It hadn't taken long to saw the log, and even though moving the rounds had been awkward, he'd gotten the job done. Now he could bring in supplies more easily.

And so could Shae.

Shae, who'd been in the bunkhouse the entire time he'd serviced the chain saw. What in the hell was she up to? What plans did she have for a building that up until now had held nothing but good memories for him? As kids, he and Cole had spent hours playing there while his dad had mowed and baled the meadow hay, playing hide-and-seek, building forts out of the odds and ends of lumber stored there, talking about the ranches they would own one day. Well, he owned a ranch now and couldn't do one damned thing with it.

He walked up the weed-choked path leading to the front entrance of the building and stopped in the doorway. Shae glanced up as his shadow fell across her, then laid out a metal measuring tape along the wall next to him as if he wasn't there, hooking the end on a crack in the corner molding. She got half-way across the room when the tape slipped free and bounced sideways, ruining her measurement. He saw the muscles of her jaw tighten before she locked the tape, strode back to the corner and once again wedged the end of the tape in the crack. As she returned to where the spool lay, Jordan put his thumb on the metal end, holding it in place. The disconcerted look on Shae's face when she realized what he was doing almost made cooperating with the enemy worthwhile.

"Thanks," she muttered. She jotted down the measurement and then retracted the tape. She measured the adjacent wall without mishap, then measured the distance to the window and up to the sill.

"What plans do you have for this building?" he asked.

"Nothing definite," she said. Her eyes didn't quite meet his, telling him that she did have a plan, though. He liked this old building as it was. Miners had lived there a century ago while working their nearby claims, cowboys had bunked there during roundups, generations of kids had played there, dreaming big dreams, and none of them had involved a dude ranch.

He took a slow step forward, the floor creaking under his weight. She stiffened as he approached.

"This is wrong, Shae." He spoke sincerely, rubbing the underside of his jaw with his ruined left hand. Shae's eyes cut to it, then back up to his.

"Are you going to play the sympathy card now?" she asked.

Jordan felt as if she'd taken a swing at him. The last thing he ever played was the sympathy card. "I was hoping to appeal to your humanity. Guess that's a lost cause."

"Yet you sound surprised," she said coldly, "after

making it clear last night that you didn't think I was particularly empathetic."

"With cause," he added.

"You know nothing about me."

"I know what I saw when we rodeoed. The way you treated people. And Shae? It wasn't pretty."

"It was also a decade ago."

"You've changed," he said flatly, disbelievingly.

"Haven't we all?" she asked in a cool voice.

He didn't know if she was talking scars or temperament or what, but Jordan had had enough. He turned and strode out of the building without another word. It was time for him to do something. Take action. Stake a claim to his property. For that he needed a plan, and some money wouldn't hurt, because he was probably going to be paying Emery a boatload of the stuff.

SHAE CROUCHED TO take another measurement, then set down the tape and sat on the dusty floor instead. She was ashamed of herself for her last comments, but how was she supposed to do battle with this guy? Was she supposed to acknowledge his scars? Ignore them?

They were there. They made her distinctly uncomfortable, but as she ran her fingers over her forehead in an attempt to calm herself down, she realized that it wasn't entirely because of how they'd so radically changed his appearance. It was also because she couldn't stop wondering about what he'd gone through. How horrible it must have been to re-alize his fingers were gone, his face and other parts of his body forever damaged. Shae's lips curled slightly.

Empathy, Jordan. I'm feeling empathy.

He'd never believe it.

She got back to her feet and walked to the window, watching through the filthy glass as Jordan disappeared into his house. Just how badly scarred was he? Did worse injuries lurk beneath his clothing? And how damaged was he mentally? He seemed to hold his own in their confrontations, but there was no missing that faraway, haunted look he got now and again. Was he all there? How could he have gone through what he had and not suffered lingering damage?

The kicker was that this put *her* at a disadvantage. How was she supposed to deal with a guy like this on a daily basis? How was she supposed to work around him?

JORDAN HADN'T BEEN anywhere near serious when he'd told Emery he was going to stop by Claiborne's to see if they had any rank colts. After training his last batch of potential widow-makers for the man, he'd sworn never again. But he hadn't been desperate for a way to make money and stay on his ranch before now. He needed to be there. Guard his interests. Hope against hope that Shae wouldn't come up with a viable proposal, although he knew, realistically, that Miranda would probably make a dude ranch there even if it lost money—just to teach him he couldn't mess with her.

As if he'd started it all.

Nope. She'd started it and he'd ended it, almost as abruptly as he'd dumped Shae on the barroom floor not that long afterward. And now he wished like hell that he'd told his old man what his perfect new wife had tried.

He couldn't have done it. As far as he knew Hank had died a happy man, content with his life and his marriage.

Jordan pulled into the driveway of the Claiborne place. It hadn't changed much. Beautiful yellow horses of all ages filled the fields and corrals. Buckskins, palominos, yellow duns. Claiborne bred for color and conformation and, unfortunately, his foundation stud had a nasty disposition that he'd passed along to his striking get. They could become fairly decent horses with the proper start… and therein lay the rub. There were too many foals produced each year to start properly and Claiborne was constantly playing catch-up, trying to find time to train the older horses first, before they got too old. Meanwhile another crop of foals was born.

Jordan parked and steeled himself for the inevitable averted glances. Part of his life now. He wasn't disappointed. When Claiborne came to the door, his head jerked back when he saw Jordan's face.

"Jordan," he said after clearing his throat. "This is a surprise."

"I imagine so," Jordan said. "Maybe I should have called first."

"No, no. That's fine," Claiborne said, stepping back and holding the door open so Jordan could come inside. "What brings you here?"

"I'm looking for work."

Claiborne's gaze shot down to Jordan's hand and he grimaced slightly. "Around the place here?" he asked.

"No. If you have any colts to start, I'd like to work at the High Camp. And if you don't, I thought you might know of someone who did."

"Can you work colts…like that?" Claiborne asked.

"I can," Jordan said giving the man points for candidness while taking away a few for having no faith in his abilities.

"I, uh, might have a couple I can throw your way."

"What's your hesitation?" Jordan finally asked. "My hand isn't what it used to be, but I can still use it."

"Are you alone at the High Camp?"

"Why?"

"I don't want you to get yourself in trouble up there by yourself with my colts."

"Are you worried about liability?" Jordan asked, flabbergasted.

"Some. They're my colts, after all."

"You never worried before."

"You were…whole before."

And there it was, laid out for him. He wasn't whole. Screw this. "I'm whole in the ways that count," he said. "But I'm not here to twist your arm." Jordan got to his feet.

Claiborne also rose. "I'll give you three fillies… if you sign a release saying you won't come back at me if my animals injure you."

Jordan turned back. "Whatever."

"What's your rate?"

"Same as before."

"That's low now."

Like your expectations of me? Jordan held the words in. He wanted some income, not to correct Claiborne's feelings about him.

"If this goes well, the rates will go up," Jordan said.

"Agreed." Claiborne gestured to the door. "Want to see what I have?"

"Yeah." Jordan followed the man out the door, slowing his steps when he caught sight of a short, rotund pig that was waiting for them on the porch. It sniffed Claiborne's pants as he walked by, then fell into step behind him, trotting along like a dog.

"Pet?" Jordan asked.

"My son's girlfriend wasn't aware that potbellied pigs don't stay small," the older man said on a note of disgust. "She thought they were micropigs or something. My son's in love. He gets the girl. I get the pig."

Jordan smiled a little and it felt odd, smiling. He never smiled anymore.

Claiborne ended up showing him ten young horses and told him to take his pick. Generous for Claiborne, but then Jordan wasn't "whole" anymore. He ended up taking two halter-broke three-year-olds and a rank five-year-old palomino mare that'd been started by Claiborne's son's last girlfriend, who hadn't had any idea what she was doing.

"You sure about this?" Claiborne asked.

"Yeah." Jordan figured if he could make headway with the five-year-old, then he could probably write his ticket with Claiborne, taking a few animals every sixty days until the man ran out of horses…which probably wasn't going to happen anytime soon.

"Can you deliver to the High Camp?" he asked. "I don't have a trailer yet."

"I can do that, but it probably won't be for a couple days. That okay?"

"That will be fine."

AFTER LEAVING CLAIBORNE'S place, Jordan drove straight to Emery's, hoping against hope the old guy had come up with something. Emery met him on the porch again, ushered him inside, and Jordan decided that even if he didn't have the news

he wanted, it was good to see the old man. Good
to have someone in his life who was on his side.

"I've been waiting for you to stop by," Emery said
after serving Jordan a cup of coffee that was the
antithesis of the iced tea—pale and weak. Jordan
preferred it to the overly strong tea. "It's impossible to call you up there at the ranch. Thought I was
going to have to drive over if you didn't show soon."

"Call about what?"

"Well, Miranda is correct in her assertion that
'operations' are not limited to farming," Emery
said. "And I apologize for Jasper's oversight."

"Who would have thought that someone would
use the place for anything else?" Jordan said, sounding more philosophical than he felt. No sense raging
at Emery for something that had happened while
his wife had been dying.

"She can use the land as she pleases as long as
she gets the proper permitting. She can build a
structure as long as she either removes it at the end
of the lease or turns it over to you. However—" the
old man smiled a little and Jordan found himself
leaning forward in anticipation "—while she has
access to the buildings—the barn, tool and equipment sheds and the like—she can't change them. If
she wants to make capital improvements like, say,
adding a bathroom, or cooking facilities, she needs
your approval. All she can do is repair them."

Jordan felt a smile start to spread across his

face—the second in one day. "Shae's measuring buildings as we speak."

"All she can do is repair them," he repeated. "No renovations. No tearing down walls or anything like that."

"I see." Jordan tapped the tips of his fingers on the table. Things had just gotten so much better. He couldn't kick Miranda off the place, but he could probably affect how she used the bunkhouse, which was no doubt intended to be part of the unique experience Shae had mentioned.

"So what now?" Emery asked cautiously.

"Guess I'll share the good news with Shae."

"You want me to give Miranda's attorney a call so that we're on the same page?"

"Yeah. Do that. And I'll let Shae know." Jordan rolled his shoulders, popping out the kinks. "This is the best I've felt in a couple months."

"This is nowhere near over," Emery cautioned.

"Oh, I know. But at least I've won a little ground." Jordan picked up his coffee. "There's nothing in the lease about me using my own corrals, is there?" There'd better not be, since he was going to need them.

"You have the corrals." Emery picked up a pen and flipped over an envelope. "The lease is specific." He drew a rectangle that represented the High Camp acreage. "Your dad leased everything south of the fence that separates the upper part of the property from the lower, which unfortunately includes all the buildings except the house. You have access to those buildings, but can't use them for anything that interferes with Miranda's operations."

"Which in her opinion would be everything I want to do."

"The corrals, if I recall, are on the north side of the line, so you can do anything you want with those and she can't interfere."

"So the north pasture is mine, too."

"It is."

"Then I foresee a long future between myself and Claiborne."

Emery sat his cup down with a thunk that sloshed the coffee over the side. "I was kidding when I said you should start colts for him."

"It'll be fine."

Emery stared down at Jordan's hand and it was all he could do not to pull it back. Hide the reason everyone thought he was less than capable. "The hand is not that big of a deal. Lots of guys train who have more of an infirmity than this."

"That wasn't what I was thinking."

"What were you thinking?"

"You said you'd never again touch a Claiborne colt after that last batch. And you were eight years younger then and a hell of a lot less beat-up."

"I need to do this. If I can send out decent Claiborne horses, then I can get all the business I need."

"And if you can't…what then?"

"Maybe I can get a job on a guest ranch. I hear there may be one close by." Jordan clenched his good hand into a fist on the table. "But regardless of what happens, I'm not leaving the High Camp."

Emery shook his head as if Jordan's answer pained him. It probably did. No one liked to see someone beat their head on a brick wall until it was bloody.

"I'm going to focus on the horses, Emery. Try to ignore what Shae's doing, which should be a hell of a lot easier now that I know she can't renovate the buildings."

Emery fell silent, his gaze focused on Jordan's two hands—one loosely fisted, the other with stumps where his fingers had once been. Only his thumb and his index finger to just beyond the first knuckle remained.

"I want to reclaim my ranch," Jordan said. "I'm living there and making it my home for just as long as I can. It's the only way I can think of to fight back."

"I think you're on the right track if you plan on staying," Emery said slowly, as if trying to convince himself rather than Jordan. "Make the ranch back into a home. Get yourself some livestock. A few chickens. A dog."

"I have one."

Emery lifted the cup to his lips before he said in an undertone, "Kind of." He swallowed, then set the cup back down, a smile spreading across his face.

"Chickens? Hell. Get peacocks. The most annoying domestic bird known to man."

Jordan gave the man a satisfied nod. "I like the way you think."

CHAPTER SEVEN

THERE WERE HEAVY tire tracks on the road going into the High Camp. Uneasy for reasons she couldn't pinpoint, Shae stepped on the gas and Killer bounced over a rut, jostling her sideways. Jordan had made himself scarce over the past several days—three, to be exact—leaving the ranch shortly after Shae arrived and not returning home until after she left, and Shae had started to wonder if he'd made peace with the idea of the High Camp becoming a guest ranch.

Unlikely. So why did it appear that he'd just given up?

She'd told herself that he was probably looking for work. Or had found work. But whatever the reason for his absence, she should be glad he wasn't there, purposely making her feel self-conscious. Instead she felt uneasy. The Jordan Bryan she'd known in high school wouldn't have backed down so easily. A guy who backed down didn't become a top-notch bronc rider…although it was possible that the accident had changed him in that regard, too, affected his determination and drive.

It hadn't affected his work ethic, though. During the evening hours, while she'd been back at her apartment, dealing with the bills that kept pouring in and making calls and calculations, he'd been working around the ranch. Every morning when she walked the property, she noticed new repairs, like loose boards nailed back on the barn and outbuildings. And he'd started working on the corral attached to the barn. He had to be working to keep from going crazy from boredom during the long evening hours. She figured he certainly wasn't doing it to help her in any way.

Shae had taken advantage of the repaired barnyard corral yesterday and brought in her little bay mare, Belinda, so that she could ride the trails she'd marked out on the aerials and determine how much grooming was necessary. There'd surely be windfalls that she'd need to deal with and areas of washouts and overgrowth.

When Shae drove past what was left of the windfall, she realized that there were several sets of trailer tracks, as in more than one trip had been made. She wasn't expecting any kind of deliveries yet, so this was all Jordan. As soon as she came in sight of the ranch, she spotted three horses in the pasture—a buckskin, a dun and a palomino— banded together at the far end. Belinda stood at the corral gate, head high, trying to no avail to get the attention of her brethren.

Horses Shae could deal with—it was a guest ranch, after all—but she hadn't expected Jordan to get livestock. And why did one man need three horses?

She pulled her truck to a stop close to the Subaru and got out, stopping in her tracks when a black-and-white-spotted pig wandered out from behind the house. It saw her and made a beeline for her, snorting and grunting as it charged. Shae took a backward step, then scrambled back into the truck as the pig picked up speed, slamming the door shut as the animal rushed toward her. Porky slid to a stop at the truck and looked up at her with beady, marblelike eyes barely visible between the rolls of fat on its forehead. Tufts of hair wavered in the breeze between its ears as it studied the truck, as if trying to figure out a way to get in.

Shae pressed her palm to the window, plotting strategy. *It's just a pig.* A super-ugly pig. How fast were pigs? Did she care to find out? But it wasn't as though she could spend the day in the cab of her truck. The pig snorted as it disappeared under the truck.

Damn Jordan Bryan.

Speaking of the jerk—Shae spotted him at the old round pen, his yappy dog trotting beside him as he carried a board toward the round pen. Shae rolled down the window and the pig reappeared, snorting and snuffling. "Why don't you go eat that poodle?" Shae muttered. Should she yell for help?

Oh, hell, no. That was exactly what he wanted. Shae debated and then, while the pig was still in view on the driver's side, she scooted across the seat to the passenger side, thrust the door open, jumped out and ran for the house. The pig followed, and while it didn't take long for Shae to realize that the animal was no sprinter, she didn't slow down. She jetted across the porch and into the house, slamming the screen door behind her. Only then did she turn and see the pig come to a stop at the steps, which were apparently too much for the chubby beast. It let out a hefty breath, then snorted its way along the edge of the porch, snout down in the dirt, looking for who knew what.

Shae leaned her forehead against the doorframe, waiting for her heart rate to return to normal. A pig. Really? If Jordan Bryan thought a pig was going to slow her down, he had another think coming... although it was going to slow her down until she caught her breath.

Turning back to the room, Shae was surprised to see signs of habitation. A stack of paper plates sat on the kitchen counter next to the sink, and while the living room was still dusty, the kitchen had been cleaned. There were gallon jugs of water next to the sink and a cooler next to the oak table, which had been scrubbed. Curious, Shae walked down the short hall to the two bedrooms. One of them had also been cleaned and Jordan's sleeping bag was laid out on an old-fashioned metal bed frame, a pair of running shoes neatly lined up under the window, an open duffel bag next to them. A couple of prescription bottles sat on the floor next the bed, along with a tube of scar cream. Shae bit her lip for a moment as she tried to imagine what his life had been like since the explosion. What he'd been through. But that was past. They were in the here and now and she was part of that here and now.

She went back to the living room and looked out to where he was repairing the round pen. The pig wandered past the window, snout still to the ground. That was going to be a problem. And she was trespassing. She needed to get out of there.

If Jordan could be outside with the pig, then so could she. It was probably friendly, even though it had looked as though it wanted to maul her. She watched the animal as it went on its way, cheerfully doing its pig thing, until it disappeared behind the house. Only then did she go to the door and step out onto the porch.

Shae trotted down the steps, keeping an eye out for Miss—or Mr.—Piggy as she headed for the round pen. She had absolutely no idea what she was going to say once she got there, but was unable to stop herself from braving the pig and confronting Jordan. If nothing else, she was going to assume that the animal was not a man-eater.

Jordan looked up from where he was leaning on a drill, screwing a plank back on, and Shae instantly blanked out her expression. "You have horses," she said, stating the obvious and wondering if he'd seen her hundred-yard dash from her truck to the porch…or if he was aware she'd been in the house.

"Mmm-hmm," he said past the long screws he held between his lips. He picked up the old-fashioned bit-and-brace drill and used it to put another hole through the plank into the fence post, holding the brace steady with the palm of his injured hand while turning the drill with his other. It was slow going and once finished, he set the drill on the ground and put the plank in place, holding it with his knee as he took a long screw from his mouth.

"And a pig." The word was barely out of her mouth when an earsplitting cry came from behind her. Shae jumped a mile, then whirled to see a peacock strutting along the edge of the corral, its tail dragging in the dust behind it. "What the *hell?*" she muttered before turning back to glare at Jordan. "Do I have one bit of color left in my face?" she demanded.

His expression shifted, as if she'd amused him and he was fighting a smile, which he no doubt was.

"Peacocks?"

"Great for snakes," he said.

"I didn't realize we had a snake problem," Shae said, fighting to get her heart rate back to normal. "Where'd you get the horses?" *And is your pig as dangerous as it looks?*

"I called around to see if anyone had any horses that needed the kinks taken out of them."

"Because…?"

"Because," he said, speaking slowly, as if she'd have difficulty understanding, "that's how I plan to make my living."

"Taking the kinks out of horses."

"Claiborne horses have a lot of kinks."

"Claiborne horses?" Oh, yeah. It would be lovely having those nasty-tempered yellow horses cohabitating with her nice, gentle trail horses. Wasn't going to happen, but that wasn't something she was going to fight about now.

"Ah." Shae approached the pasture gate and the horses' heads instantly came up. The biggest horse, a palomino mare, snorted and stamped her foot. Shae closed her eyes, willed herself not to react. "Aren't you worried about that pig eating your dog?" she asked.

"No. She's more of a people person."

"And you don't think having her around is going to interfere with what I have to do?"

"She's friendly and has no teeth."

"No teeth?"

Jordan shrugged and picked up the battery-powered drill that lay beside the bit-and-brace. "By the way, I had my lawyer check over the contract," he said as he put the bit into the top of the screw and squeezed the trigger. The drill whined. Shae clenched her teeth, waiting for him to tell her the rest. He finished with the screw and then let the hand with the drill fall to his side, smiling a little as he did so. It was the first time she'd seen him smile, but it wasn't a pleasant expression, being more predatory than friendly. "You can't make changes to the buildings without my permission."

"Miranda—"

"You can clean, repair and use them. You can't make significant changes without my permission."

Shae felt blood beating in her temples. "That's what your lawyer told you?"

"Unless Miranda managed to change the contract, which she couldn't have done without my consent, I'd say that the bunkhouse is going to get a good scrubbing and that's it."

She started to speak, then stopped. What the hell could she say?

"Anything else?" she asked, just to have the last word.

"Yeah," he said. "Give Miranda my love when you talk to her."

Oh, she'd give Miranda his love all right. Choking back a growl, Shae stalked away from the round pen. He was lying. Miranda would have looked into this before letting Shae onto the property. Of course she would have.

But Shae still felt a little sick as she walked toward the bunkhouse and the four cabins nestled behind it. If he wasn't lying, then she'd wasted a couple days of her contracted time making plans for the bunkhouse that would never come to fruition. Time she couldn't afford to waste. And they were great plans. She was going to knock out walls, changing the tiny cells into much larger bedrooms. The rest of the building would be a comfortable dining and meeting area with a centrally located wood-burning stove as the focal point. The setup would be rustic and unique—just as Miranda had ordered.

He had to be lying.

Shae yanked at a tall weed as she walked by it, then instead of going to the bunkhouse, she walked straight to Killer. The pig charged as she approached the truck, but Shae didn't slow down. "No!" she commanded, pointing a finger at the beast.

The pig slid to a halt, but Shae barely noticed. She got into the truck, fired it up and after checking to make sure the pig was far enough away, put it in gear. Miranda needed to know what was going on, which meant she had to get into cell reception range. Hopefully in an hour or so, she'd have a better idea as to how to proceed.

"Now, LET ME get this straight," Miranda said. "Jordan says that we can only use the buildings in their current condition?"

"He said we could repair existing conditions, but can't improve or renovate."

"Repair, but not renovate."

"Exactly." She'd gone over the conversation enough times in her head as she'd driven to the cattle guard, where her phone finally showed some bars, that she probably could have repeated it verbatim. "Before I go forward, I thought clarification was in order."

"Just assume he's lying," Miranda said.

"I've already done that," Shae said drily.

"I'll contact Noel, but until you hear from me, continue as if we have full rights to do whatever we want."

"But what if we don't have full rights?"

"Was I not clear?" Miranda asked mildly.

"You were clear," Shae replied, wishing she'd said nothing. "Continue as if we have rights." That was going to be interesting.

"Make your presence felt. Do not let him buffalo you. Trust me, once it's settled, Jordan will play ball."

"All right," Shae said, more hesitation in her tone than she'd intended. "I'll do my best."

Miranda let out a soft sigh then, as if realizing how harsh it sounded to be strong-arming her injured stepson. "You need to understand, Shae… there's so much more to this situation than I can tell you about. Old history I don't want to dig up. Suffice it to say that if Jordan had really wanted this ranch so badly, he would have come home sooner. He had the option and turned it down. It wasn't until Hank died and I was left alone that suddenly the ranch became all-important to him." She paused as if searching for words, then said, "He blames me for a lot of things I had no control over and he wants to make me suffer. But once he realizes I won't back down like his father always did, I think he'll give up. It's time to prove to him that I won't keep rolling over. That's where I need your help and I know you're capable."

"I'll make my presence felt," Shae promised. Somehow she was going to have to establish dominance. It was apparent her boss expected no less.

"Excellent," Miranda said, even though she still had shades of doubt in her voice, as if wondering if Shae was the right person for this job. "And I'll get back to you as soon as I hear from Noel."

JORDAN SPENT THE day working on the round pen in relative peace, reinforcing and replacing boards. Shae had driven away shortly after he'd broken the bad news to her—off to see Miranda, no doubt, to get counsel—and had not returned. Jordan enjoyed the respite, even though he knew it meant Miranda was gearing up for the next assault.

How many battles would they fight before this was settled one way or another?

Even if she ended up getting her way, Jordan was going to make her pay for every small piece of her victory.

The sun was setting when he finally put his tools away and then came back out of the barn to lean his arms on his newly repaired fence and watched his horses graze in the south pasture—the one that Miranda would probably soon lay claim to, forcing him to move the horses to the north pasture. But until then he was keeping the horses there, close to the barn and his tack. Every movement, every small noise brought their heads up and they were still spooking every time Clyde trotted through on his hourly rounds. Oh, yeah. He had his work cut out for him, but at least he had something to do.

The pig came out from behind the house, saw him and came running. Clyde hugged closer to Jordan's legs, still uncertain about his new playmate, and Jordan reached down and scooped up the dog. The pig honestly had no teeth and when Jordan had borrowed him, Claiborne—who allegedly hated the animal—had given careful instructions for making mash that a toothless pig could choke down.

It was a pain in the ass, but it was worth making mash to torture Shae. He pushed open the rickety back gate and started for the house, wanting to light the lanterns before it got dark, only to stop when he saw headlights cutting through the deepening twilight.

Really?

Someone from Cedar Creek? Perhaps the queen herself, Miranda, there to confront him about this new legal wrinkle? He couldn't help but think that not being able to transform the buildings had to put some kind of kink into her master plan.

But it wasn't Miranda. Shae's old Chevy truck drove past her usual parking place next to his Subaru to the rear of the bunkhouse, where she parked out of sight. With a nasty feeling in the pit of his stomach, Jordan started toward the bunkhouse, getting there just as Shae climbed out of the vehicle. She reached inside to pull out a couple of duffel bags and an electric lantern, and then the headlights went out.

No.

She ignored him and headed for the door of the dark bunkhouse. Fast. As if avoiding a pig or something. The lantern clicked on once she got inside and closed the door, leaving him standing alone. A few seconds later he exercised his right of access and pulled the door open.

"What are you doing?" he asked. He knew what she was doing, but hadn't been able to stop himself from asking the question. Or maybe he hoped he only thought he knew what she was doing and was way off base.

Shae sent him a blank look. "I think it's pretty obvious what I'm doing."

"You're going to stay here." Jordan glanced around the room. She'd tidied it up so that she could work there, but the place was still a shambles. Even he wouldn't want to sleep there with the thick dirt and spider webs, and he'd lived in the Kuwaiti desert.

"I have some work ahead of me," Shae agreed, following his thoughts. "Feel free to dive in and help. It's your place, after all." She dropped her duffels on either side of her, raising small clouds of dust that swirled in the bright lantern light, challenging him with her eyes as she waited for the clouds to settle. Jordan wasn't biting.

He turned and walked out the door. What now?

"Watch out for pigs," Shae called.

Jordan yanked the door shut behind him with a satisfying bang.

SHAE WENT BACK to the truck and got out the second electric lantern she'd brought and the cot she'd borrowed from her brother. She carried in a bucket and mop and broom, her iPod and headphones. Tonight she was going to do as much cleaning as possible without water, set up her cot, then sleep in the truck. There was no way she was risking a night with mice and since she'd parked on the far side of the bunkhouse, out of view of the house, Jordan didn't need to know where she slept.

Slowly she started sweeping by the light of the lantern, concentrating on cleaning the floor without raising a cloud. There were no mouse droppings to be seen, which made Shae feel better. It was one thing to make a point and another to dash shrieking out into the night because something small and furry was running across the sheets.

Make your presence felt. She smiled grimly as she moved the broom. Miranda had loved the idea of her moving onto the ranch.

Shae set up the cot, positioning the bed against the wall, then stood back to study her new home. It was…rugged. The closed doors of the twelve cell-like rooms she'd hoped to make into four bedrooms by knocking out walls were downright creepy in the night, and unlike Jordan, she didn't have a poodle—or a pig—for protection. She wished she hadn't shut all the doors the last time she'd been in the building.

Time for bed, as in time to get out of there. She shut off the lanterns and pulled the small Maglite out of her pocket, feeling an even more urgent need to get out of the building once the room fell dark.

You're not eight years old and afraid of the dark.

No, she was twenty-nine years old and leery of the dark.

Shae crept out around the bunkhouse. She already had her sleeping bag laid out on the backseat, so she shucked out of her jeans, planning to sleep in her T-shirt, opened the truck door and slipped inside, tossing her jeans and moccasins onto the front seat. One of the blessings of being short was that one could sleep on a truck seat fairly comfortably—she'd done it a time or two during the rodeo season. Regardless of what people thought about her, Shae was capable of roughing it. To a point. As long as there were no mice or major discomforts involved.

As soon as she was convinced there were no mice in residence, she'd sleep in the bunkhouse—but the doors to those twelve tiny rooms where the miners had once slept were going to be wide-open.

JORDAN WOKE UP feeling as if he hadn't slept—mainly because he hadn't. The nightmare had come early, before midnight, despite taking his last pill, and he'd woken up thrashing. As far as he knew, he hadn't shouted out—if he had, and Shae had heard him, she hadn't felt the need to come to his rescue. No surprise there. Clyde had crept up onto his chest and lain there, offering comfort, and eventually Jordan had fallen back to sleep in the early-morning hours, only to wake up feeling like shit.

He took the path to the ponds and had a quick wash in the cold water, then headed back to the house for coffee and cold cereal, fully aware that he might run into Shae at any time. He hated having her there, hated losing his morning solitude, but he was going to roll with it. Focus on making his ranch a home for himself and Clyde.

A peacock screamed as he headed for the pastures to separate out the dun filly he was going to start working that morning. Emery was correct—peacocks were the most annoying bird on the planet. Nice to look at, hell to listen to. He rounded the corner of the bunkhouse, intent on his mission, then skidded to a stop when he found himself face-to-face with Shae standing next to the truck clutching a pair of jeans to her midsection. Her mouth opened and closed and then she snapped her back straight and gave him that haughty Shae expression, which lost some of its impact, what with her having no pants on. And then it struck him—she'd slept in the truck.

"Jordan," she said.

"Shae." He felt like smiling as he continued to regard her, rather enjoying the stains of color on her cheeks. Being a guy, he noted that she was wearing a bra under her T-shirt, but that still left him facing a woman with miles of leg and the remnants of a stunned expression on her face. "Sleep well?"

Still holding the pants in front of her with one hand, she brushed back her tousled hair with the other. "Fine, thank you."

"The bunkhouse wasn't comfortable?"

"I wanted to mop before spending the night," she said with a faint sniff.

"Ah." He smiled. "That makes sense." He touched his hat and walked on, whistling lightly. He'd never been a big whistler, but the occasion seemed to call for it.

SHAE LET OUT a frustrated breath as Jordan walked away whistling. The bastard. Catching her in her panties had not been on the agenda…and neither had the way he'd looked her up and down as if he'd suddenly realized that she was a woman. *News flash, Jordan.*

Why did nothing she did around this guy work out?

Grumbling under her breath, she pulled on her pants, shoved her feet into her moccasins and headed for the outhouse—the existence of which she was pretty certain was a violation of EPA

regulations. She'd have to look into that—just as
soon as she didn't need it anymore.

When Shae had come up with her brilliant plan to
make her presence felt, she hadn't counted on just
how uncomfortable it was to start a morning without running water. Until the power was turned on,
the pump wouldn't operate and there was no water
in the lines. Jordan had at least ten gallon-size jugs
stored in the kitchen while Shae had two, which
she'd planned to drink and use to brush her teeth.

But there was the old hand pump at the trough
behind the bathhouse.

Shae walked around the building, hoping she
wouldn't bump into Jordan just yet, and started
pumping the handle. Nothing. Then she remembered priming—they'd had to prime the old pump
at Mel's place. Grabbing the galvanized bucket next
to the trough, she scooped water out and poured it
into the top of the pump. Success. Freezing-cold
water started to flow after a few pumps—enough
to wash her hands and face. She pulled the towel
off her shoulder and patted her face dry, wondering just where it was that Jordan bathed. Surely he
didn't soap up here at the trough. But if he did, he
might well have an audience in the future, which
again made her wonder what the extent of his injuries was. Was his arm the worst of it?

She'd probably never know, but she wanted to.
He'd been so damned perfect back in their rodeo
days—all lean, hard muscle and get-it-done atti-

tude. There was something about confidence that Shae found sexy—one of the reasons she'd made that bet. His reserved, can't-get-to-me quality had been another. Shae did love a challenge.

Now the challenge was different, the circumstances vastly changed. It wasn't the time to be wondering about naked Jordan. Or to be lamenting his injuries. She did love perfection, though, and the fact that he was no longer the specimen of manhood he'd once been did bother her. How shallow was she for that?

Pretty damned shallow, she admitted, pursing her lips as she studied her reflection in the trough. Shallow and petty—which was exactly how he saw her. Mel, her brother, Jordan. All had recently been very free in pointing out *her* imperfections. And maybe they had a point.

Shae pushed the thought aside, but it edged back almost instantly. Three people, two of whom she cared about, had judged her harshly. Four if she counted Reed.

Later. She'd confront these issues when she wasn't trying to save her professional ass. At the moment, she had a job to do and a few things she needed to straighten out with Jordan now that this was her home away from home. Pulling her hair back into a barrette, she stepped out into the sun. Where was the man? In the barn? In the pastures? Had he circled around while she'd washed her face and gone back to the house?

The pig spotted her as she walked toward the bunkhouse and came galloping toward her. Shae froze, telling herself the animal had no teeth and the worst she could do was knock her down—which she tried to do, sideswiping Shae as she ran by, then turning to jog back as Shae caught her balance.

"No!" Shae commanded, just as she had last time, and again the pig slowed to a stop.

Shae cocked her head.

"Stay," she said firmly and the pig stood its ground as Shae took a couple steps back.

A trained pig. Did Jordan know? Probably. And hadn't told her.

Shae walked around the pig and then turned to face it, walking backward toward the bunkhouse. The animal didn't move and Shae smiled to herself. Cool.

"Uh…" she said once she was in the doorway, wondering how to release the animal. "Run free…." She waved her arms. "Shoo. Go do pig stuff."

One of the words worked and the pig started snuffling along the ground again. She went into the bunkhouse and changed her clothes, stuffing her old clothes into a duffel bag she'd brought for that purpose. She thought about taking a few minutes to put on some makeup and then decided that while she was here, she wasn't going to bother. Even if she felt kind of naked without it.

Now to deal with Jordan—if she could find him. She'd seen his dog at the barn, so that seemed like the place to begin the search. When she slid open the heavy barn door, she was greeted by the thud of hooves and a sharp curse as the horse that Jordan had been in the process of haltering shied violently and shot out the gate to the pasture. He sent her an angry look, but Shae only shrugged.

"Nice animal," she said as the mare sped across the pasture to the far corner to join her friends. Belinda whinnied from the adjoining corral.

"Yeah," Jordan replied, making Shae wonder how long he'd worked to get close to the horse.

And then she noticed what she hadn't noticed when she'd faced off with him in her panties—he looked like hell.

"Did you sleep okay?" she asked.

"Always," he said with such heavy sarcasm that Shae realized she'd touched a sore spot. "You?"

"You inquired earlier if you recall, but for the record, I slept splendidly."

"Well, now that we're done lying to each other, what is it you want? Because I don't think you purposely came down here to scare off my horse and I doubt you came down to say good morning."

"No. I did just want to say good morning."

"Bullshit," Jordan said matter-of-factly.

"I want to have the power turned on," she said, expecting him to balk on general principles.

"Pay the deposit."

Shae frowned at him. "That's why you don't have power? The deposit?"

"I don't need it right now."

"You don't need plumbing?"

"There's an outhouse."

"I prefer plumbing," Shae assured him. "And the EPA frowns on outhouses now."

"Well, the plumbing is in the house and that's not part of your domain, even if the water was turned on."

"I can make plumbing part of my domain," Shae said mildly. "There're facilities in the bathhouse." A toilet sitting in the corner of the room that had four shower spigots coming out of the wall and one big drain in the floor. Every bit of plumbing was from the 1930s, when the bathhouse had been built during the last small gold rush in the area. "I'll just repair existing facilities in the bathhouse."

She sauntered closer as she spoke, noting the way he drew himself up in response, as if preparing for an assault. Because he despised her? Well, he might despise her, but that hadn't kept him from giving her a good once-over not that long ago.

"That's legal, isn't it?" she asked.

"I need to talk to my attorney."

"Well, while you do that, I'm calling a plumber."

SHAE'S PLUMBER ARRIVED in the early afternoon. As soon as he opened the door, the pig charged, but Shae held the animal off with a quick command.

How the hell had she figured that out?

Shae smiled as she approached the wary-looking

guy, spoke briefly to him, then turned toward where
Jordan was working on his corral. Even at a distance he could see the smug expression on her face.
He also saw the plumber give her a good once-over,
his gaze lingering on her ass for longer than Jordan thought necessary. And although Shae wasn't
looking at the plumber, she was aware of what was
going on. Jordan was sure of it. Women like Shae
were born aware of the power they had over other
people. And Shae enjoyed the power.

No. There wasn't a lot to like about her.

Which was probably why it was killing him that
he was finding her more fascinating than he should.
It'd been ages since he'd been laid, and yeah, she'd
looked damned good in her panties, but that was no
excuse. Not when he knew what kind of person she
was. How many people had he seen her run roughshod over during high school? And she'd appeared
so freaking oblivious. That was what had really
fried him. She hurt people, pushed them around,
and didn't seem to notice the effects of her actions.
Hell—that was exactly what she was doing to him
now with this guest-ranch business.

He watched her lead the way to the bathhouse,
smiling and talking to the plumber, confident in
herself and her ability to control all situations.
There were a lot of similarities between Miranda
and Shae—they were both attractive, charming,
manipulative and used to getting their own way—

and it behooved him to remember that. Especially when it was his own eye being drawn to her ass.

Disgusted with himself, Jordan focused back on the fence.

It would kill him to have Shae think she was getting to him. That he found her attractive on any level, because then she would try to work him…or rather, try harder to work him.

He wasn't going to let that happen.

CHAPTER EIGHT

SHAE'S PLUMBER WAS PLEASANT, helpful and mildly flirtatious. He also had to break the news to her that the septic system for the bathhouse was nonexistent due to age. To get the system up and running, she'd have to have a new septic tank installed and then have extensive work done on the pipes. It was possible she'd have to get Jordan's permission to dig up what was left of the old septic system. Not the answer she'd hoped for, and if she was not mistaken, Jordan looked pretty damned smug over in the round pen, where he was pointedly ignoring her and the plumber as he brushed down the buckskin filly he'd worked that morning.

Shae walked with the plumber, who'd insisted she call him Cody, back to his truck, smiled and shook her head when he asked if she spent much time in Missoula, then shooed the pig away when he started the engine. Damn, damn and double damn.

Once the dust from Cody's truck had settled, Shae unfolded the written estimate he'd given her. Repairing the plumbing had been an area she'd pegged as a high-budget item, but she hadn't realized that none of the existing system could be used. The figure was about four times what she'd estimated, she still had no facilities and Jordan was probably not going to give her his go-ahead.

She was going to do it anyway. Miranda had said to proceed and she was proceeding. She now had one estimate for plumbing repair in the bathhouse and she planned to get at least two more. She'd also get estimates for making changes in the bunkhouse and the cabins that she'd yet to fully explore.

Even if Jordan had more rights than Miranda was willing to concede, the High Camp would become a guest ranch. Of that, Shae had no doubt. She'd gotten the strong feeling during their last meeting that Miranda would operate it at a loss if she had to, just to show Jordan he couldn't continue to harass her. It was more than apparent that he did have some kind of vendetta against his stepmother, and she against him, and Shae was going to have to walk a thin line to stay out of the middle of it. The thought nagged at her for most of the morning. All she wanted was to do her contracted job, not to be caught up in a family drama. Especially not this family.

Finally, close to noon, she got into her truck and drove down to the cattle guard to make a few calls. She hung up from the last one, a contractor who specialized in restoring historical buildings, who'd thought he might be able to squeeze in a trip for an estimate within the month, and then dialed the Cedar Creek Ranch and asked for Miranda.

"She's not at the ranch," Ashley said with a snip in her voice. "She's due back late tonight."

"Thank you," Shae said. "Would you please tell her that I'm staying at the High Camp, so I have no phone service? I'll check in every day or two."

"Noted." Ashley, who was not the forgiving sort, gave a small sniff and asked if there was anything else.

"Nothing for now," Shae said and then ended the call without saying goodbye. For a moment she sat in her truck, staring straight ahead, the siren song of a hot shower luring her to drive on toward Missoula. Shae fought with herself for another few seconds, then put the truck in gear and made an illegal U-turn across the highway, heading back the way she came. She still had work to do. The shower, as lovely as it would be, could wait.

She'd just crossed the cattle guard when the Subaru came around the corner and she and Jordan swung to their respective sides of the road, the vehicles brushing past each other. She glanced in the rearview mirror as he pulled back onto the road and smiled with a touch of satisfaction.

He'd probably thought she'd be gone for the day. Well, now he was going to have to contend with her being on his precious ranch without him. She brought her eyes back to the road.

Maybe while he was gone she could figure out just where it was that he bathed.

THE PHARMACIST SHOOK his head after typing Jordan's name into the computer. "I'm sorry. The prescription's yet to be filled. We never got verification from your former pharmacy."

Jordan stared at the man, telling himself this wasn't happening. Not when he'd just taken his last pill the night before. "Could you check again? When I talked to the assistant here last week, she said transferring wasn't a problem."

"Well, there was a problem," the pharmacist said. "Too many refills in too short a time. According to the note here, we tried to call you, but your phone was out of service."

"I live in a nonservice area," Jordan muttered, digging in his wallet for his physician's card. Once he found it, he shoved it across the counter. "Can you call my doctor, please? See what you can do?"

"Certainly, but we don't keep this drug in stock. It takes an extra day to fill, since this is not a common prescription. It's normally not a problem, once the patient knows to order in advance."

"I thought I had."

The pharmacist looked over his glasses, clearly commiserating but unable to do anything about the situation. "Once we get through to your doctor and he gives the okay," he said patiently, "we can have the medication here by one p.m. tomorrow."

Jordan cleared his throat. "Fine. Do you mind if I wait until you make that call?"

"If you'd like."

Ten minutes later Jordan left the store, telling himself that he'd slept without the pills in the past without issue. He was taking them as a precaution. No need to be concerned...except there'd been no one around to hear him if he did have a nightmare. Now there was.

Get a grip. He'd already had one nightmare with Shae there. Obviously the chances of her hearing him, or doing anything if she did, were nil if she spent the night closed up in the truck again. It couldn't have been that comfortable sleeping in the truck...though he had to admit that he was kind of impressed she had gone that far to prove a point.

She had to be either pretty damned angry or pretty damned desperate to prove her worth as Miranda's right-hand woman.

Jordan unlocked his car and got inside, running a hand over Clyde's head. The dog curled up between Jordan's chest and the steering wheel, his body warm and comforting. "You can't ride there," Jordan said. Not if he wanted to steer effectively.

As if he understood, Clyde slunk off his lap and sat beside him, his little chin tilted up, looking out the window. Jordan put the car into Reverse. A quick stop for groceries and water, another for a mineral block, then he could get back to the ranch, where Shae was enjoying some undeserved alone time. He hated the thought of her being there without him.

Hell, he hated the thought of her being there *with* him. It froze him up, sharing his space, even if he did have the opportunity to see her half-naked. And if he felt like this with one person around, what was he going to feel like with a crew of enthusiastic vacationers tromping all over the place? Did he seriously think he was going to be able to work his horses with people standing at the fence asking questions?

He would deal with that when he had to. Right now he was going to keep his heels stubbornly dug in and hope he could somehow win this battle.

And what if you can't? What then? The stubborn voice refused to silence itself as he drove home and by the time he crossed the cattle guard, his head was throbbing. All he'd wanted when he'd started his cross-country journey a few weeks ago was to go home and heal.

Miranda and Shae were making that an impossible thing to do.

IT DIDN'T TAKE long after she'd trapped the pig in the backyard and closed the gate for Shae to find the trail through thick brush and trees from Jordan's house to the ponds several hundred yards away. She'd spotted the connected dredge ponds on the aerials, knew they were remnants of the placer operations that had flourished between 1890 and the

1930s, but she hadn't realized just how picturesque they were. As they were located on Forest Service land, anyone could have access to them, but the area was so remote that they were virtually untouched. Shae kicked her shoes off and waded in, the icy water sending a shiver through her. If Jordan bathed here, he was a stronger person than she was. Shae stood for another moment on the smooth gravel bottom, telling herself it wasn't that cold. But it was, so she waded back out. She could bathe tonight in Missoula while she waited at home for Miranda's call.

She was on her way to the barn to saddle Belinda for her first trail reconnaissance when the sound of a diesel engine stopped her. She reversed course as a new red Dodge drove into sight. The Cedar Creek Ranch trucks were white and the woman who climbed out of the cab after parking was unfamiliar.

"Hey," she called, waving cheerfully. "I'm Devon. You called my dad today about a renovation?"

"Hartley Renovations?" Shae asked as she crossed the distance between them.

"Yeah. Dad realized I was in the area and asked me to stop by and take some photos for him. He knows you're on a schedule and thought if he had some information it'd make it easier for him to work up an estimate for you."

"Great," Shae said. "I'll show you the buildings and get you a copy of the measurements." Miranda's copy, but she'd make another tonight.

They went inside the bunkhouse and Shae explained that she didn't yet know how extensive the renovation might be. "I'll be in touch with your father within the next week or two and let him know what we've decided on before he makes the trip out."

"Budget issues?" Devon asked as she lowered her camera.

"Among other things. But I'm certain the project will progress no matter what."

"Cool," Devon said. "Can I see the other buildings?"

"Sure." Shae heard the Subaru drive in as they stepped outside, but ignored it and led Devon to the bathhouse.

"We could turn this into a really nice sauna," Devon said, snapping a picture and moving forward to open the door. "We've refurbished a couple buildings like this on other ranches."

"I'd love a sauna," Shae said. She'd love a bath. Anything except an icy swim.

The Subaru door opened and closed and then Jordan called his poodle back with a quick command. Devon looked out from the bathhouse, but Shae refused to turn around. If all went well, Jordan would disappear into his house and she could get through this impromptu consultation without incident.

JORDAN CARRIED IN his groceries, dumped them on the counter and then went to stand near the living room window, arms crossed as he watched the invaders making plans for his place.

They stood on the path directly between the house and the barn—exactly where he wanted to be since he'd yet to work the dun—but there was no way he was running that gauntlet. Not after suffering a sleepless night and then discovering that he had no drugs to get him through the night ahead of him. For one thing, he didn't know if he could hold his temper, since everything in him wanted to order the two women off his place and tell them not to come back, and for another, he'd had enough stares and double takes for one day.

He'd trained himself months ago to ignore the looks, although there were times he would have loved to have been his former self—a guy who could walk into a pharmacy and not get startled looks—but today the stares and sidelong looks had become irritating. He was not subjecting himself to more. So instead he stood at the window and watched as Shae gestured and the other woman nodded, hating them both for what they planned to do to his ranch. All he wanted was peace and quiet, to train horses and come to grips with his life as it now was.

What did he get instead? Shae McArthur doing Miranda's dirty work. And once she was done, she'd move on, leaving him with a ranch full of staring strangers. He, who'd never liked being the center

of attention, would be living in a veritable circus
ring if she and Miranda got their way.

Jordan turned away from the window as the two
women started walking toward the red pickup, and
rubbed his hand over the scarred flesh at the back
of his neck, every nerve in his body feeling as if it
were close to exploding.

She hasn't won yet.

He closed his eyes, steadied his breathing. Or
tried to, anyway. He was so damned close to losing it.

Too close.

*Catch a horse. Go to work. Forget that bitch
Miranda and what she's trying to do to you.*

It was the only thing he could do. Jordan opened
his eyes, and with a quick intake of breath headed
for the front door.

SHAE WENT BACK to the barn after Devon drove
away. She still had time to put in a couple hours
on the trails before driving back to Missoula. She'd
be dealing with her parents later today, and much
as she loved them, she was feeling guilty about
the amount of money she'd allowed them spend on
the wedding. Money she'd convinced herself they'd
wanted to spend, until she'd spoken to Brant. They
had wanted to spend it, but she shouldn't have taken
so much.

The barn door wasn't latched, and as Shae pulled
it open, she realized that Jordan was inside, gath-

ering his gear to work one of the horses. He shot her a sideways look when she walked inside, then went back to coiling the rope he held, every line of his body radiating tension.

"Are you all right?" Shae asked, eyeing the jerky movements of his hands.

He didn't answer, but she could see the muscles tighten in his jaw, as if he was holding back the words he wanted to say.

"I was just asking," she said as she reached for Belinda's halter.

"Don't," he snapped.

Shae propped a hand on her hip, telling herself to let it go.

She was so bad at letting things go.

"I get that you don't want me here, because you don't want the place to become a guest ranch, but this feels personal," she pointed out. "What is it about me that you find so heinous? It can't all stem from our past, which was pretty damned sketchy at best. So what is it? Do I remind you of someone you hate?" One corner of her mouth quirked up. "Like, say, Miranda?" She could see from his face that she'd gotten it in one. "I'm not Miranda, you know. I just work for her."

"Well aware," he said stonily, but still, she wondered. He turned his back, effectively shutting her out, which was his right, but it pissed her off.

"You've got issues, Jordan."

He rounded on her, his expression fierce. "No

shit. Did you come up with that all by yourself? Yes. I have issues. Big ones. And now you're here adding to them." He advanced a couple steps. "You asked why I came back? I don't know. But it had to do with survival. I was dying back there in Virginia. I had to get out. Get back home where I could—" He stopped abruptly, as if suddenly realizing what he was saying, and to whom.

"I—"

"Don't," Jordan said roughly, cutting her off. He gathered up the halter and whip and strode out of the barn, leaving Shae staring at the weathered wooden door as it slammed shut.

She'd planned for a lot of eventualities when they had their next confrontation. She hadn't planned on this.

JORDAN STALKED OFF, pissed beyond measure. He was so frigging stupid, pouring his gut out to Shae McArthur. Now Miranda would really have something to work with.

He left the horse in the field and walked into the round pen, heading to the far side, out of view of the barn where Shae was now saddling her horse. His breathing was shallow, uneven. What was happening to him? Yeah, the nightmares always left him shaken and irritable the next day, and not getting the prescription as planned had thrown him, but he'd never blown like this.

He leaned back against the lodge poles, folded

his arms over his midsection, the good one over the bad, tilting his head down to study the ground. He never used to lose it. He'd always held things inside. It'd worked for him. Even the deal with Miranda he'd kept to himself. The only time he'd let go had been during therapy, because he'd come to understand that the therapist had been telling the truth when he'd said some things didn't go away on their own. The guy'd been right. And after the group therapy had helped a little, he'd gone into special therapy involving eye movements and reliving the trauma. Shortly thereafter he'd weaned himself off the prazosin and discovered that the nightmares had stopped.

Not keeping it in had worked right up until a few months ago, when everything had gone to hell again. No dreams—not until he'd hit the road back to Montana—but an overwhelming feeling of being trapped, yet not belonging anywhere. Of not being able to hang onto anything. Of emptiness. And he'd hated his useless job, sitting behind a desk, doing things a chimp could do. A made-up job for a guy who wasn't quite whole. He'd come to resent it with everything in his being and that had exacerbated the emptiness.

Well, he didn't feel empty anymore, and maybe in a sick way he had his former stepmother to thank for that. Miranda had given him something to live for. His mouth twisted ironically as he felt the stubs of his left hand digging into his right upper arm.

So was it better to feel hate than emptiness?

He'd have to say yes to that. At least he felt somewhat alive now.

AFTER HER TRAIL RIDE, Shae drove to Missoula and spent the rest of the day in her apartment, far away from Jordan but still unable to concentrate. That damned conversation kept playing in her head, drawing her off task. She could understand him transferring his resentment of Miranda to her and had already figured something like that was behind the personal nature of his attacks. But that wasn't the part she was having trouble with. It was what had followed. His words about why he'd come back.

It had to do with survival. I was dying back there in Virginia. I had to get out...

Unguarded, pain-filled words, soon regretted.

And not even close to the picture Miranda was painting of a vengeful stepson coming back to harass her. Shae couldn't shake that thought. Something was off.

Don't get involved. Make your plan, gather your estimates.

Make a plan. So much easier said than done when her mind was elsewhere—which was what had gotten her in trouble with Miranda in the first place. Shae spent the rest of the day online researching tents, just in case she found that she wasn't able to use the existing buildings to the extent she wanted. She looked at wall tents, cook tents, shower tents.

Tents with wooden floors and half walls. All very expensive and not at all unique. And the entire time she was researching, she dealt with the two conflicting trains of thought. One was that she wanted this project on her résumé, wanted to slip back into her old job and not worry about bills or fending off her parents' rescue attempts. She wanted to pay back her parents and maybe prove to them—and Brant, and herself—that she'd progressed past the spoiled-princess phase of life.

The other train of thought was that she wanted to know more about what was going on in Jordan Bryan's life…and why he and Miranda had it in for each other. As Miranda's employee, she had no business looking into such matters, but after Jordan's explosive words that day, she felt as if she had to know more before continuing with the project.

Shae printed the last of several tent price sheets and set it on top of the stack, then leaned her elbows on the table and stared blindly at the computer screen until it clicked into power-save mode. How was she to proceed?

JORDAN WAS IN the round pen working the five-year-old mare when Shae drove in. The horse had for all intents and purposes been ruined and it was his job to undo the damage Claiborne's son's girlfriend had done. A little knowledge was indeed a dangerous thing. Pal, as Jordan had started to call the palomino, was headstrong and had learned that by pushing hard enough, she could get her way. Kind of like Shae, who thankfully had spent the night in town and therefore didn't hear him when he woke up shouting.

Jordan stopped the mare and attempted to mount. Although she was saddle-broke, it had taken most of the session for Jordan to mount the animal without her walking away the second his foot left the ground. By the time the session was over, he was exhausted from stepping back onto the ground and sending the horse around the round pen at a canter, then stopping her and attempting to mount again. After half an hour, she had begun to take him seriously, but even then her attitude was less than respectful.

Jordan eventually quit a winner and was on his way to the house when he noticed that the porch light was on. Shae must have taken his suggestion and paid the electrical deposit. He had not intended for her to do that. In fact, he'd intended to keep the electricity off for as long as possible.

So much for that inconvenience.

He'd heard banging noises in the bunkhouse when he'd gone by, but hadn't bothered to look in and see what she was up to. Because he was tired? Or because he was still self-conscious about their last encounter?

Or was she wearing him down? Was he ready to accept the inevitable?

No. He walked into the house, blocking the pig,

who'd finally figured out the stairs, with his leg so that Clyde could slip inside, then snapped off the porch light. It occurred to him that he could probably check out the indoor plumbing in the house now that the pump had juice, but he decided a cold swim was a better idea. Nothing like dunking under frigid water to knock aside all thoughts of a frustrating, long-legged intruder to whom he'd said too much.

JORDAN'S TRIP TO town that afternoon went without incident. He picked up the prescription and a few plumbing parts to fix the valve in the toilet he didn't know leaked until Shae had turned on the power. Did he feel bad about having a real bathroom while she still had to make do with the outhouse? No.

He got home in plenty of time to put his hours in on the palomino. Patience was the name of the game and Jordan had learned some hard lessons about patience in the hospital, which helped as he wondered just how many times he was going to have to go over the same lesson with the mare. Or if it was even worth it. But whether he thought the horse was worth a rat's ass was beside the point—he was being paid to do a job. He'd be honest with Claiborne about the horse's potential—that she couldn't be trusted and he'd think twice about using her as a broodmare—but he was going to damned well do the best he could during his sixty-day stint.

The one positive was his sense of satisfaction after each training session—a feeling he'd never

gotten with the government job. He was putting his
talents to work, accomplishing something and while
he was training he almost felt a sense of peace.
The instant he left the round pen and saw Shae, or
evidence that she was there, working to change his
place, the stress came barreling back.

After twenty minutes of ground work, Jordan
mounted and started the tedious process of asking
the stubborn horse to give her head, putting pressure on one rein until she moved her nose in the
right direction, then letting up. And invariably, the
palomino would try to take control, jab her nose up
into the air and lean away from the pressure, losing
her balance and stepping sideways to catch herself.
And then Jordan would start again. A little pressure
followed by a release.

Finally the palomino gave in both directions and
Jordan was about to dismount when the horse ex-
ploded. The next thing Jordan knew, he was on the
ground, lying in the mud created by the previous
night's rain, covering his head as hooves flew by.
He scrambled to his feet once he was clear of the
horse, then picked up his carrot stick and started
the horse moving, ignoring the mud and dirt that
covered his side and back. He kept the horse moving until they were both exhausted—him mentally,
the horse physically—then he got back on, his heart
hammering. He didn't want to take another fall,
didn't know how his recently healed bones would
take it. But he had to follow through. The palomino

tightened her muscles, then when Jordan relaxed, she relaxed. Slowly Jordan put pressure on the reins and slowly the mare responded. First right, then left.

Good enough. Jordan dismounted and unsaddled the horse. He brushed her down and released her. He was still covered with mud. It flaked off his shirt and jeans and was caked onto his arms and face. Jordan slapped his hat on his leg, knocking the dirt off, then started for the spring-fed pasture trough, peeling off his shirt as he went. Even sore and covered with mud, he felt better than he had sitting behind his desk in Virginia.

SHAE HADN'T MEANT TO SPY. She'd heard the commotion in the corrals and Clyde's distressed yaps on the way back from the meadows, but by the time she'd gotten to a vantage point, Jordan was on his feet, covered with dirt and once again working the horse.

He'd obviously just been dumped and Shae was certain he planned to get on the horse again before the session was over, so she settled herself in the tall grass, out of sight unless he happened to be looking for her, and waited until he finished. Yes, she could have gone to the corral to see if he was all right, but he obviously was, and she didn't want to embarrass him—which was strange, because she'd never before thought much about embarrassing people. Maybe because until recently she'd never been easily embarrassed herself—right up until her near-miss wedding. That was when the concept of deep embarrassment had become very, very real.

Finally, Jordan released the horse and Shae shifted position, intent on slipping away unseen once his back was turned, but she froze when he turned and began to peel off his shirt as he walked to the water trough not that far away from where she was sitting.

Oh. Man.

She needed to turn away, sneak back out the way she'd come, but she couldn't seem to pull her gaze away from the patchwork skin of his back. The burns spread up from his arm, red and ugly, across his back, up the side of his face, puckering and twisting the skin. He leaned over the brimming trough, cupped his hands and brought water up to scrub his face. Once, then twice. Then his arms and chest. When he was done, he dunked his head, then shook the water off his hair before reaching for the shirt he'd hung over the railing. Any moment he was going look up and spot her.

Then what?

She'd apologize, that's what, but it'd be much better if he never knew she was watching, so she kept stone-still.

A second later, he started patting his injured arm dry with the shirt, then stopped, keeping his eyes down as if listening. Shae held her breath, silently letting it back out again when he continued drying himself. He turned around and pulled his damp

shirt on as Shae quietly made her way back to the
trail, then disappeared toward the meadow.

ONCE SHAE HAD DISAPPEARED, Jordan leaned on the
edge of the trough, head down. He hoped she'd enjoyed the show. He'd planned on grossing her out
with his burns from day one, so why did he feel so
damned unsettled now? As if her judgment mattered?

How long had she been there, sitting in the tall
grass, watching him?

Why hadn't she said something?

Let it go.

But he couldn't. He hated being spied on, hated
thinking that he wasn't free to do anything on
his own property without being gawked at. It'd
be worse once the "guests" came. He could only
imagine the spectacular hell his life would be then.

Miranda was winning. He felt his hold on the
place slipping away, so when Shae came back down
the trail almost half an hour later, he was waiting
for her at the corner of the barn.

"You should have said something," he said in a
deadly voice, feeling less satisfaction than he'd expected when the skin over her cheekbones colored.
"Why didn't you?"

"I didn't want to embarrass you."

"In the future, embarrass me, okay? I prefer it to
being spied on."

"I stayed in case you got dumped again," she

said, tilting her chin at him in a challenging way. "And I didn't say anything because I figured if I did say something, you'd go all macho and send me on my way, then the horse would stomp you into the ground again and no one would be the wiser, except for Clyde the Wonder Dog."

Shae pushed past him then, but Jordan reached out and took hold of her shoulder, stopping her. Her gaze jerked down to where he was touching her and Jordan instantly released his grip. "Did you think it was my bad hand?" he asked.

"I was thinking you had no right to touch me, period."

Jordan felt his expression shift from self-righteous to chagrined as her words sank in and then he stepped back, shaking his head. "You're right," he said, shoving his good hand in his back pocket. "You're right."

"You *know* what I meant."

"And I agree." He looked past her. "Totally agree." He met her eyes briefly, pressed his lips together tightly for a moment. "I was out of line."

"Yeah. We both were." She gave him a look, then brushed by him and headed toward the house, leaving Jordan wondering just what the hell was going on. With him. With her.

With everything.

CHAPTER NINE

JORDAN'S PAINED EXPRESSION when she'd made it clear she didn't want to be touched stayed with Shae. He'd totally misinterpreted what she'd meant and that bothered her. Not because he'd thought she was grossed out by his hand, but because it showed the direction of his thoughts. He thought *he* grossed people out.

He probably did, to a degree. A rotten thought, but true. Shae could still recall her stomach tightening in a sickening way the first time she'd seen him a few weeks ago. And she remembered staring. She'd stared openly, trying to equate the Jordan Bryan who was standing before her with the physically perfect guy she remembered. How had he taken it? Had he assumed she was studying him like a freak in a sideshow?

That hadn't been her intention, even though she'd been openly stunned. She'd been trying to process and for that she'd needed information, so…she'd stared.

Damn it, Shae. Get a clue.

How would she feel if she had an injured face and people stared openly at it?

She wouldn't like it one bit. She and Jordan might not be each other's favorite people, but she hadn't intended to hurt him. And the odd truth was that his injuries didn't bother her so much anymore. Not in the way he thought they did, anyway. When she'd seen his back today, sympathy had been her chief emotion. That and perhaps a touch of empathy, which no one seemed to think her capable of. The pain he'd gone through had to have been tremendous...and now here she was adding to it.

Something to think about, but she knew that even if she gave up this contract, Miranda would bring someone else in. Someone who wasn't beginning to feel a growing concern about Jordan's well-being.

It was well after midnight when Shae finally dozed off, only to be brought bolt upright in her makeshift bed in the truck by an anguished yell followed by a silence so heavy that for a moment she thought that she'd dreamed it.

Ears straining, Shae sat perfectly still. No noise other than the brush of the pine boughs against one another in the night breeze. But she hadn't imagined the yell. Jordan had cried out.

Shae forced herself to get out of the truck, the damp grass uncomfortable on her bare legs. Silently she pulled her pants on and then slipped her feet into her shoes. She approached the house, which now had one light burning in the room that had to be his bedroom. The window was open so she called out.

"Jordan…?" There was no answer, so she called again, more loudly. "Jordan! Answer me."

"What?" His voice was thick and raspy.

"Are you all right?"

"Yeah. Fine."

"For real?"

"Leave it alone, Shae."

"Fine. Whatever," she called back. "Scare the crap out of me and then tell me to leave it. I don't care. Just part of the package." She stalked back to the truck and got inside, pulling her wet shoes off on her sleeping bag, heedless of the wet grass and soil sticking to them.

But once she was back in her sleeping bag, she lay awake, listening. The night remained silent except for the pine boughs and occasional night noise, but she couldn't sleep. Jordan must have had one hell of a nightmare, but wouldn't allow himself any comfort—at least not from her. That she understood. What she didn't understand was her need to offer that comfort.

Since when had she been the comforting kind?

JORDAN WORKED THE buckskin early the next morning, then took her out for a long ride along the same trail he and Clyde had hiked the previous evening, prior to the nightmare. It seemed like a decent plan since he was awake before dawn, unable to go back to sleep. And it wasn't the nightmare that kept his

184 ALL FOR A COWBOY

mind revved—it was the fact that Shae had heard him and come to check on him.

That he couldn't deal with.

The buckskin sensed his tension and mirrored it, dancing unnecessarily as she made her way down the trail, spooking at objects she'd walked by the day before with no concern. Jordan made a concerted effort to relax and the horse relaxed, too, but finally he called it quits and headed home. Maybe if he pulled the shades, he could sleep this morning, make up for the sleepless night. But he'd damn well close the window...or better yet, maybe Shae would go back to town. She'd never stayed for more than two nights in a row, so it was time.

When he got back to the ranch, Shae was waiting for him at the corral, where she was grooming her mare, and he quickly deduced from the way she was brushing the horse with quick deliberate flicks and not looking at him that she was deep in thought. It didn't take much to figure what she was thinking about. She kindly waited until he had unsaddled and brushed down the buckskin before she approached and stood behind him, waiting for him to acknowledge her.

Leave it. Don't ask me to talk.

Too much to ask for, of course.

"What happened last night?"

What if he just told her? What if he simply said, "I have nightmares. I can't control them"?

Yeah. What if he did that?

He couldn't face feeling that vulnerable. Not around someone who had the power to hurt him. And he wouldn't risk Miranda finding out. Hell, she'd probably try to get him kicked off the property as a danger to paying clients. He wouldn't put anything past her.

Shae leaned against the edge of a stall, watching as he untied the buckskin. "You have nightmares."

"What of it?"

She shrugged one shoulder. "Understandable." A humorless half smile curved one side of her mouth. "You mentioned going to hell. I imagine that sticks with a guy."

For a moment he couldn't come up with an answer. Finally he said, "It does," and walked by her, leading the buckskin, hoping it was the end of the conversation. But it wasn't. Shae followed him to the gate.

"You don't need to feel self-conscious about it... I understand." She hesitated for a split second before saying, "I used to have nightmares, too."

"Somehow I don't think it's the same, Shae," he said bitingly.

Her face instantly blanked out. "No. Of course not," she said in a way that made him feel like a jerk because, well, hell, she'd been trying to make nice and he'd hurt her feelings. A month ago he would have said that wasn't possible, but here she was looking as if he'd just slapped her. "I'm going to Missoula this evening. I won't be back tonight."

She gave him a falsely bright smile. "Lucky you. You have the place to yourself." Then she turned and started toward the bunkhouse.

"Shae." He called her name before he could stop himself. She turned back, frowning, giving him a fleeting impression of vulnerability before she brushed the windblown hair out of her face and politely arched her eyebrows. It'd never occurred to him that Shae was at all vulnerable…not until a few minutes ago when she'd tried to connect and he'd slapped her down.

"Thank you for your concern," he said, "but nothing happened last night."

"Yeah. Got it. Nothing happened."

And with that she walked away, stopping to reach down and scratch Miss Piggy's head before she continued on to her truck, leaving Jordan feeling like even more of a jerk than before.

MIRANDA CALLED TO cancel their evening meeting just as Shae hit the Missoula city limits, so she called her parents and invited herself to Sunday dinner, the first they'd had as a family since the wedding had been canceled.

"Are you enjoying the chicken?" Vivian asked cheerfully several minutes into the oddly silent meal. She was always cheerful with Shae—more so even than with Liv, her own daughter. Cheerful, accommodating, eager to help. Whatever Shae wanted, Vivian helped her get. And Shae hadn't been shy about asking for stuff. But the upbeat tone was forced today.

"Excellent as always," Shae said, making an effort to dig in and do the meal justice.

"And are you okay?" Vivian asked tentatively a few minutes later.

Was she? No. But not for the reasons her parents probably assumed. Issues she'd never given much thought to were shoving themselves to the front of her mind…such as the effect she had on other people's lives. People like Jordan, and her parents. How much of a strain had she obliviously put on their resources over the years? She couldn't begin to tally all the ways they'd helped her out financially—particularly during the wedding planning. But Vivian was looking at her expectantly, waiting for an answer.

"I'm making headway on my contract," she said honestly.

"How's Jordan Bryan handling the matter?" her father asked in a tone that told her that this had already been a topic of conversation in the McArthur home.

"He's quiet and keeps to himself. Just like he always did." *And he has nightmares.* The thought of him reliving whatever had happened to him over and over again disturbed her.

"So he's okay with this?" her father asked.

Shae could hedge, but she couldn't flat-out lie.

"Not exactly, but Miranda holds the rights of operation and so he doesn't have a lot of choice."

"He's not belligerent or anything, is he?" Vivian asked in an uncharacteristically brusque tone.

"No," Shae said on a note of surprise. "I couldn't say he's warm and welcoming, but he does his thing and I do mine."

Her father sent Vivian an I-told-you-so look and her stepmother rolled her eyes. "There's nothing wrong with being concerned," she said to her husband, then turned to Shae. "I was in the Northtown Pharmacy the other day when he came in and let me tell you…he looked wild."

"Wild?" Shae asked.

"Yes," Vivian said carefully putting her fork down next to her plate. "I was startled by the scars, of course, but that wasn't what concerned me most. He looked like he was going to lose control as he spoke to the pharmacist. I understand that he's been through an ordeal, but sometimes things like that affect people permanently. And you're up there *working* with him."

"Around him," Shae correctly absently.

"What?" Vivian asked with a perplexed expression before Shae's father reached out to run a hand over her shoulder in a reassuring gesture.

Shae considered her words carefully before she said, "I think Jordan may not put his best face forward in public right now, but when we're alone…"
What? The tension ran high, but she didn't feel

threatened? She was starting to notice things about him she hadn't noticed before? He had her thinking about him more than she wanted? "...he's fine. I think you're right about him dealing with issues from his injuries, but—" she lifted one shoulder "—he's fine," she concluded lamely.

Vivian did not look convinced, but her father seemed confident in her abilities to handle the matter, probably just as she'd handled every other obstacle in her life—by putting her head down and plowing through it.

"Hey, did you hear about how well Brant did last weekend?" her father said, shifting the subject in a none-too-subtle way.

"Tonight, as a matter of fact," Shae said with a smile, grateful to not be discussing Jordan any longer. "But I haven't heard from Liv lately." Which wasn't surprising. They'd never been all that close and she'd put her stepsister through the wringer during the wedding planning process.

Again Vivian and David exchanged glances, making Shae want to say, *Really, I'm doing okay now.* But she didn't, because it was still hard to talk about. Better to change the subject one more time.

"Hey, Dad," she finally said. "How about those Montana Grizzlies?"

Her father caught his wife's eye one more time at the mention of his favorite college football team, then took the bait, expounding on the team's chances during the upcoming season. Shae made all the proper responses as she ate and Vivian stared unhappily at her plate.

Family dinner was not what it used to be.

SHAE SWISHED THE mop across the last stretch of floor. The interior of the bunkhouse was probably cleaner than it'd been in several decades and Shae felt as though most of the dirt was now stuck to her damp skin. She brushed the hair off her forehead with the back of her hand as she leaned against the mop and surveyed her handiwork. She'd stored all the tools and boards and whatnot into two of the small rooms and closed the doors. The other ten doors were open, the rooms airing out. The only thing that still concerned her was mice. Shae simply couldn't handle sleeping with wildlife, so even though she'd yet to see a sign of them, it was the truck again for her.

She was supposed to go back to town tonight for a phone conference with Miranda, who was still on the other side of the state, but she had no intention of being home to take that call. Not until she'd had some time to think. Before she steamrolled over Jordan, refurbished cabins and buildings she might well have no legal right to refurbish, she wanted more information, like why she was beginning to wonder if Miranda was as much about harassing Jordan as she alleged he was about harassing her. Something wasn't right.

Shae picked up the bucket of filthy mop water

and carried it out the door, glancing around to see if she could spot Jordan. The palomino that'd dumped him a few days ago was back out in the field with her cronies, so that meant he could be anywhere. She emptied the water then glanced around as she let the hand with the bucket fall loosely to her side. No dog. Only the pig, snorking along the backyard fence.

Where was he?

The ponds, maybe?

She wanted to meet with him to settle a few things. To try once again to establish a middle ground—a plan where both he and Miranda could coexist, because the situation with him was eating at her. It floored her, but she felt guilty actively working against him. He didn't like her. Made no secret about that, but she couldn't stop herself from feeling as though she had no business adding to his private hell, whatever that might be. And that floored her even more.

How long had it been since she'd given a lot of *deep* thought to anyone's feelings? She'd thought about Reed's feelings, or at least she had until the wedding had taken over her life and she'd become oblivious to everything else and essentially written *finis* on their relationship. She couldn't fix that situation; she'd realized almost as soon as he'd broken it off that it was better if she didn't even try, but that hadn't kept her from mourning and hurting or the wedding bills from rolling in. She'd screwed up and was paying the price. She wasn't going to screw up again.

She needed to talk to Jordan.

Smoothing back her hair, she took a quick glance in the truck mirror. Who was the bare-faced brunette with the freckles scattered over her nose and the smudge of dirt on her cheek staring back at her?

She was the woman who was going to figure out a way for Miranda to have her ranch—because there was no way in hell she was giving it up—while causing Jordan the minimum amount of aggravation. Somehow. If he would talk to her about what he could accept and couldn't, then maybe they could find a way to compromise. But first she had to find him.

Shae wiped the smudge off her face, then headed for the house, where she coaxed the pig into the backyard and closed the gate before walking down the path to the ponds. No sign of Jordan, but the water looked so inviting after more than an hour spent washing filthy windows and mopping the bunkhouse. Impulsively she kicked her shoes off, wondering if it was as cold as she remembered.

A fish broke the surface on the far side of the pond, snapping up a bug as Shae curled her bare toes into the damp, silty sand. Another fish rose, tickling a memory, reminding her of how her dad had taken her and Brant fishing at similar ponds when their mom had still been alive and recovering from chemo. Shae had not been a fisherman, but she'd liked being by the water, sitting with her mom and watching Brant and her dad pull in sunfish. She smiled at the memory, the first time she'd smiled in a couple of days.

Shae stepped into the pond, her breath catching as the cold clear water swirled around her toes. She brought her hands up to her cheeks, felt the traces of grime, then took a breath and dived in, surfacing a second later and shaking the water out of her eyes as her toes touched the graveled bottom of the pond. The water was so cold that it was hard to breathe, but she was no longer covered with sweat and dust and as she waded back out, she realized that she felt better for having taken the impulsive plunge.

No towel. Bad planning on her part, but the day was warm and felt even warmer now that she was out of the icy water. She and Brant had played in the pond after fishing time ended, fully clothed, just as she was now, then stretched out on the grass to dry.

Family time.

She missed family time. After her mother had died, her father had gone out of his way to provide for her and Brant—not so much experiences such as fishing or picnicking or camping, but things. They'd gotten lots of things, and the opportunity to do whatever they wanted. They'd been spoiled rotten.

She wouldn't have believed it back then, but more camping, fishing and picnicking might have been good for her, good for the family.

And that was when Shae realized that she had a viable option for her much-needed plan B for the ranch.

Shae spent the next few hours first in the meadows, scouting locations, then sketching possible tent campsites on photo overlays. After that she searched the baseboards of the bunkhouse for possible cracks through which mice might get in. Tonight she was sleeping in the bunkhouse instead of in the mouse-proof truck. She'd seen no signs of mice after the initial cleanup and she couldn't expect guests to sleep there if she wouldn't.

Close to dark, about the time Shae was seriously beginning to worry, since his car was there and he was not, Jordan finally showed up, walking into the ranch along the trail leading to the mountains. Clyde lagged behind him with his tongue hanging out, his gait less dainty than usual. The pig rushed to meet them and Jordan said a few words to the animal before continuing to the house. He'd been hiking? Shae shrugged. Why not? It's what she expected her guests to pay to do.

WHEN SHAE GOT UP the next morning, Jordan was already working one of the horses—the small buckskin that he seemed to be making the most headway with—by the time she finished washing up at the pump. He put a couple hours a day on each of them, starting with groundwork and then getting into the saddle. From day one Shae had recognized that the buckskin was frightened, but wanted to trust. Well, Jordan had succeeded in bonding with the animal and now the filly was willing to depend on him to save her from whatever scary situation she found herself in. The lineback dun was not so trusting yet, but Shae had spent enough time watching Jordan and the horse to see signs of improvement. The older palomino was a strikingly beautiful animal that, in Shae's opinion, should go directly back where she came from. The animal was not to be trusted.

But Jordan kept working her, dodging trouble and working some more.

Stubborn man.

Shae worked on her notes and maps, filling in the details of plan B while tweaking plan A, as the stubborn man put in his hours on the buckskin, released the animal, and then, instead of catching the lineback dun, as was his habit, put away his gear and headed for the house, Clyde on his heels. Shae stepped back from the bunkhouse window, but he looked straight at her as he walked by, making her wonder if he knew how much time she spent watching him.

Too much time. But she couldn't get him out of her head.

It did appear, however, that he was avoiding her. Soon after going to the house, he and Clyde headed back down the mountain path again.

Catching up with Jordan was becoming a whole lot harder than she'd thought it would be.

Finally she ran him down in the late afternoon as he walked down the path from the ponds toward his house, damp hair brushed back from his forehead and a rolled-up towel beneath his arm. She couldn't help herself. She called his name and when he stopped, she jogged over to where he stood.

"You have running water, you know," she said once she caught her breath. She would have given just about anything for running water.

"I like swimming."

"That water's like ice."

"You've been to the ponds?" he asked.

"I've been everywhere," Shae said, her gaze traveling over his face and down his neck, where the angry scars showed. Was it her imagination or did he stiffen? "You know…" she said slowly, not wanting a replay of the horse-trough incident, "…when people look at your scars, they aren't necessarily being unkind. They just need to process."

Something flickered in his blue eyes and for a minute she thought he was going to say something, but in the end he just pressed his mouth more tightly shut.

"I have some ideas I want to run by you."

Instant suspicion flared in his eyes. "Why?"

"Because you need to know what's going on," she said. "Do you want to go to the bunkhouse, or can we talk in your place?"

"The bunkhouse," he said after a moment's pause. "Give me a few minutes. I have some things to take care of."

Shae paced the bunkhouse as she waited for Jordan, wondering if he was going to pull a power play and not show.

He'd show. He wanted to know what she planned to do, and sure enough, a few seconds later he opened the door.

THE BUNKHOUSE SMELLED of strong disinfectant. The ancient flooring had been scrubbed clean, the beaded-pine wall panels had been washed and ten of the small bedrooms had been emptied of their contents and cleaned. The two remaining doors were closed, which, Jordan imagined, was where he would find his tools.

Shae motioned him over to a small folding table, where she spread out an aerial photo of the meadow with small rectangles inked in.

She looked up at him, her expression serious. Gone was the bravado, the apparent confidence that everything she did was right, and if it wasn't, that she'd make it so.

"One of the plans I'm proposing to Miranda is that we use the bunkhouse only as a gathering place. A common area. Nothing else. I'm proposing that we invest in wall tents with wooden floors, which we'll set up in the meadow seasonally. I'm proposing changing the marketing focus from the one-percenter appeal—"

"One-percenter?"

"This was supposed to be a unique yet rugged experience. Only a few people at a time. Guided fishing trips, hunting trips. Everyone would share the bunkhouse. There'd been excellent food and good beds—which there still will be, even with the tents—but it'd be a very intimate experience and we would have charged top dollar."

"How intimate and rugged could it be with me living here? With a poodle and a potbellied pig."

Shae drew in a breath. "Exactly," she said in a more reasonable voice than he'd ever heard from her. His barriers started to go up. Why was she being reasonable? "So I'm suggesting more of a family camping experience."

"And is that supposed to make me feel better?"

"I thought it might be more palatable than a bunch of wannabe Jeremiah Johnson types swaggering around."

"These are your potential guests, Shae. Should you be talking about them that way?" he said snidely.

"Are you going to tell on me?" she asked, holding his gaze. As the seconds ticked silently by, Jordan became more and more aware of the fact that at that moment he was seeing a different Shae. A Shae he hadn't even known existed.

A Shae who made him feel decidedly uneasy.

"If we go with this option, I have no plans to renovate," Shae continued in a reasonable voice. "I'd like to update some things, but it's just cosmetic. And the camp will be in the meadow over the rise. Out of sight, so you'll have more privacy."

He frowned at her. "Why?"

"Why what?"

"Why the sudden concern for my privacy?"

For the first time in the conversation, Shae appeared evasive. "Because I thought it would be easier to make peace than to be at each other's throats, as awesomely fun as that is and all."

"You want to make peace."

"Yes."

He moistened his dry lips, then asked the question that had been nagging at him for the past few days. "Why is this project so important to you?"

"It's my one chance to get my job back," Shae said matter-of-factly, but he could see that it hadn't been easy to make that admission. And maybe that was why he decided to tell her the truth as he saw it.

"You won't get your job back."

Her eyes flashed to his. "How do you know?"

"Because Miranda is working you, like she works everyone. She's using you." He leaned on the table, bringing his face close to hers. "I'd say that the chances of you getting hired back on after completing this project are nil."

"I think you're wrong," she said.

He made a dismissive gesture. "You'll find out the hard way."

"No," she said, laying a polish-free hand with short utilitarian nails—a far cry from the fancy manicure she'd sported her first days on the ranch—down flat on the photo as she leaned toward him now. "I won't. I got fired because of a mistake I made. The fact that Miranda agreed to give me a second shot speaks volumes."

"What kind of mistake?" Jordan asked, his eyes narrowing as he realized that Shae was admitting to being less than perfect.

She met his gaze dead-on. "I don't want to talk about it," she said, carefully enunciating each word. She looked down at his scarred hand, then back at his face. "Some things are private."

He looked her straight in the eye as he said, "As long as we both remember that, all should be well."

AFTER JORDAN LEFT, Shae slowly rolled up the aerial photo, wishing Jordan had taken her peace offering as just that, rather than assuming she had an ulterior motive. For once in her life she didn't. She simply wanted to do the best job she could here at the ranch without making things worse for him, and she wanted to go back to work at her old job, matching people and ranch properties. If she got that job back, she'd treat it so damned seriously.

Shae leaned on the table for a moment, thinking about the times she'd spent most of the workday on the phone with caterers and florists. Yes, she'd done her work at home later on, but she could see now how disruptive it must have been to Mel and those around her.

Mel, whom she hadn't spoken to in weeks. Did her friend find that alarming or freeing?

Shae had to admit that she could understand if it was the latter.

She walked to the window, stared out into the growing twilight. The lights were on in the house.... *Thank you, Shae... I appreciate you turning on the electricity for me....* Except he didn't. He probably could have gone on indefinitely without electricity, swimming in the icy pond and visiting the illegal outhouse. He'd probably kept the power off as an inconvenience to her and here she was, living a more rugged lifestyle than he was.

And she still wasn't going home. Miranda was going to have to leave a voice message tonight, no doubt wondering why she'd missed their phone meeting. She'd come up with an excuse in the morning, but right now she wanted more time to figure out what was right, what was wrong...and walk that thin line that allowed her to get her job back without screwing Jordan over too badly.

CHAPTER TEN

JORDAN WAS A SURVIVOR—he might not be in top form, but he was a guy who didn't give up—and he didn't want Shae's help or concern. He'd made that more than clear and she needed to step back. But as she showered and dressed for her meeting with Miranda at the ranch in two hours, Shae found it next to impossible to stop thinking about how he'd said he'd come home because he was dying back east. He'd come home to a place where he felt safe. Where he could be alone to heal. And she and Miranda were keeping him from doing that.

If you don't work on the High Camp proposal, then someone else will.

And that person probably wouldn't care any more about Jordan's recovery than she had in the beginning. The best thing Shae could think of to do was push the same proposal to Miranda that she had to Jordan—a wall-tent camp, with a cook tent and shower trailer, which was easier to manage than a shower tent. The only option that left Jordan a modicum of privacy. Plus, it was the most cost-effective option, something that usually perked Miranda up. But not this time.

"A shower trailer?" Miranda said, her voice edged with distaste. "What happened to renovating the bathhouse? I spoke to Noel and he says we can repair anything that's already in place that we have access to, and the septic system counts as repair. As does refurbishing the bunkhouse."

"The plumbing and septic will be expensive."

"I think we'll make it back in no time. And these wall tents you're talking about—"

"Yes," Shae said quickly, passing Miranda a brochure across the desk. "As you can see, with wood floors and half walls, they're quite nice."

"And a dime a dozen in this part of the state." She tapped her forefinger on the desk impatiently. "I asked for rustic and unique."

No...that was my pitch to you.

"I thought this was supposed to be an exclusive experience," Miranda continued in a deadly voice. "One-percenters, I believe you said."

"Yes," Shae said, dragging the word out. "That was my initial intention."

"And that has changed why?"

Shae raised her eyebrows. "After spending time at the ranch, I realized that I needed to rethink my initial idea. I think we need to market more toward family camping excursions. There are some excellent ponds nearby where kids can fish—"

"We offer that at the Cedar Creek."

"But this is smaller, and the wall tents will make it more like an actual camping experience. Also, we have the gold mining in the area. I was thinking of some panning…"

Miranda rolled her eyes. "I want to use the bunkhouse, the bathhouse, the small cabins and the barn. I want this to be a remote *ranch* experience. Not a family campout." Miranda leaned back away from the desk, studying Shae with a deep frown. "Tell me how my stepson has influenced your thinking."

"Excuse me?" Shae said, wondering if she'd heard right.

"Jordan. How has he managed to affect your decision making?"

"He hasn't."

"You're staying on the ranch together. You must talk."

"Not much," Shae said. "He keeps to himself, works his horses and ignores me."

"Works his horses?"

"He has the right to keep livestock."

"Says who?" Miranda asked softly.

"His lawyer. Emery someone." Who Shae hoped was correct in his assertion.

Miranda's mouth tightened. "You and Jordan seemed to have had some lengthy legal discussions while you were not talking."

Shae fought to keep her frustration level from showing. "I hadn't realized the horses were an issue, but I should have said something. You asked me to work around him and that's exactly what I'm doing."

"Yes." Displeasure practically dripped from the single word, making Shae's throat go dry.

"Jordan keeps to himself. We don't talk."

"You know that he has issues," Miranda said softly. "From the accident."

"The occasional nightmare is understandable given the circumstances," Shae said, feeling the need to defend him.

"Are you afraid to be around him?"

"No," Shae said, shocked. "Not at all." She was slipping into trouble here and it was getting worse, so she went for the hard sell for the tent camp. "Here are just a couple more things to think about concerning the upscale wall-tent camp. You have the cost analysis there and if the tents don't work out, there is a resale market and you're in a prime position to take advantage of it. The only investments will be the tents and the cooking and shower facilities—all of which have a resale market and some of which can be rented. It honestly makes sense to dip our toes in the water using this strategy."

The silence was deafening. Shae slowly rose from where she'd leaned on the table to make her point and waited. Miranda tapped a short polished nail on the table a couple times, then shook her head.

"You are not accomplishing what I asked for."

"I'm delivering other options, as I always do when initially presenting a project."

"I'm not interested in other options. By the end of this week, I want detailed plans drawn up for the repair of each cabin. We will proceed with the original plan. We may not be able to knock out walls and build suites in the bunkhouse, but we can still use it. Adding appliances does not count as capital investments, since we can remove then when the time comes. Upgrading electrical—that's a repair."

"All right," Shae said. "I'll work up the rest of the costs."

"And you may as well start clearing out those cabins. We're using them."

Shae was beginning to get a sense of where Jordan was coming from. She'd never had issue with Miranda until she'd gotten fired, and the woman had a reputation as being tough but fair. Shae was beginning to wonder about the fair part. What on earth had happened between Miranda and Jordan to foster such mutual hatred?

She could only think of one thing and she had to admit she didn't like it.

Had they had an affair?

Not cool, but such a scenario would certainly account for the current drama.

"And sketches. I want sketches."

"Done," Shae said woodenly. Damn. She used to be able to fake things better than this.

"I plan to meet with Jordan, give him a rundown of what I can and cannot do, according to Noel."

And he'll no doubt say that you can go to hell.

Shae started gathering her materials, wondering how things had gone so wrong so fast. Damn

Miranda and her vendetta against Jordan. Apparently a tent camp set in a meadow wasn't disruptive enough to his lifestyle for her tastes.

And it ticked her off to be caught in the middle of a private war.

"I'm wondering," Miranda said, "if you need an assistant."

"What?" Shae asked, startled. "I'm handling the workload just fine."

"Another set of eyes."

A spy. Egad. She slowly fed the rolled map into the cardboard tube. "I don't need an assistant, although I appreciate the offer."

Miranda inclined her head. "Fine. When you see Jordan today, would you please tell him to contact me soon, or I'll have to pop on over to the High Camp and contact him."

Oh, yeah. He'd love that.

"I'll tell him," Shae said.

"And I'll be in touch with you later."

Dust was coming up from the round pen when Shae drove into the High Camp. The pig peeked its head out from around the house as she parked, then trotted over to greet her as she walked down to where Jordan was working the lineback dun, sitting deep in the saddle as he took the horse through a slow spin on her hindquarters. He looked over as she approached, his expression less than welcoming, then took the mare in a circle around the pen, stopping next to where she stood. Seemed she couldn't please anyone today.

"Don't worry, I'm not hanging around," she said. "I have a message from Miranda. She wants to talk to you."

"When hell freezes over."

"If you don't see her, then she's coming here."

"Fine. She can see me here."

Shae shrugged. The message was delivered, her job was done.

"Why?" She turned back, tilting her head at him. "Why does she want to see me?" he asked. The mare impatiently pawed the earth with a front foot and Jordan moved her forward a couple of steps.

"I don't know," Shae said truthfully. "Wish I did." With that she turned and headed to the bunkhouse, where she sank down on the cot she didn't use, resting her elbows on her knees. She'd put together such a decent package. Why was Miranda being so difficult about it?

Because Jordan was still on the ranch. That wasn't Shae's fault. He did own the place, after all, and she'd worked around him as ordered, but apparently that wasn't good enough. Shae closed her eyes, pressing her fingers into her temples. Footsteps sounded on the porch and Shae instantly jumped to her feet, not wanting to look as if she were teetering on the edge of depression, even if she was. Jordan knocked, then came inside.

"The meeting didn't go well?"

Shae studied her hands for a moment before saying, "There are a lot of variables to consider before Miranda can make a decision on which way to go here."

"She's only interested in going the way that will make me the most unhappy. If you want to sell your idea, just tell her that it'll make me miserable."

"I think she wants you to be more than miserable."

Jordan's eyes met hers with a startling intensity. "Are you going to help her?"

Shae didn't have an answer for that. She wanted this project to be a go and to have it on her résumé. And she wanted to have a steady paycheck. "I don't want you miserable," Shae finally said, "but I think there's room for compromise here. I just need some time to convince her."

"There's no middle ground. Not for her."

"I hope you're wrong," Shae said.

He simply shook his head. "I'm not."

JORDAN WALKED BACK to the round pen, where he'd left the buckskin tied, Clyde tagging along at his heels. It appeared that Shae finally understood that Miranda was out to cause him pain—and she didn't seem to be in favor. That surprised him...and also made him feel oddly unsettled, as if facts had suddenly shifted and he no longer knew what was true. Not that long ago he'd thought Shae and Miranda were soul mates, caring only about themselves and no one else. Now…now he wasn't so sure about that. There was more to Shae than he'd first assumed. Who would have guessed that she had a vulnerable side? Because if there was anyone he'd met that he would have pegged as bulletproof, it was Shae.

Yet she'd tried to connect with him concerning the nightmares and of course he hadn't let her because he felt too vulnerable in that regard. No heart-to-hearts there. And then she'd tried to make peace by making her proposed guest ranch more palatable to him. A lost cause, but she'd made an effort.

Okay…he'd concede that the jury was still out on Shae. But what about Miranda and her recent maneuverings?

Did he force her to come here? Or did he meet her on her turf?

Her turf, because then he could leave.

THE RECEPTIONIST IN the bolo tie and crisp white shirt was behind her desk when Jordan walked into what had at one time been his own living room, but the burly cowboy wasn't around. Miranda either had him on call or she'd decided that Jordan wasn't going to go off on her.

And he wasn't. He'd promised himself that.

"I'm here to see Miranda."

"Is she expecting you?"

"In a way."

It was obvious that the girl found his answer disturbing—perhaps something to do with the last time he'd visited, but she reached for the phone and punched in a number, keeping her eyes on Jordan the entire time. "Your stepson is here to see you… Yes…All right, I'll tell him." She hung up and fake smiled at Jordan. "You can go up."

"Lucky me," he said. The girl's mouth twisted as if she didn't comprehend his irony. "And don't call me her stepson, all right? The name is Jordan." He started for the stairs, feeling as though he was stepping into a trap-door spider's lair.

"Jordan, welcome." Miranda smiled broadly and waved him to a seat—the same one he'd sat in the last time she'd attempted to screw him over.

"Thank you," he said instead of *Cut the bullshit and get to the point.*

Miranda smiled slightly, then perched on the edge of her desk. "I'm going to get to the heart of the matter. I'd like to make an offer on the High Camp."

As he'd suspected. "We've already covered this territory."

"But I don't believe you thought I was serious about developing it." Jordan said nothing and Miranda went on. "I am very serious about operations there. The ranch will be receiving guests before the year is out."

Jordan still said nothing, but he kept his eyes on Miranda, doing his damnedest to keep his expression neutral, not to let her punch his buttons, which she was clearly expecting to do. It was how she always controlled him—trying to get him to lose it.

"I'm prepared to offer you an adequate price, which would allow you to buy elsewhere." Jordan tilted the injured side of his face toward her, watched her eyes slide away. "You may not find a place with as much acreage as the High Camp, but you'd have the solitude I know you crave." Miranda sucked in a breath. "Well?"

Jordan smiled a little, glad that she'd been the first to blink, because he was having one hell of a time hanging on to his temper. "Go screw yourself, Miranda." The exact same words he'd uttered when she'd tried to get him to screw her. And from the look on her face, she remembered. He got to his feet. "Anything else?"

"Sit down."

Jordan gave a short laugh. "I don't think so."

"I promise that you're going to be sorry if you stay on that ranch."

He wanted to answer her threat, but bit his tongue. Every word he said gave her a chance to find a point of weakness.

"I know this is difficult for you. I know that you have issues from the accident. Things you're still dealing with…nightmares and the like. I commiserate, but you can see where having someone with post-traumatic stress on the premises could be a liability and interfere with operations—which the lease contract specifically prohibits." The muscles in Jordan's face tightened and he swore he saw a brief glimmer of satisfaction in Miranda's pale green eyes. "I understand why you seek solitude, but you need to do that in a place where you can make a fresh start, Jordan. Not a place full of memories of a past you'll never see again. You need to move on so that you can heal."

Jordan started for the stairs. He'd had enough. He was at the brass chain barrier by the time she'd said the last word and instead of bending down to unlatch it, he put his foot on top of it and snapped the end off the wall.

"Violence," Miranda said softly from the top of the stairs, "never solved anything."

By the time he reached his car, his breath was coming in short huffs and his head was pounding. He jammed the key into the ignition and turned. The engine sputtered and for one hellish moment he thought the car was going to fail him, but then it came to life and he jerked the gearshift into Reverse.

She'd won again. Instead of doing the smart thing and telling her he'd think about it, he'd snapped. Not as badly as before, until he reached the stupid chain, but he'd snapped.

Issues from the accident. Nightmares.

There was only one way she could have known about those.

Shae. Shae had been discussing him with Miranda.

SHAE WAS WARMING soup on the hot plate she'd bought for the bunkhouse on her last trip to Missoula when she heard Jordan drive in. She turned off the burner and went to meet him, along with the pig and the poodle. But for once Jordan ignored the dog when he got out of the truck.

"What happened?" Shae asked as he closed the truck door harder than necessary.

Jordan turned angry eyes toward her. "What the hell do you think happened? She played the mental-health card. Next she'll be trying to prove me incompetent or something and take the ranch away from me."

"What?"

"'I know you still have issues from the accident,'" he mimicked, his expression so fierce that Shae started to move away from him before she realized what she was doing and stopped. "Nightmares, to be exact."

"I don't understand."

"Give me a break," he said. "How did Miranda happen to know about the nightmares?"

"I..." Shae stopped, realizing that she'd essentially told Miranda about the nightmares.

"You told her."

"Not maliciously."

"But you told her."

Yes, she had. And it was obvious that Jordan wasn't buying any excuses, so she did the only thing she could. "Guilty," she said softly.

"Why?" There was a note of pain beneath the anger. "Why couldn't you have just kept that one thing quiet? What the hell happened to all of your talk about finding the middle ground and making peace?"

"You aren't interested in a middle ground, Jordan, any more than she is."

"But you had to give her more ammo."

"There's no ammo in nightmares, Jordan. None. You're just sensitive about them because it's one more thing in your life that you can't control."

"So sayeth the queen of control."

"Meaning?" she asked coldly.

"Have you ever encountered anything you haven't been able to control, manipulate and turn your way? Has anyone ever told you *no* in your life and had it stick?"

"You mean like my fiancé telling me no, he didn't want to marry me, just before the invitations went out? You mean something like that?" Her eyes narrowed. "I'll admit that I've had my way more times than not, but you know what? It didn't do me any favors. So don't you dare start flinging judgments at me." She pulled herself up and said, "I didn't judge you."

"Not much, anyway."

"Not any more than you deserved."

"All right. I'm judgmental. I call things the way I see them. I can't apologize for that."

"Is that all?" Shae asked, ice dripping from her

voice even though she felt tears starting to sting the corners of her eyes.

He looked as if he wasn't through, as if he wanted to say more, but as Shae held his eyes, willing herself not to give in to the stupid tears, he finally said, "I'm done," before heading toward his house, the dog trotting behind him.

And once he was gone, the threat of tears seemed to have passed, too. Shae rubbed the back of her wrist under her eyes. She wasn't a crier by nature—never had been until Reed had broken off the wedding, and then she had discovered tears in a big way. She swallowed and walked back down to the bunkhouse, where her dinner was growing cold. Screw it. She yanked the pan off the burner and walked outside to dump it. Food seemed like a very bad idea with her stomach knotted up as it was. Then on second thought, she turned around and poured the lukewarm broth into a coffee mug. She hadn't eaten all day and had been ravenous before Jordan had come back.

Mechanically she sipped the soup, swallowing without tasting. She made it through half the mug before she set it aside.

Where did he come off judging her?

And why did it hurt so freaking much? He was just the guy living here. The guy making her job harder than it needed to be. The guy she was supposed to be easing off the property, according to Miranda.

He wasn't supposed to be the guy who made her feel something.

It had to be the result of too much going on in too short a time period. She'd spent more than a year centering her existence around a wedding that never happened, only to wake up to find her life a wreck because of everything she'd let slide. She'd always had difficulty with focus—as in she tended to ignore everything except what she was focused on—and trouble with knowing when to stop.

Well, things had stopped. Stopped and left her reeling.

Had anything *not* gone her way prior to the wedding cancellation?

Nothing major. She'd *always* gotten what she wanted and she'd wanted a lot. She asked, and received, and that had pushed people away.

Shae put a hand to her head and squeezed her forehead. It had pushed a lot of people away. She remembered once trying to tell Mel that she wished people didn't hate her for what she had and the uncomprehending blink she'd gotten in return—and this was from Mel, who was brilliant and understood everything.

She'd felt pretty damned alone after that conversation. Just as she felt pretty damned alone now. But this was her life and she was going to make it a success despite the roadblocks popping up. And Jordan could go to hell—or rather, back to hell.

THE EARLY-EVENING HIKE had become a sanity saver for Jordan, helping him fall asleep, though there was no guarantee against nightmares. He explored trails he hadn't been on since he was a kid, scouted out new places to take the horses. And he worked out frustrations. Many frustrations.

Clyde hadn't been too sure what to think of the wilderness the first few hikes, but after that he'd become an enthusiastic chaser of squirrels and chipmunks and anything else small that would run from him. He started venturing out far enough that Jordan had taken to tying neon flagging to his collar so that he could spot him more easily. But tonight Clyde seemed to sense that Jordan wasn't himself and stuck close to him, offering moral support—right up until the red squirrel scampered down a tree to sit on a rock close to the trail and chatter at the dog. Clyde instantly challenged the squirrel, which flipped its tail before scampering off across the rocks, and the chase was on.

Despite his foul mood, Jordan smiled a little as the poodle appeared, then disappeared, his whitish head popping up out of the brush as he followed the squirrel through the undergrowth and around the granite boulders, yipping excitedly. The squirrel would stop, taunt the dog, then scurry on. Jordan sat on a rock and waited for Clyde to exhaust himself.

The sun was getting low, but Jordan wasn't ready to go back. He was pissed at Shae, pissed at himself. Needless to say he was most pissed at Miranda, but she, at least, hadn't changed. Shae…he'd started to trust. To think that maybe his read on her had been wrong, and it was more than just his dick talking.

And it bugged him. He used to be pretty good at reading people, at looking through the layers, but now…now he had trouble looking through his own layers. Why wasn't he getting better?

Another squirrel ran across the trail close by and Jordan got to his feet, whistling for Clyde. He waited, then whistled again. All he heard was the chattering of the squirrel that had now climbed a tree and was scolding him from the branch just above his head.

"Clyde!"

The dog had never gone so far that he didn't instantly respond to Jordan's call.

Jordan started over the rocks in the direction Clyde had been running the last time he'd seen him. Now that he thought about it, he'd never let Clyde go this long without calling him back. Maybe the dog had figured he was good to go until he heard the signal to come back.

Jordan called again, then stopped to listen. Nothing.

Heart beating harder, he made his way through the brush and around the boulders. What if Clyde had run into a coyote or bear or wolf? He'd never forgive himself for taking a city dog out into the woods and letting him fall prey to—

A faint yapping caught his ear.

"Clyde?"

Again, the yapping, distant and hollow sounding. Jordan started climbing over the granite rubble, calling Clyde's name then stopping to listen. The barking grew louder, echoing off the rocks. Jordan stopped climbing, trying to home in on the direction the sound was coming from. It wasn't until he was almost on top of it that he saw where Clyde had fallen into a deep narrow crevice. Too deep for him to reach down into.

Jordan tried anyway, first lying on his belly and reaching down with his good hand in an attempt to snag Clyde's collar. He wasn't even close. He scrambled around and, getting as good a handhold as possible on one of the larger boulders at the edge of the opening, eased himself down as far as he could fit, reaching for Clyde again with his injured hand. He was still a good ten inches shy.

Jordan let his forehead rest against the rock. He couldn't leave the dog there, yipping and yapping alone, ringing the dinner bell for some hungry predator. And, other than spending the night out there, keeping his eyes on his dog, he could think of only one solution.

SHAE DECIDED THAT as long as things were in limbo, she had no reason to stay at the ranch, making both herself and Jordan crazy. Okay, she didn't mind driving Jordan crazy, especially after his verbal attack, but she was drawing the line at herself. When she'd proposed this project, her only goal had been to save herself professionally. She hadn't counted on getting sucked into this family mess and she hadn't planned on doing battle with a guy who had no qualms about openly insulting her to her face.

The battle wasn't over, but she could at least retreat for a bit, enjoy a hot bath, a dinner out. Call Mel and see how she was doing.

No. Scratch that. If she called Mel, then she'd have to say how *she* was doing, and she didn't have a ready answer for that.

After packing her dirty laundry in one of the duffels, she grabbed her purse, snapped off the lights and headed for Killer. She'd just opened the truck door when she heard Jordan call her name. He came jogging toward her from the direction of the barn.

"I need your help." Shae shoved her duffel into the truck without answering. "Clyde fell into a crevice."

The note of desperation in his voice stopped her from climbing into the truck. Slowly she turned back to face him.

"I can't reach him," Jordan said in a taut voice. "He won't stop yapping. I don't want him to be dinner to a bobcat or something."

Shae let out a breath. "Where is he?"

Jordan apparently sensed that the less said the

better and gestured toward the trail leading to the meadow. Shae gave a solemn nod and reached under the truck seat to pull out a flashlight, which she held out to Jordan. He took it, his mouth twisting slightly as he did so.

Humble pie ain't no fun, is it?

He headed off down the trail past the barn, walking so fast that Shae had to jog to keep up with him. She might be pissed at him, but she didn't want anything to happen to his dog. By the time Jordan turned off the path to start climbing through the boulders and rocks that had once been part of an ancient landslide, Shae was winded, but she sucked it up and followed Jordan up the mountain. The flashlight bobbed up and down and Jordan climbed.

"Clyde!" Jordan yelled and a sharp yap followed.

"He's down there a ways," Shae said joining Jordan at the edge of the crevice. The dog was at least six feet below them.

"I couldn't come up with a way to reach him," Jordan said. "I can't climb like I used to be able to, and the rock gets too narrow."

"Yeah," Shae said. "If I squeeze down there, I might be able to grab him." She swung her legs over the edge and started easing herself down into the crack, wedging her feet against the opposite sides. She slipped and was startled by an ironlike grip on her wrist.

"Thanks," she said without looking at him as she regained her footing and started working her way down until she reached a point where she could wedge herself into a crouching position and lean down. Her fingers brushed curly fur. "Come on, you little mutt," she murmured. "Here, Clyde. Nice Clyde."

The dog stood on his hind feet and licked Shae's hand. She let out a breath and reached lower. Her shoulders scraped against the rock as her thighs started to shake from the effort of bracing herself. She stabbed her hand down, once again touched fur, stabbed again and caught his collar with one finger. "Hold…still…" She managed to lift the little dog just enough to slip another finger, then another, under the web collar.

Slowly she worked herself back up to a crouching position, her shoulders rubbing painfully against the rough granite, pulling the squirming dog up into her lap as she collapsed back against the slab behind her. Clyde jumped to his feet as Jordan reached down with his good hand to take the dog from her.

Shae started climbing back to the top, taking hold of Jordan's wrist and allowing him to pull her up over the edge. "Thank you," he said once she was on her feet. Clyde was leaping up and down at Jordan's side and he reached down to scoop him up. The poodle licked his face joyously and Jordan smiled as he ruffled the dog's fur. "No more squirrel chasing for you," he muttered, holding the dog close for a moment. He met Shae's eyes after he put Clyde back down on the ground.

"Maybe you should carry him to avoid, you know…" Shae gestured toward the crack.

Jordan picked the dog up again and held him under his arm. "Are you all right?" he asked, shining the light so he could see her face.

"Fine," she said. "I need to get to town."

Jordan stepped back and she started climbing back down toward the trail. Jordan followed, moving more slowly as he maneuvered around the rocks while holding Clyde. Once she reached the trail, Shae didn't slow down to wait for him or the light. She wanted to get out of there. Away from Jordan, away from the way he made her feel.

"Shae!"

She didn't slow down. She'd helped him out, done her duty. She was out of there. Apparently he didn't get the memo, because he jogged until he caught up with her, the poodle still under one arm.

"Wait."

Rolling her eyes, Shae slowed, then as he caught up with her, she stopped and turned. Once she was no longer moving, he seemed uncertain. Well, so was she. "I'm glad I could help. I like your dog. But I have to get to town."

"Tonight?"

"Yeah. Tonight."

"It'll be late when you get there."

"I have things to do in the morning."

They started walking and Shae couldn't remember another time when she'd been so very conscious of a man she wasn't touching.

"I said some things today—"

"That you meant at the time and you don't mean now because I helped rescue your dog." She didn't want to get into this now, not when she was so aware of him. Not when she could still feel what his grip had felt like on her wrist, or how solid his chest had felt when he'd helped her off the rock. "Understood."

"Shae."

She didn't slow down. She covered the last yards to the truck in silence.

"You're bleeding," Jordan said when she jerked the truck door open, moving to where he could see the back of her white T-shirt by the truck's interior light.

"That's just lichen and moss," she said looking over her shoulder at the dark stains on her shirt, although now that she saw it, she had to admit it hurt.

"And blood. Come on," Jordan said, gesturing toward the house with his head. "Let me at least help you clean up. That's a hard area to reach."

Shae pulled in a shallow breath and willed herself to resist this temptation, but the pulsing awareness between them made her feel as if she couldn't move. Couldn't move, couldn't think straight.

She *had* to move. To get out of there.

"I'll take care of the blood when I get back to

my apartment." She brushed past him to get into the truck.

"Will you be back tomorrow?" he said, taking a step back but keeping his hand on the door as he waited for her answer.

"Of course," she said in a voice that didn't come close to echoing the wild thoughts that were swirling through her head. "But we're going back to the way things were. You working your horses and me making plans to ruin your life."

"Thanks for helping me with Clyde," he said, ignoring her dig.

"What else could I do?"

"You could have said no."

She let out a breath, shook her head. "I shouldn't have told Miranda about your nightmares," she said, surprising the hell out of herself. "I need to go."

Before they traveled any further down this road. Before she said, *yes, take care of the scrapes on my back. Just let me just take my shirt off....*

Jordan stepped away from the truck. She closed the door, started the engine and snapped on the headlights, the beams cutting the darkness. Jordan stood off to the side with Clyde while she swung the truck in a circle and then slowly started up the drive, wondering why she felt as if she'd just made one hell of a mistake.

What *would* it feel like to be touched by Jordan Bryan in a caring way?

CHAPTER ELEVEN

JORDAN DIDN'T HAVE a nightmare, but he didn't sleep, either. Yesterday he'd let his hatred for Miranda spill over and poison yet another part of his life. He'd verbally attacked Shae, instantly assumed that she'd maliciously reported his nightmares to Miranda. Frigging Miranda had probably worked it out of her.

Or so he hoped. He was startled by how badly he didn't want Shae to have discussed his nightmare with Miranda.

He owed her for Clyde. And more than that, while they'd been arguing at the truck last night, he'd wanted to touch her. To take her into the house, treat the scrapes she'd gotten helping him. To put his lips on her skin, make it better. The thought rocked him and ruined him.

Jordan lingered over coffee instead of heading directly to the round pen—coffee made on Shae's hot plate since his ancient stove had chosen that morning to give up the ghost. It was about twice as old as he was, bought new by his grandmother, so it was time. Just not a convenient time. He'd deliver

the fillies back to Claiborne in a few weeks, and
he'd hoped to use his paycheck for something other
than a stove.

He saw the rooster trail of dust come up over
the rise before he heard Shae's truck and got to
his feet, his pulse rate bumping up as he set down
his cup. The pig poked her nose through the front-
yard fence and Jordan pulled the gate shut as he
walked through, shutting both her and Clyde inside. Clyde gave a yip, but Jordan didn't slow down
as he headed for where she'd parked next to the
bunkhouse. He wanted to get this over with, and
he hoped that once he was face-to-face with Shae,
he'd figure out just what it was he wanted to say.

Shae pulled her backpack out of the passenger
seat as he approached, then stilled as she caught
sight of him. Her hair was clipped up and she wore
makeup, but he could see the lines of tension around
her eyes. She hadn't slept any better than he had.
Yesterday had been hard on her, too. She reached
out to swing the truck door closed, then stood where
she was, waiting for him to make the first move,
somehow sensing that it was his turn to do something…if only he knew what it was.

So what did he say now? *How* did he make the
peace?

He finally said, "You made some valid points
yesterday." Lame, but truthful. Robert Brown-
ing he wasn't. She nodded but said nothing in re-

sponse, which kind of left the ball in his court. "I just wanted to tell you," he added.

"Is that kind of like an apology?" she finally asked with a clip in her voice.

"Yeah. I wanted to…apologize…before you go to work for the day—"

"Destroying your ranch?" The words were sarcastic, her expression a mixture of anger and vulnerability.

This other side of Shae was getting to him in a way he hadn't expected—a way that wouldn't play out well for either of them, he ventured to guess. "Your words," he said.

"No. Yours. More than once."

"Guilty." He echoed what she'd said to him yesterday, hoped she took it the right way.

She looked down at the ground for a moment, her slim fingers lightly gripping the leather strap of her backpack, as if debating a course of action. When she looked up at him, her expression was once again candid. "I've been thinking things over. For most of the night, actually." Her lips tightened as she brushed her fingers under her eyes. "It shows, doesn't it?"

"You look good, Shae." He didn't know where that came from or why he said, but it was true.

Surprise crossed her features, and then she said, again with a touch of wariness, "Thank you."

It was nothing but the truth. She did always look good. But whereas she'd looked shellacked before, now she looked…real…as in real damned good. And it wasn't makeup or the lack of makeup or anything like that…it was deeper than that. She could gussy herself up and her hair could be perfect, like today, and he'd still see a different woman—the one who was now staring at him.

"What were you thinking about?" he asked.

"How much I dislike being in the middle of this… thing between you and Miranda." She adjusted the backpack's shoulder strap.

"If I could have gotten a job elsewhere in my field, I wouldn't be." She fingered the strap again. "Maybe I should have been more patient…and I might have been if there hadn't been other circumstances."

"What kind of circumstances?" he asked.

"Private ones," she said just before the sound of an engine brought their heads up. Jordan stepped back to where he could see the drive, a deep frown forming as he recognized a Cedar Creek Ranch truck.

Apparently he was about to fight another battle—this one on home turf. Shae came to stand beside him, close enough that their shoulders touched, sending an unexpected jolt of awareness shooting through him as the truck parked on the opposite side of the Subaru.

The door opened, but instead of Miranda, as he'd expected, a neatly dressed young woman wearing a white shirt and jeans got out, standing for a moment with her hands on her hips, surveying the place, apparently looking for signs of life.

Shae put a palm to her chest. "Gee," she said softly. "Too bad the pig isn't out.

"WHAT'S SHE DOING HERE?" Jordan asked. Shae found herself moving even closer to him, drawing strength from his proximity.

"Heaven only knows," Shae said, watching as Ashley, who hadn't yet spotted them, started for the house, then stopped dead at the gate when she caught sight of the pig. "But I'm not getting that good-news feeling." She shot him a quick glance, then with a fatalistic shake of her head, started toward the house.

"Ashley. Hi," she called. The expression on Ashley's face didn't help relieve any of her growing tension.

"Hello," the girl said cautiously, glancing at the pig, then back at Shae. "Sorry about the surprise arrival, but it's impossible to call, you know."

"Yes. Unfortunate."

"Miranda has sent me over to act as your assistant until the project is complete," Ashley announced in an I'm-the-new-teacher's-pet voice.

"She mentioned she might do that," Shae said, doing her best to play the game and look pleased to have help.

"Yes. This way Miranda will get nightly progress reports."

"Whoa," Shae said lightly. "That almost sounds like a threat."

"Excuse me?"

Shae curved her lips into an ironic smile. "A joke, Ashley. I was making a joke." Except that she hadn't been. If Miranda was sending an assistant for a job that didn't call for an assistant, then her career with Cedar Creek Enterprises was probably on very shaky ground. Why? Had Jordan said something to make Miranda think her loyalties were shifting? Had she? Was this a test to make certain she was a Jordan adversary?

"So," Ashley said brightly. "Do you want to bring me up to speed?"

"Certainly," Shae said, opening the gate and letting the pig out. Ashley froze as Miss Piggy sniffed at her pant leg, squinted up at her, then went about her business. "Let's go to the bunkhouse. I can show you the plans, then we can tour around."

Ashley glanced over her shoulder a couple times as they walked toward the bunkhouse. Shae thought about telling the girl that the pig didn't have teeth, but decided against it.

"First, let me explain the general plan and then we can get to work on the cabins." Shae wrinkled her nose at Ashley's shirt. "You probably shouldn't wear white here."

"Oh. Uh, yes," she said looking down at the pristine shirt. "I didn't know I was coming until a little while ago."

By the time they left the bunkhouse, Jordan was working the palomino in the round pen, cantering slow circles before he set out on his hour-long daily trail ride. Ashley stopped to watch him, her eyes narrowed thoughtfully.

"Does he bother you much?"

"I ignore him. Miranda said to work around him and that's what I do." Shae led the way to the cabins she'd put off tackling. If she had an assistant, why not take advantage of it?

"Where does Jordan keep his livestock?" Ashley asked, sounding as if she had a mental list of items to check off.

"The horses in the north pasture, the pig in the yard." Shae gestured for the woman to precede her into the cabin.

"Does he keep livestock in the barn?"

"The barn is leased to Miranda."

"So his horses have no shelter."

"Well," Shae said slowly. "They are horses, and it is summer."

"What about the horse that's in the barn corral now?"

"She's mine." Any doubts Shae had about whether or not Ashley was there to spy were now rapidly dissipating. "We need to clear enough stuff out of the cabins to get some accurate measurements, check for rodent infestations and water damage."

"The roof looks good," Ashley murmured.

"It's fairly new," Shae agreed. "Jordan's dad took care of the place." She pointed across the room. "We also have to measure all the windows—nothing is standard size in these cabins. They even vary a lot from one to the other. And doors. They'll probably have to be custom-made if we can't use the originals." Which would run into the pricier range—not that Miranda cared as she proceeded on her seek-and-destroy-Jordan mission. Shae walked over to the pile of dusty lumber sitting in the middle of the room. "Why don't you take that end and we can stack these boards outside one at a time."

Ashley, who'd obviously not planned to move lumber, gave Shae a dubious look.

"Would you like to borrow a shirt?" Shae asked.

"Uh...no." She bent down and gingerly took hold of the dusty board. Shae did the same and they awkwardly carried it outside the cabin. After setting it down, Shae led the way back in the cabin to move the next board.

"So, Ashley," Shae said as they walked, "what is your education? What prepares you to do this job?"

Ashley set down her end of the board, then attempted to brush dirt off her white shirt without rubbing it in, which was futile. "I have a two-year degree in resort management and now I'm studying prelaw."

"Your parents must be proud."

"Are you mocking me?" Ashley asked cautiously as they walked back into the building.

"Why would I mock you?" Shae asked on a note of surprise. *Other than to express my general distaste of someone sent here to spy on me.* She smiled at Ashley. "No. Really. I have a friend studying law. I know how intense it can be, especially in tandem with another job."

"Yes," Ashley said, somewhat mollified. "It can be. I don't plan on going to law school until I get some experience in the business world. I want to go into real-estate law."

"Then you only work for Miranda during the summers." Like three-fourths of her staff.

"Full-time during the summer, yes. I've been with the ranch for five summers now. I won the Cedar Creek Ranch scholarship."

So you're beholden to Miranda. How wonderful. "How long will you be here today?" Shae asked, pulling the tape measure off her belt.

"Until five or six."

"I'm going back to Missoula early this afternoon. I have an appointment with a contractor."

"I'll leave when you leave." She glanced over at the round pen, making it obvious that she didn't want to be left alone with Jordan. Miranda had done a number on the girl and Shae wasn't going to do anything to undo it, recognizing a lost cause. Ashley was probably hoping to move from part-time employment to full-time very soon. All she had to do was take over the High Camp.

Jordan worked his horses for about twice as long

as usual and Ashley kept a close eye on him all morning long, asking questions that Shae either answered, hedged on or flat-out lied about. She was not going to give this woman any more ammo than necessary.

Unfortunately, a small amount of ammo was necessary, otherwise Ashley would have reported to Miranda that Shae wasn't showing the proper amount of animosity toward Jordan.

"So it really doesn't bother you, being here alone with him?" Ashley asked after they'd finally finished measuring the cabin and were walking back to Ashley's truck.

"Should it?" Shae asked.

"Well, he does have post-traumatic stress disorder."

"Where did you hear that?"

"Miranda," Ashley said. "She told me to watch myself."

"Always wise when you don't know someone," Shae murmured.

"Do you know him?" Ashley asked.

Did she? Excellent question. She knew that he hurt in ways he didn't seem to be able to resolve. She knew he was at heart a decent man with some serious wounds. "We went to high school together. We weren't close," Shae said shortly.

Ashley drove away, leaving Shae standing in the driveway watching the dust settle. She tilted her head back and stared sightlessly up at the sky. Her job was slipping away from her. Miranda no longer trusted her. And she had a choice now: doing damage control and/or starting a new job hunt and hoping that Miranda hadn't poisoned Shae's professional reputation.

Jordan was still out on his last trail ride of the day and Shae wished he was back. Not because she would pour her guts out to him—she'd never been big on baring her soul, since it tended to clue people in to the fact that she did have worries, she wasn't quite perfect—but just because she needed some company.

Standoffish, self-contained Jordan for company. That was something.

But it worked for her.

She smiled a little as she rubbed the back of her dusty neck and started for the bunkhouse. Never in a thousand years would she have dreamed her thoughts would drift toward him on a regular basis. Not in the way they were drifting now, which had little to do with empathy and a lot to do with how very attractive he was.

Yet another unknown to figure out before she left this place.

JORDAN WAS SO damned glad to see that the Cedar Creek Ranch truck was gone when he rode the buckskin through the far pasture gate, but he didn't unsaddle his horse in the barn as usual, just in case the wench was still there. Instead he tied the dun to

the corral fence, took off the saddle and then lugged
the gear up to the house. Odd that he was thinking
of protecting Shae.

Shae, who was nowhere to be found. Not in the
bunkhouse, not in the barn. Not in the house, although he hadn't expected to find her in his domain.

The ponds?

Had she gone for a swim after her assistant left?
One of the cabin doors was open, the building airing out, and if she'd spent the day there, well, a
swim was in order. He smiled to himself as he
walked into the backyard, a can of iced tea in hand.
He liked the idea of her working her new assistant
in the dirtiest environment she had to deal with.
Nothing like jumping in with both feet on the first
day of a new job.

The pig was sitting in the backyard, staring down
the trail, confirming Jordan's suspicion of where
Shae had gone. He wouldn't have minded joining
her after a full day in the saddle—except that then
he'd have to bare everything that made him feel
self-conscious. Even he didn't like to look at his
injuries or to touch the odd-feeling skin that had
healed into thickened ridges in some places and
was overly smooth and shiny in others.

Shae could have her swim. He'd catch up to her
later. But that didn't mean he wasn't going to think
about her in his pond, soaking wet.

When Shae eventually came back down the path

239

toward the house, Jordan was sitting on his porch with Clyde. They had forgone the evening hike partially due to the previous night's adventure and partially because Jordan wanted to talk to Shae.

"How'd it go with your new assistant?" he asked.

She came over to the fence and he noticed that although there was a towel around her neck, her hair was dry.

"Just great," she said. "Can't wait to get subtly interrogated tomorrow. How was your day?"

He wanted to ask more about Ashley, but decided to go a different route. "I kind of enjoyed the extra time with the horses. The palomino is coming along."

"Finally."

He raised an eyebrow and she said, "I've been watching you." A beat of silence followed her announcement and then she clarified, "Not like a stalker."

He laughed and she smiled back. "Your hair is dry."

Shae lifted a handful and pretended to inspect it. "Yes. It is."

"Didn't you go to the pond to swim?"

"That was the plan."

"Didn't pan out?"

"That water is freaking cold," she said with a shudder. "I couldn't do it. If I didn't feel fairly certain that Ashley will soon be taking my place here, I'd buy a solar shower."

He didn't like the thought of Ashley taking Shae's place. Of battling it out all over again. But as long as Miranda was in the picture, that was how his life was going to be.

"You could go back to your place."

"I could, if I wanted to drive an hour and half home, then an hour and a half back tomorrow morning to deal with Ashley." She sent him a mock stern look. "Otherwise you get to deal with her."

"Use my shower," he said.

Shae's eyebrows lifted and held for a moment, as if she was trying to figure out whether or not he was serious, and then a wide smile wiped all signs of caution away. "Thank you. I've been itching from cabin dust all day."

"I only have one extra towel," he said. "But maybe I could talk you into doing laundry on your next trip to town."

"Or you can come to Missoula with me and do it yourself."

"I hate laundry." And he had a hard time picturing himself and Shae going anywhere.

"Me, too." Shae smiled again and Jordan felt himself warm inside. "Besides, I have a towel," she said, pulling it from around her neck. "So if you have the shower, I have everything else I need."

And he was beginning to wonder if she didn't have some of what he needed, too. It'd been a long,

long time since he'd felt anything close to light-hearted and, like working the horses, talking to Shae just now had made him feel a touch more like his old self.

JORDAN STAYED ON the porch while Shae showered in his old-fashioned bathroom. She could hear him outside the window she'd cracked open, occasionally murmuring something to the dog about being a good boy. What was his life like, living here along with just the animals for company? What would it have been like if she hadn't come up with her brilliant proposal at just the wrong time? Would Miranda still have sought him out, attempted to make his life miserable?

Shae ducked her head under the blessedly hot water. So much better than the pond. How on earth did Jordan swim there?

But maybe the cold water felt good on his damaged skin.

Would he go all silent if she asked him? He wasn't exactly open to questions, but things were changing between them. Was it too personal? Perhaps, but Shae wanted to know more. She'd ask later, because at the moment she didn't want to risk alienating the one person who had a glimmer of understanding as to what was happening here. So strange to think of Jordan as an ally.

Ashley showed up early the next morning, almost before Shae had finished rinsing her toothbrush at the old-fashioned pump. Jordan had offered her the use of his bathroom, but he'd done so with just enough hesitation that Shae wondered if he regretted letting her use his shower…or more likely that he regretted opening up to her.

He still didn't trust her. And why should he? She worked for Miranda. But he was attracted to her. She was pretty damned sure about that, and equally unsure about how to handle it.

Ashley was wearing brown today. Good thing, because Shae was looking forward to another industrious day in the cabins. If Miranda was hell-bent on repairing them, then Shae was going to work Ashley hard. She was beginning to feel a lot like Jordan, battling what was probably inevitable, but refusing to go down without a fight.

Pride had always been Shae's downfall and it was not an easy vice to part with.

"Good morning," Shae called when Ashley got out of the truck. She stayed right where she was, next to the pump, towel around her neck.

Ashley frowned as she came closer. "You're here early," she said, casting a long look at Jordan's house as if wondering if that was where Shae had spent the night.

"Yeah. I'm after that worm." Ashley's blank look told Shae what she'd started to suspect yesterday: irony was lost on the woman. "The early bird gets the worm?"

Another blank look and Shae finally shook her

head, albeit with a polite smile. "I slept in the bunkhouse. Just give me a second to grab my coffee and I'll be right with you. I hope we can get two cabins done today."

"Yes, about that...the dust affected my asthma yesterday."

"Then I can't see that I have a whole lot for you to do today. As my assistant, I mean. It doesn't make sense for Miranda to pay you to sit here and watch me."

"She wants me to stay and help."

And Shae was damned if she was going to clear out the cabin alone while Ashley watched.

"Here's the deal," she said matter-of-factly. "You're my assistant, so you either help me or you leave. That's that."

Ashley's mouth pursed for a moment, then she turned and walked back to her truck, started the engine and put it in reverse. Shae stood next to the pump, toothbrush still in hand, amazed that she'd gotten rid of her that easily.

"Whatever you said, say it to Miranda next time you see her," Jordan said from behind her. Shae turned to see him walking toward her from the porch, holding a cup of coffee. He gestured toward the rooster tail of dust. "Gone for good?"

"Off to tattle," Shae said, sticking her toothbrush in her shirt pocket as the brake lights of Ashley's truck came on briefly before she rounded the corner and disappeared from sight. The dust was still settling from where she'd first pulled out.

"Just what *did* you say to her?" Jordan asked as he came to a stop. Something seemed different in the way he looked at her. It took her a second to realize it was that he was looking at her…not through her, the way he did when he was angry.

Shae cleared her throat. "I just did what I always do when faced with conflict. I told her it was my way or the highway."

"How wise was that?" he asked.

"Very, very foolish," Shae said, holding his eyes, but very much wanting to look down. To his mouth, to be exact. That maddeningly firm mouth that she'd wanted to feel against her skin before he'd dumped her on her ass. The mouth that she'd then sworn would never get anywhere near her, even if he begged.

Shae was starting to think that never was too strict of a parameter.

She needed to come back to earth. Jordan might be loosening up toward her, but that was a long way from trusting her…or even kissing her.

Damn.

Shae looked away, toward the cabin. She'd had her way with a number of men, but Reed had been her one and only for over three years and toward the end, due to stress, things hadn't been the greatest.

She'd been dumped. She was lonely. Her confidence had taken a hit and it was time to get back in the saddle.

Yeah.

But when she cut a quick sideways glance toward Jordan, took in the scarred skin stretched over his cheekbone, she was hit by the realization that maybe it was more than being lonely. Or getting her confidence back.

Maybe it was Jordan.

SHAE SPENT THE day cleaning the cabins and Jordan had halfway considered helping her—but he couldn't bring himself to do anything that would ultimately benefit Miranda. The cabins were unique and not in too bad shape for enduring as many winters as they had, but they were so damned close to his house. Why would people pay money to stay in a setting that was basically in someone's backyard?

There was no accounting for taste. He'd been on the Cedar Creek enough times since Miranda's transformation of the place to know that vacationers didn't mind being close to a residence, but if he was paying that kind of money, he'd want the place all to himself.

He'd never been a people person. Shae, on the other hand, seemed perfectly at home with people. Probably because she had so many years of practice getting them to do what she wanted. It was as much confidence as manipulation: she believed they were going to do what she wanted, so they did.

But it had all caught up with her.

Midafternoon, just after Jordan had caught the palomino, Ashley's truck drove back in. Miranda might have the lease, but Ashley was parked on his part of the property and he was going to involve himself in this—if for no other reason than because she was bothering Shae. Jordan tied up the horse and headed for the house at the same time that Shae came out of the cabin, covered with dust. Jordan couldn't hear the words, but he could read the body language as he approached. Ashley was trying to assert authority and Shae was basically looking down her nose at her.

Way to go, Shae.

As he approached he heard her say, "So you're back, ready to help, now that I did the heavy lifting?"

In response, Ashley held out a piece of paper.

"A note?" Shae asked, unfolding it.

"The phones don't work here," Ashley said shortly.

Shae glanced over the paper, then back at Ashley. "Fine."

Jordan stopped a few feet away from the two, touched his hat mockingly when Ashley looked his way. "What's your business?" he asked.

"I'm assisting Shae."

"She seems to be doing a great job of messing up my life by herself. Why does she need you?"

"Because I need the experience," Ashley snapped, basically telling Jordan what was in the note.

"You will if you work for Miranda," Jordan said. He caught Shae's eye for a brief second, had no idea what he read there, then turned and headed back to the palomino.

CHAPTER TWELVE

THE DAY DIDN'T go well for either of them. Shae swallowed her resentment toward Ashley and, on the off chance that she could salvage herself professionally, after measuring the cabins and inspecting them, she showed Ashley some preliminary sketches she'd made of the interiors.

"We have to be careful about how much we do," she said. "Otherwise it leaves the realm of repair and becomes capital improvement."

"I'm familiar," Ashley said.

"That's right. Prelaw."

"And a long conversation with Mrs. Bryan," Ashley said with a touch of smugness.

Shae was about to reply when a commotion in the round pen brought her head around. She and Ashley turned in unison to see the palomino giving Jordan a serious test, head down, all four feet coming off the ground as she bucked hard.

Shae took a step forward, her hand pressed to her chest, then forced herself to stop. This was Jordan's forte. He rode broncs. And he rode this one until she finally gave a few final hops and then came to a jarring stop. He instantly moved her forward into a trot and kept her trotting around and around the pen and then in figure eights.

"Something has to be done about that," Ashley said once it was clear that the show was over. "He can't do this with guests around."

"I think people pay money to see things like that."

Ashley gave a small sniff. "It's dangerous."

"We don't control those corrals." Shae swore she heard Ashley mutter, "Yet," under her breath, but she ignored her, concentrating on getting her heart rate back to normal.

Twenty long minutes later Ashley got into her truck for the second time that day and headed back to the Cedar Creek Ranch to report to Miranda. Shae went down to the round pen, where Jordan lingered even though he'd released the palomino.

"Here to check on me?" he asked as she approached.

Shae shrugged. "I saw the mare test you."

"It turned out better than the last time." He leaned his arms on the fence, watching the mare, but Shae wondered if he even saw her. Everything about him read *stand back, keep your hands off* and she didn't think the mare was responsible.

"Well, you are a bronc rider," she said, leaning her arms on the fence beside him.

"Was."

"You looked good."

"Don't placate me, okay?"

"And don't take your frustrations out on me," Shae said, stepping away from the fence.

She was on the verge of leaving, letting him have his space so that he could feed his anger in peace, when he suddenly folded his arms, as if protecting himself, and said, "I always knew you were telling the truth when you said that if you didn't work on the place, that someone else would...but that Ashley chick..." He shook his head. "That's the kind of people Miranda plans on surrounding me with, doesn't she?"

"Only if she knows it bothers you."

He studied her for a moment, his dark eyebrows drawn together in a slight frown. "You've finally figured that out?"

"Yeah. You two truly hate each other. Why?"

Jordan's expression instantly shuttered. So much for the direct approach.

"Sorry," Shae said. "None of my business."

"It's not," Jordan agreed. "Not one bit of your business." He pressed his lips together. "But there's really no need to keep things secret. Not with Dad dead. It's just become such a habit...."

Shae leaned back on the fence, looking out across the field where the poodle was bounding around, chasing field mice. She held her breath, wondering if he was going to continue.

"Probably not too difficult to connect the dots," he said, leaning his arms against the fence again so that they were side by side, facing opposite directions.

"No," she said softly. "Something happened between you."

"It didn't happen," he said. "But not for want of the bitch trying. And when she realized I was serious when I said 'no,' well, that was probably a hit to her ego, but beyond that, she had to make sure the old man wouldn't believe me if I told him."

"Was she successful?" Shae asked softly.

"He loved her. Was enamored of her. Honored to have her as his bride."

"Enough said."

IF SHAE WAS shocked at his half-assed confession, she didn't show it. Jordan had no idea why he'd opened up, let loose the secret he'd kept for so many years, except that maybe it was time. There was really no reason to keep quiet any longer, although he didn't want people laughing at his old man. Despite everything, he didn't want Hank Bryan to be the butt of barroom jokes. But with the situation the way it was between him and Miranda, who would believe him?

Shae. She'd believed him. If he wasn't mistaken, she'd already guessed the truth.

Had other people done the same?

He doubted it. Miranda was subtle in her maneuverings—at least until she got him alone.

His temples were starting to throb. He needed some space.

"Are you spending the night?" he asked.

"I'd rather not make the drive."

"Just so you know," he said, "sometimes when things get stirred up like this…" He let out a breath. "Short version—if you hear anything during the night, no need to concern yourself. Just me wrestling demons."

"Connected to Miranda?" she asked curiously.

"Hell, no." His response was instant and adamant, which was in itself telling. "Just…stress."

"Do you have the dreams often?"

"Often enough," he said in a tone that did not invite further confidences. Shae ignored the signal.

"After your accident, you must have talked to people."

"Therapy?"

"Yes."

"I did."

"Did it help?"

"I think time helped."

"But you still have nightmares."

His barriers were rising and it took a moment of struggle to say, "They stopped for a while. With the therapy. I thought I was past them, then they started again."

"When?"

Jordan pressed his fingers to his forehead. When he looked up, he saw that Shae was studying his other hand, or what was left of it, resting on the fence. She raised her eyes without one hint of self-consciousness.

"When?" she repeated.

Jordan moistened his dry lips. "When I was driving back to Montana."

"So what's the connection?"

"I, uh…" She propped an elbow on the fence as she waited for him to finish. He grimaced, shaking his head slightly, as if to clear it. "I thought it was just the stress of doing something stupid. Quitting my job and heading home. Choosing to live on disability rather than continue doing what I was doing."

"Which was?"

"The computer-age equivalent of pushing paper in a cubicle. I pushed a lot of paper." And hated it. "It was a simple job, but it got to where I couldn't focus. I got things wrong. It got worse and worse."

"But no nightmares?"

He shook his head. "But I wasn't all there."

"You're all there with the horses." He shot her a look. "You focus when you train," she said. "And you're all here now."

"For the most part," he said drily.

"You were in the wrong job in Virginia," she said.

He gave a short laugh. "It's not as simple as that, Shae."

"I know." She leaned forward and shocked the hell out of him by touching his damaged hand. He jerked it back. Her breath caught as her eyes flashed to his and for a second he thought she was going to call him on his knee-jerk reaction—she seemed to be calling him on everything else. She didn't. Instead she continued as it nothing had happened. "But it's one aspect of the situation that was making life more stressful than it needed to be. Some—" she gestured as she sought out the word "—primitive instinct kicked in and you bolted. Self-preservation, like you said."

"Probably," he agreed on a condescending note, but Shae was not insulted. She simply tilted her head, pressing her lips together thoughtfully, as he'd seen her do in the past when other people didn't act the way she wanted.

"Okay, that's an oversimplification," she said, "but sometimes, Jordan, people looking in from the outside can see things you can't."

"I've had enough therapy, Shae. What I want is to be left alone to work this out." What he wanted was to not slip into the danger zone with her. He was edging toward wanting her in a way that probably wasn't possible.

"In that case, you'd better take Miranda up on her offer."

"Isn't going to happen."

"Then being left alone isn't going to happen, either."

True. Very true, although at the moment Jordan didn't know just how alone he wanted to be.

He looked down at his hands where they rested on the fence rails. The strong, tanned one on one side, the mangled one on the other. Were these the kind of arms a woman wanted around her? The kind a woman like Shae would want around her?

He might be drawn in by this side of her that he'd never dreamed existed, but he needed to remain grounded in reality. He had issues, wounds, inside and out. He was not unworthy, but he felt unready.

He didn't know if he'd ever be ready.

JORDAN'S EVENING WAS SHOT. When he usually spent time at the ponds or hiking with Clyde along the deer trails, tonight he hung around at the house, where there was no danger of running into Shae. Or of having to talk again.

Maybe his dealings with Miranda hadn't been that big a deal in the larger scope of things, but the memories still brought up the feelings of outrage and shame he'd had at the time—at her and at himself. As if he'd done something to encourage her.

He paced through the house, unable to settle, and then, around nine o'clock, he heard Shae's truck start. He went to the window, saw the red glow of taillights as she drove away.

A respite.

He had no idea why she'd left, but since she was gone, he didn't need to worry about waking her up by yelling—or sleeping with the window shut on a hot summer night to keep her from hearing. Given the state he was in, the way thoughts of Miranda and Shae were crowding his mind, the nightmare was sure to come.

And it did, despite the drug. He jerked upright in bed just after midnight, his breath coming in short gasps, startling Clyde, who crept up along the blanket on his belly and set his chin on Jordan's chest as he settled back and his heart rate slowed.

He let out a long, low breath, then rolled over onto his side, scooping Clyde up against him and closing his eyes. These nightmares, the ones he'd had since starting home, were different than the ones he'd had before his PTSD therapy. He didn't remember images or situations as he had when he'd first dealt with the dreams—just the feeling of being engulfed. Overwhelmed. But they were triggered by the same thing. Whenever he was stressed or felt vulnerable, the dreams came. Just living in the same state as Miranda was enough to make for nightmares. When he'd been traveling, the closer he got to Montana, the more frequent the dreams had become.

Except that while he'd been traveling, he hadn't known that Miranda was going to screw with him. Hadn't known that she planned to breach his sanctuary. He'd been coming home to escape and heal. Why would that make the nightmares come back?

SHAE ENJOYED WAKING UP in the comfort of her own bed, with no worries about errant mice or washing up with freezing water, but she still wished she was at the High Camp.

Staying there hadn't been an option. Jordan

needed his space, just as he'd said. He regretted confessing to her, even if he hadn't exactly blurted out the facts, and he needed time to deal with it—without worrying about her crowding him. And then there was the attraction between them....

How were they going to deal with that?

Shae started the shower and stood for a moment regarding her reflection. She probably shouldn't have pulled the amateur psychology number on him, but she'd wanted to help. Wanted him to nail down the source of his problem.

As if that wasn't obvious, she thought as she turned away and tested the water before walking under the spray. It'd left him with massive scars that he was self-conscious about. He'd jumped a mile when she'd impulsively touched his damaged arm, which in turn had made her heart break. But it was more than that. The other issue in his life—his deep hatred of Miranda—wasn't helping matters.

Shae reached for the shampoo, holding the bottle for a moment as the spray tapped hollowly on the plastic. Would he ever be able to move past hating the woman? The signs didn't look good, and if he stayed at the High Camp while she built a guest ranch around him...not a chance.

She was drying off when the phone rang and she walked through the dining room to the glass coffee table to pick it up, toweling her hair as she walked. She was hoping for Mel, but instead it was Vivian, her stepmother.

"Finally!" Vivian said when Shae answered the phone. "I didn't know if I'd ever get through to you. I was starting to get concerned."

No doubt, judging from the number of messages Vivian had left checking on her. "Sorry I haven't returned your calls, Viv. I've been out of service range."

"You're still staying at the High Camp, then?"

"It's easier than driving back and forth."

"How is the project coming?"

Shae gave Vivian a highly editorialized version of the project, focusing on the few positives as much as possible and leaving Jordan's name completely out of it.

"And Jordan?" Vivian asked, the omission not getting past her.

"We've found a middle ground," Shae said matter-of-factly. It might be uncomfortable, but they were communicating. "We're talking and…actually getting along quite well."

"I see," Vivian said, obviously still dwelling on his "wild" appearance when she'd seen him in the pharmacy.

"How's Liv?" Shae asked, changing the subject the best way she knew how. She still felt a pang of jealousy when she thought about her stepsister, but now it was because that Liv had figured out a few things about life that Shae was still getting a handle on. Liv always had been the smart one.

"Doing well," Vivian said cautiously, as if not

wanting to remind Shae about the bad thing that had happened after Liv's wedding.

"I'm happy for her," Shae said.

"I know you are," Vivian said in a voice that made Shae want to say, *No, really. I am.* She didn't.

"I think Reed did the right thing walking away when he did."

Vivian gasped. "Shae!"

"It helped open my eyes to a few things…like the fact that I walked all over him. And he let me."

"No—"

"I don't think we loved each other," Shae said. Because if they had, she wouldn't have been more devastated by having so many bills only a couple weeks after the breakup than she was by losing the relationship. "We liked each other. A lot. But I think I ruined that."

There was a long silence and then Vivian said, "If you truly feel that way…then maybe it was—" she cleared her throat, perhaps remembering the months of hell Shae had put her through "—for the best."

"I'm so sorry," Shae whispered into the phone.

"For what?"

"Everything. And I'm paying you guys back."

"No—"

Once again Shae cut her off. "Yes. It'll take some time, but don't try to tell me not to. I really, *really* need to do this."

"I'll talk to your father."

"So will I," Shae said.

ALONE WASN'T WORKING. Shae wasn't there, Ashley had yet to show up, but the anticipation of their arrivals had Jordan on edge.

Alone hadn't worked in Virginia, either. Not that he'd been physically alone for a good part of the day, but he'd stayed in his cubicle, worked on his computer and kept to himself, content to be the PTSD guy whom everyone kept their distance from. For all intents and purposes he'd been alone at work, and he'd still be overwhelmed by a need to escape. The mind-numbing job hadn't helped, but it'd been more than that. He'd needed to be alone in an environment where he felt at peace, so he'd followed the urge, came back home…only to find you can't go home again.

Miranda had seen to that. But he also found he couldn't leave. The woman had drawn a line in the sand and he was stepping over it as many times as it took for her to get it through her head that he was staying. She was not winning.

Did he want to live his life like this, on edge, waiting for the Cedar Creek employees to show up every day?

No. But he was going to.

He whistled for Clyde, who came running from the backyard. The pig also came running, stopping when she saw that Jordan had the door of the Subaru open. She'd made the connection that when the car was involved with whatever Jordan was doing, she was not. Clyde shot into the front seat and sat facing the windshield, shooting a superior look at the pig, who was now snuffling toward the bunkhouse.

Jordan drove toward the cattle guard, thinking that he really had to find a way to invest in a truck. He could haul mineral block and the occasional bag of pig mash in the Subaru, but he wasn't going to pull the old ranch trailer with it—once he got the tires replaced, that is. As it was, the trailer was going nowhere.

As he reached the end of the drive, his cell phone buzzed and he picked it up to see a reminder to reorder his prescription. And there was also that annoying number one over the voice-mail icon, reminding him that he'd yet to return his cousin Cole's weeks-old call. But he couldn't bring himself to delete the message. Which, as he thought about it, was telling. Maybe he couldn't go home, but he could reconnect with the small bit of family he had left. All it took was one phone call.

Even if it was going to be awkward.

An hour later Jordan made that call.

Cole was obviously surprised to hear from him— possibly because Jordan hadn't answered the voice message he'd left over a month ago—but immediately suggested that he buy Jordan a drink at their one-time favorite watering hole on the outskirts of Missoula. Neutral ground. Jordan agreed.

Cole was waiting when Jordan got there, and as he made his way to where his cousin sat at the bar, recognition of the fact that he'd been a major asshole amplified with each step.

He stopped in front of Cole, waiting for the words of apology he'd been working on to surface, but before they came out, Cole pushed a stool out with his foot.

"Have a seat."

"Sorry for being an asshole," Jordan said as he pulled out his wallet, then sat.

"No problem," Cole said. "I know you've had some deep shit to deal with."

"Miranda or the other?"

"Is Shae the other?" Cole asked and Jordan laughed in spite of himself.

"I was thinking more about—" he lifted his left hand for Cole to see "—which is usually what people are referring to when they ask me about my troubles."

"Not me. I was talking about the women in your life." The bartender ambled down the bar, stopping in front of them with a bright smile that faded fast when she saw the scarred side of Jordan's face, but he had to give her credit for professionalism when she almost instantly pasted it back on again. "Gentlemen?"

"Whatever nonalcoholic beer you have," Jordan said. Cole grimaced and ordered a draft.

"You've changed," Cole said.

"Had to. Alcohol and painkillers...not good."

"Do you still have to take many drugs?"

"Enough to keep me on the wagon."

There was an awkward lull as they watched the bartender pour Cole's draft and uncap Jordan's Kaliber and then Jordan broke the silence.

"I'm sorry," he said abruptly. Cole shifted his gaze from the bartender back to him, a questioning frown drawing his eyebrows together. "That you wasted that plane ticket. When I was in the hospital."

"I understand," Cole said. "I might have done the same." He smiled at the bartender as she set the drinks in front of them. "Nobody knows how they'll react in a situation like that."

"Yeah. But all the same... Shae mentioned your trip once when we were talking—" *arguing* "—and I realized I never apologized."

"You getting along all right with Shae?" Cole asked, seeming glad to have a new topic to grab onto.

Jordan shrugged with more nonchalance than he felt. "We're doing okay, considering."

"Considering what?" Cole asked with a half smile.

"Considering how I dumped her off my lap in the bar that time."

Cole laughed. "I forgot about that."

"She didn't."

"Yeah. She's probably sensitive about the word *dumped* right now."

Jordan felt his throat close a little, but it didn't

keep him from asking, "What exactly happened there?"

"Well," Cole said slowly, "Shae was engaged to a real nice guy, spent about two years planning the wedding of the century, even had a deal for a regional magazine spread, and then he called it off." Cole took a drink and wiped the foam off his upper lip. "Guess old Reed wanted a wife more than a wedding."

"Shae never was a halfway sort."

"Recall how she once managed to get all of the rodeo royalty decked out in lights for the grand entry of the state finals?"

Jordan nodded. He recalled. At the time he'd disgustedly thought it was another look-at-me tactic on Shae's part, as it might well have been, but he'd never thought about why she needed people to look at her. Approval of others had never seemed to matter to her—she'd always been supremely confident—so he had to assume now that it had had something to do with approving of herself.

Deep shit, this. They were a pair.

"What's going on with Miranda?" Cole asked after once again pulling his gaze away from the bartender.

"Where to begin," Jordan said with a soft snort. Then, as he slowly sipped the beer that wasn't quite a beer, he described the situation, starting with Shae making the proposal and then Miranda following through with a vengeance, determined to develop something on a property she hadn't cared about until he showed up again.

"Sounds like she's skating on thin ice with some of this. Renovating the cabins?"

"Right now Emery says there's not much I can do as long as she's merely repairing the property." He settled his elbows on the bar. "What screwed me was Dad putting in that recreational clause so he and his buddies could still hunt there if…you know…something happened to me overseas and Becky inherited."

"What screwed you was letting Miranda inherit."

Cole's words stayed with him as he drove home. His dad had screwed him. And then he'd died.

"I HAVE ESTIMATES for the windows," Ashley said as soon as she stepped into the bunkhouse, where Shae was halfheartedly marking trails on a map as part of the permitting process and wondering where Jordan was.

"I didn't realize you were getting the estimates," Shae said coolly.

"Miranda's idea," Ashley said. "When we went over the notebook, she suggested that I handle the windows and doors." She walked over to the map and stared down at it. "Permitting?"

"Yes."

"I could do that," Ashley said. "Free you up to do something else."

Like what? This was pretty much a one-man operation. "No. Thank you."

"Then what shall I do?"

Shae barely stopped herself from saying, *Go home.* Instead she said, "When I'm done with this I'm going to ride one of the trails. Perhaps you could come up with a use for these…useless cells?" she said, gesturing at the doors that lined the far wall. "Something unique. Miranda's all about unique."

"All right," Ashley said slowly, pulling out her notepad. Shae continued to mark trails. Ashley paced, paused, paced. Shae felt herself going quietly nuts. Finally she put down her pen.

"Done?" Ashley asked.

"Yes. Are you?"

"How about small retail and rental areas? We could have local souvenirs and products in one. Fishing equipment rentals in another." She started pointing at doors. "Locally made fishing rods for sale. Artwork. Maybe some outdoor gear, gloves and hats, things people might not realize they need in another. It shouldn't be too hard to come up with a theme for each one."

Shae stared at her. Great. Just great. She should have kept her mouth shut. Now Ashley was the hero.

"Yes. Work that up to present, okay? I'm going out to check the trail." She couldn't get out of there fast enough. Jordan still wasn't back from wherever he was, but when he got back, he was going to have to deal with Ashley alone.

WHEN JORDAN GOT back to the High Camp, Ashley's truck was gone and Shae's mare was not in the corral. Jordan went to the pasture and caught the dun, thinking that after groundwork he might saddle up and see if he could find her. He'd just started putting the dun through her paces when Clyde alerted and he turned to see Shae dismounting at the barn. She led her horse inside and Jordan turned his attention back to the filly, but he kept an eye on the barn.

Several minutes later the mare ambled out into the corral, but Shae didn't reappear. She still hadn't come out by the time he'd finished the round pen work, so he tied up the dun and headed to the barn.

The building felt empty when he walked inside. He stood, listening, then a small bit of dust filtered down from the rafters above him and he glanced up. The hayloft. He walked over to the ladder, reached for the rung just above his head and started to climb.

"Hey," Shae said softly when he poked his head up through the opening. He couldn't tell from the tone of her voice if she was okay with him disturbing her, so he took a chance and climbed the rest of the way up. She sat in the window with her back against the frame, the late-afternoon sun streaming over her, making the reddish highlights in her dark hair gleam. Awkwardly he stood, balancing on the loose boards covering the joists. As kids they'd never been allowed in the loft unless there was hay—too much potential for slipping through a crack and falling—and there hadn't been hay in the loft for years. His father had kept it outside, under tarps where it was easier to get at with the squeeze.

"Ruminating?" he asked as he made his way over to the window and sat beside her, his back against the wall.

"Going over a few things."

"Ashley's gone."

"I'm *not* hiding," she said with exaggerated innocence.

He cocked a knee up and rested his arm on it. "It was late when you left last night."

"I had some things to do in town and, well, I sensed that you might like some space." She met his eyes, her expression candid. "Did you have a nightmare last night?"

"Yeah," he said, surprising her by being equally candid. "I think I talked myself into it during the day."

Shae ran a hand over her knee. "What are they like? The nightmares?"

He felt his barriers start to rise, but she was honestly trying to understand, so he did his best to push them back down again. "They were flashbacks in the beginning. I'd be there, you know? Everything happening in slow motion." He swallowed. "I'd try to get away before the explosion, but my feet wouldn't move."

"Did that really happen?"

"No. One minute I was walking with two of my buddies and the next I'd been knocked down by flying debris. The weird thing was that I recall the colors and images, but no sound." He reached down to pull a cocklebur off his pant leg. "But in my dreams I hear sound and it surprises me. Every time. When I wake up, I'm the one making the sound."

"What happened to your buddies?" she asked softly.

"One was killed. One had only minor injuries. I was the middle guy."

"I'm sorry," she said automatically.

"It was bad," he admitted. "I had issues. But I thought I'd worked through most of them in therapy. It got to where I was going months at a time without having a nightmare. But I was still damned unhappy at my job and felt so disoriented and empty. So…I headed home. Then, like I told you before, the dreams started again on the trip. Stress, I guess, but…" He hesitated before confessing, "I hate backtracking."

"And feeling that it could get worse?"

"Feeling that I have no control. I want to be back in control."

Shae nodded then turned her head to look out across the meadows, the sunlight casting shadows under her cheekbones. What had happened, he wondered, to make her so pensive? Had Miranda attacked again?

But he didn't want to bring up Miranda. Not now. So instead he reached out with his boot to nudge the toe of her shoe. "You said you had nightmares," he said when she looked up.

She nodded, her forehead knit into a frown. He wondered if she was going to answer after the way he'd shot her down before, but after a few silent seconds, she said, "For a couple years after my mom died. She had cancer, and we knew she was dying, and it was so damn hard, but I didn't have the dreams until after she went, so I don't know what I was dreaming about." She looked off toward the horizon. "But I was angry, you know?"

"Angry?"

"She left me. I couldn't help it, and I hated myself for it, but I couldn't get over my outrage that she would...die on me, instead of somehow fighting and carrying on."

Jordan wanted to reach out and touch her, but instead he curled his good hand into a loose fist on his knee. "My dad compensated by always giving me whatever I wanted," she said. "And my stepmother...she went overboard. So I would accept her, I guess. I pretty much only had to ask and wish granted." She was silent for a moment. "I don't think that was the best strategy."

"How so?"

She gave a short laugh. "Nothing makes people hate you like getting whatever you want. Being spoiled." She leaned her head back against the window frame, looking up. "I've always been confident, so I didn't really care. Or told myself I didn't care. I think it was more that I didn't understand." One corner of her mouth tightened. "Being spoiled doesn't help a person develop a lot of empathy for others…but I'm working on it."

"I'd say you're moving forward."

She smiled at him with a touch of self-consciousness. "I know this sounds minor compared to what you went through, but…"

"It's not minor if it eats at you." And he could see that this bothered her—being hated for having it all. Or at least appearing to have it all.

"It does eat at me," Shae said, once again leaning her head back and staring at the window frame above her. "As does the fact that I never thought that much about the effect I had on other people." She bit her lip as she continued to stare upward. "Pretty damned callous, eh?"

"We can all be callous, Shae."

"But I made it an art form."

"No," he said softly, catching her attention once again. "My ex-stepmother has made it an art form."

"I don't want to talk about Miranda," she said abruptly.

"Neither do I." Their gazes connected then and Jordan became very aware of the fact that he couldn't bring himself to look away from her. He didn't want to look away from her. He wanted to reach out and touch her.

"Once upon a time," Shae said slowly, her expression intent, "you dumped me on my ass."

"I remember that."

She raised her chin a little as she said, "Would you do that now?"

Hell, no. "A lot has changed since then."

"Other than your accident?"

His throat felt dry as he said, "Yes. Other than the accident."

For another long moment their eyes held and Jordan could see she was debating about saying more, but instead she got to her feet, brushing herself off.

"I need to go and see what trouble Ashley has caused me," she said before making her way across the boards toward the ladder. She didn't look back as she started to climb down, escaping, leaving Jordan alone in the loft.

Alone wasn't working.

SHAE COULDN'T BRING herself to go back to the bunkhouse, so she headed down the trail that Jordan walked every evening, the trail that led to the place where Clyde had gotten his curly self into trouble and thus brought the situation between herself and Jordan to a head.

Her attraction to the man was troubling, as was her situation there at the ranch. Could she stay and continue as she was, actively working to make Jordan's life uncomfortable?

How could she not? She had a contract to fulfill,

whether Miranda was going to ax her eventually or not. At this point she felt she almost needed to be at the ranch for damage control. To see if she could deflect some of the impact of what she'd started.

The bunkhouse was getting dark by the time she returned from the walk, no clearer on a strategy than when she'd left, but Shae couldn't bring herself to turn on the light. If she did, then she'd have to face the cost analysis that she'd been halfheartedly working on before she'd abandoned it to go for a ride on Belinda. And after the ride she'd gone to the loft to escape her demons—and discovered even more.

She had to deal with the cost analysis and she had to deal with Jordan...or at the very least commit to keeping her distance, for both their sakes.

She walked to the window, stared out into the twilight, then gave a start as a shadow went past. A second later there was a knock on the door. She crossed the room to open it, stepping back without a word to let Jordan walk into the room. Even in the semidarkness she could see the tension in his expression and had to stop herself from reaching up to touch his face, smooth her fingers over the harsh lines there. She opened her mouth to speak, to tell him she'd get the lights, but before she got a word out Jordan leaned in, covered her mouth with his, pulling her close, kissing her long and hard.

Shae stiffened for all of a nanosecond, then as his tongue demanded a response, she pressed against him, her hands sliding up around his neck, pressing into him, kissing him back. Too soon, he took a couple steps back and she could see the conflict in his face.

He wanted her, but he wasn't sure. She could only imagine what it had taken for him to come here, do this.

He rubbed a hand over his forehead, glancing away for an instant. "I...uh..."

"I get it," she said softly. And part of her was relieved. The other part was beating her with fists, demanding that she get some more of what she'd just experienced.

Shae eased back another step, her hands sliding down his arms until they reached his hands, both of them. And Jordan wished with all of his heart that he was still whole. That he could touch her with two good hands without wondering if she was turned off by what he had to offer her.

It'd been so long since he'd touched a woman in an intimate way. Been touched. He wanted to grab her, haul her off to his bed... He wasn't ready. He wasn't ready because he didn't know what he could give and he didn't know what Shae needed.

He didn't know what he needed.

And she knew that. He could see it in her face. She understood and it rocked him.

"Go to bed," she said softly.

"Would you come with me if I asked you?"

"Probably." For one long moment they stood, neither able to move. "Definitely. But you're not going to ask me, are you?" He didn't answer. Didn't know how to say that she was right—he hadn't yet moved past his insecurities. He didn't have to. Shae reached out to touch the scarred side of his face, her palm flat against the damaged skin, her fingertips grazing his temple, where the nerves still worked. "Go to bed, Jordan."

CHAPTER THIRTEEN

SHAE HUGGED HER arms around herself as Jordan walked out the door. How damned hard had that been?

She walked to her cot and sat down on the edge, her arms still wrapped around her chest. Her heart was beating low and slow against her ribs; her lips felt swollen even though they'd only kissed once. She wanted him, but maybe for the first time ever, she knew better than to push. It wasn't about having her way. It was about waiting for the right time.

Delayed gratification.

The door scraped back open and Shae jumped to her feet, heart pounding as Jordan stepped back inside.

"Shae?"

She was barely aware of moving until she was back in his arms.

"Come to my place with me?" he asked roughly.

"Why? Mine isn't good enough?"

"Bed's too narrow."

Shae laughed and was struck by how nervous it sounded. She realized that it was because this mattered in a way things hadn't mattered before.

She nodded and took his hand, gripping it tightly as they crossed the distance to his house, woke the pig, who jumped to her feet with a snorking grunt, and safely shut themselves inside.

Jordan tugged her hand, pulling her behind him down the narrow hallway to his bedroom. The lights were out, but by moonlight so bright it cast shadows, she could easily make out the old-fashioned bureau, the metal-framed bed, the single night stand.

"Your bed isn't much larger than my cot," she said.

"We'll manage," he replied hoarsely.

Then for the first time ever, Shae realized she didn't know what to do, where to begin. Until Jordan laid a hand against her cheek, his rough palm warm against her skin. She leaned into his touch, closing her eyes. Then she covered his hand with hers briefly before stepping away and sitting on the edge of the metal-framed bed. But Jordan didn't follow. He unbuttoned his shirt, peeled out of it, and then slowly he turned, allowing her to see the full extent of his injuries in the bright moonlight.

Shae stood again, then reached out, hesitating for a moment before she lightly touched his upper back, where the worst of the scar tissue lay, running her hand over the thickened skin, wondering if he could feel her touch as she traced over the scarred area, but knowing instinctively that whether he could feel or not, he needed her to touch him there. To accept him.

She felt him tense, every muscle in his back going rigid, but he stood still beneath her touch. Shae brought her other hand up to his back and caressed, her hands moving simultaneously, one over hard-muscled flesh, the other over the thickened skin where the grafts had healed, then over his shoulders, his upper arms. From there she slid her hands beneath his arms to his waist, then around to his chest and then lower, over his hard abdomen to the edge of his jeans. She hugged him from behind, laying her cheek against the damaged part of his back.

"I'd love it if you took off your jeans," she murmured. "Or I could do it."

"You," he said, his voice thick with need. He turned and Shae hooked her fingers in his waistband, lifting her chin, inviting his kiss.

Jordan took her mouth, his tongue sweeping inside, challenging her to meet his need.

Not a problem. Her need was at least equal to his own.

She flicked open the button at his waistband with a quick twist of her fingers. The lower buttons of his Levi's weren't so easy, due to one massive hard-on pressing against them, but Shae managed to get the job done, running her palm over his tented erection with a satisfied smile.

"So you're a boxers man."

"Briefs bind," he said against her mouth before pulling her against him. Hard. Shae pressed back, meeting his kiss hungrily as she pushed his pants down over his hips, shoving them as low as she could without breaking contact with his mouth. Then she let her hand slide over the hard curve of his ass before easing it between them to run the length of his shaft. Damn. He felt as if he was ready to explode, right there in her hand.

And she did not want to waste this erection like that.

There will be others...

She started to smile, then caught her breath as Jordan brought his hands up to cup her breasts, gently squeezing them through her bra before going to work on her buttons with his good hand. She wanted to do it herself, to peel out of her clothing fast and impale herself on him, but instead she swallowed hard and waited as he popped the buttons one by one, his fingers brushing against the swell of her breasts, her rib cage. She automatically inhaled as his fingers skimmed over her abdomen, then her breath caught again as he undid the last button and moved the shirt aside, going for the zipper of her pants next.

"I want you naked," he muttered against the hollow of her shoulder and Shae almost lost it right there. Jordan Bryan wanted her naked. And she wanted the same and she wanted that mouth she'd sworn would never touch her all over her body.

In very short order she got her wish. Jordan laid her on the bed and started working his way down, tracing the tip of his tongue over her throat, dipping into the hollow between her clavicles, continuing on to lavish attention to her breasts. He didn't seem to be able to get enough of her breasts.

Shae took hold of the bars of the metal bed frame above her head, willing herself to hang on and let him do this his way instead of trying to take control. But there were areas of her body that needed attention.

"Patience," Jordan murmured, reading her thoughts.

"No," she murmured and he laughed softly against her skin.

"Yes. Because I have a feeling the second I get inside of you, it'll be all over." He raised his head, dark hair falling over his brow. "It's been a long time for me, Shae."

"I understand."

He put his head back down, continued to caress her with his good hand and his tongue, keeping his left hand tucked away. He traveled lower, lightly running his hand over her thighs, teasing her navel, then finally coming home where she wanted him to be. Oh, damn.

She bucked against his mouth and realized it'd actually been a long time for her, too, and she couldn't remember a time she'd wanted something so badly as she wanted his tongue to continue doing exactly what it was doing now.

She came before she could stop herself, gripping

the bars, arching against his mouth, then collapsing with a shuddering sigh.

Slowly she opened her eyes, trying to remember if her toes had ever gone numb like this before. "My turn," she murmured.

"Uh-uh."

"Uh-uh?" she asked, eyes widening.

"I want to be inside of you when I come for the first time in forever."

"Do you have protection?"

"Always."

"Not expired?" she said.

"Shae…" he said in a warning tone as he reached into the night stand and rummaged around.

"You said it'd been forever."

"Brand-new." He tore open the wrapper.

"You knew this was going to happen?"

He stilled and when he met her eyes she couldn't quite read his expression. "Have you ever in your life wanted something that you didn't think was possible? That seemed so impossible that you didn't think it would happen, but on a whim, prepared for it anyway?"

"Everything always happened for me," she said with gentle sarcasm, taking the condom from him and slowly rolling it down over his erection. "But I'm glad you believed in the impossible." She lay back then, pulling him with her by the shoulders, arching her hips up against him as he pushed himself slowly into her until he was all the way home.

"What now?" she murmured.

"Now," he said against her skin, starting to move, "I do the impossible."

And Shae, who'd thought she was only along for the ride, discovered that doing the impossible felt crazy good and seconds before Jordan gave his last thrust, she gasped against his shoulder, dug her fingernails in, realizing too late it was his scarred shoulder, and came again.

"Did I hurt you?" she asked once she could speak.

"What?" he asked, rolling toward her with a frown.

"Your shoulder? Did I hurt you?"

He laughed lowly as he reached out and tugged her against him, wrapping both arms, good and bad, around her. "No, Shae, you didn't hurt me. Now… let's go to sleep."

SHAE LAY AWAKE long after Jordan had fallen asleep, thinking about the impossible. Who would have thought she would have gone from sitting on her ass on a barroom floor to sharing Jordan Bryan's bed? Having some of the best sex ever.

And she'd given as much as she'd gotten.

Easing herself up on her elbow, she studied him for a moment, taking in the dark lashes, the stubble on his cheeks, the natural upward curve of his mouth. He was gorgeous and the scarred side of his face didn't detract. Not after she'd come to see it as part of him.

What was happening here? Was she actually falling for this guy? Did this go beyond raging physical attraction?

That gave her pause. She wasn't ready to fall for a guy so soon after getting dumped in a more figurative sense. Not ready at all. But she wouldn't mind more sex.

Was that fair?

Things to think about, and she wanted to be alone when she did it, not distracted by the sight, scent and feel of Jordan Bryan. She started to ease out of the creaky bed, only to have an arm drop over her in an ironlike hold.

"What're you doing?" Jordan murmured.

"I'm going."

His hold on her loosened as he asked, "Why?"

"I think…we need our space." She twisted around to nip his lower lip lightly, wanting nothing more than to stay in this bed and curl up against him, to feel him pressing against her in the morning. To make love again. "But I loved every minute of this."

"A one-time thing, then?"

"I didn't say that."

"Good." He reached up to bunch his fingers in her hair and pulled her lips back to his. Shae groaned against his mouth as she tumbled down on top of him. Minutes later she was once again beneath him, meeting his strokes, which were slower and more measured, making her even crazier than the last time.

This time she was the one who came too soon. And this time he didn't wake up when she slipped out of his noisy bed and returned to her own in the bunkhouse. As if she could sleep.

Why did *she* need to be alone? Why did she need this distance?

Because for once in her life she was not going to go full steam ahead without consideration of consequences or how she affected other people. Jordan was still dealing with issues and until he got a handle on those, they didn't have a hope in hell. She'd give him his space.

She rolled over on her side, clutching the blankets to her chest, the dampness between her legs reminding her of what it felt like to have Jordan inside of her. Right. It had felt really right.

So what now?

Excellent, excellent question, to which she didn't have even a hint of an answer.

JORDAN ATE HIS solitary breakfast, drank his coffee. Debated about what had happened the night before. He'd given in to temptation and regretted nothing. Did he want it to be a one-nighter?

His gut said no, but when Shae slipped out in the early-morning hours, when she chose to leave his warm bed and spend the rest of the night on her cot in the bunkhouse…well, that was probably his answer. One-nighter. A novelty.

She'd responded to him. No doubts there. He'd

hazard a guess that he was the first guy she'd made love to since the end of her engagement, which could explain a lot. On her end, anyway. He'd expected Shae to be a confident lover, maybe even selfish. He hadn't expected playfulness, or tenderness. Hadn't expected her to be so giving.

Or for himself to respond so deeply to what she offered.

He smiled to himself as he propped up his feet on the porch rail and tilted his chair back, enjoying the early-morning sun. One-nighter or not, making love to Shae had eased him over a very big hurdle in his life—sharing his broken body with someone else. Yeah, she'd definitely given him something.

Shae came out of the bunkhouse then, a rolled-up bundle under one arm. Jordan eased the chair legs back to the ground as she approached and then stood. Let the awkwardness begin.

But it wasn't awkward when she smiled at him, pushing her hair behind her ear with her free hand as she said, "I thought I might use your shower."

"Did you bring your own towel?" Jordan asked as she mounted the porch steps.

She came to stand in front of him, amusement lighting her eyes, but she kept her expression cool as she said, "You won't share?"

He reached out to put his hand on the curve of her hip, ease her closer to him. She moved forward until her thighs brushed against his, then pressed closer, against his growing erection. Tilting her lips up, she practically dared him to kiss her. So he did, slowly bringing his mouth to hers, parting her lips, claiming her mouth. The bundle rolled to the floor as she brought her hands up to frame his face, her fingers splaying over his scars as the kiss deepened.

"That shower is probably big enough for two."

"But is it sturdy enough for what I have in mind?" he asked against her mouth.

"I hope—"

She broke off abruptly, stepping back as the sound of an engine took them by surprise and they turned to see a Cedar Creek Ranch truck rolling around the corner and traveling toward them.

"Freaking Ashley," Shae said, reaching down to pick up the rolled clothing. When she stood back up again, she casually moved about five feet away from him, telling him that she wasn't going to be shouting about their liaison from the rooftops. Couldn't blame her there. Miranda still signed her paychecks.

"Guess you'll be taking that shower alone," he said, his eyes on the truck as it rolled to a stop.

"Probably be best," she said. "I'll just get my assistant lined out first."

"And I think I'll go work the dun."

SHAE COULDN'T TELL if Ashley had seen her and Jordan embracing. Probably not. The corner she'd come around at just the wrong moment was a distance away…and it was definitely better that she arrived when she had rather than when she and Jordan had been in the shower, doing whatever he hoped the shower was sturdy enough for...

Shae sighed.

Damn, but she wished she could have taken that shower. She was practically aching with the need to feel Jordan inside her again. Soon.

She got her wish later that afternoon, almost before the dust from Ashley's truck had settled. Shae was in the bunkhouse, changing her clothes, when he knocked on the door. Just as the first time he'd kissed her, his mouth was on hers almost before the door was open and then she was backing across the room toward the cot, which didn't seem too narrow anymore, pulling him along with her, shedding clothing as they moved. He pulled a strip of condoms out of his pants pocket before his jeans hit the floor. Seconds later Shae took the package from him, impatiently tearing it open and rolling it onto him. And then he was in her, giving her exactly what she'd been longing for since Ashley interrupted them that morning.

Later, as they lay on the narrow cot, Shae halfway on top of Jordan in order to fit—not that she wouldn't have been in that position even in a larger bed—he lifted her hand and gently kissed the knuckles.

"Come up to the house with me. Spend the night."

"This is all very sudden," Shae murmured against the hollow of his neck. He laughed, but she sensed his uncertainty as he waited for her response. She propped herself up on one elbow, biting her lip.

"What?" he asked, trailing his fingers over her bare back.

"Not that long ago I was planning a wedding." She felt his abdomen muscles tense beneath her palm, but he said nothing, so she went on. "I pushed people around to get everything just the way I wanted it to be. That wedding became more important to me than what it represented." She hesitated for a moment, then dived into what she needed to say. "I know this is poor form, but I have to say it. Reed's a good guy. He deserved better."

There was an edge to Jordan's voice as he asked, "Do you still love him?"

"Not in a way where we'd ever be together again. After he ended the engagement, and after I got done with the tears and anger, it was like the fog cleared." It sounded hokey, but it was true and she didn't know how else to phrase it. "It wasn't immediate, but I started to see what I had done, where my focus had been...why a good guy dumped me."

Jordan's hand started moving over her back, lightly, soothingly. "What I'm getting at here is that I'm pushy." He made no sound, but she felt him laugh and she smiled back. "I know, I know. It's difficult to believe, but I am."

"And your point?" he asked softly.

"I don't know where this is going, how long it'll last, but I love the way you make me feel. And when

I like something, I tend to try to take over. I want us to be on the same page. To communicate. To be honest with each other."

Jordan drew in a long breath and exhaled before he said, "As you know, talking isn't my strong suit, but I promise you honesty. I won't let you walk over me, if that's what you were getting at. And I won't walk over you."

Shae brought her lips down to nuzzle against his cheek. "That," she said against his skin, "is exactly what I was getting at. Now…let's go to the house before it gets too dark to see."

IT HADN'T BEEN easy for Jordan to invite Shae to share his bed on a nightly basis. He hated taking the pills, knocking himself out while she was there, but he didn't want to risk a nightmare. On the other hand, while they were together, he wanted to be with her. He had no idea how long they would last together—whether they *could* last after Shae's contract was done and she went back to work somewhere in Missoula—but until that day came, he wanted her in his bed.

And every night after they made love he fought with himself as to whether or not to take the pills. It was Shae who'd finally brought up the subject.

"What do those do?" she asked as he reached for the bottle.

"They knock me out." Sometimes that wasn't enough, but usually it was.

"I noticed," she said wryly. "The nightmares are still bad?"

"They suck. And they wipe me out physically."

"So do the pills." She smoothed a hand over his chest. "Wipe you out physically, I mean. I'm not saying don't take them. I was just wondering… how will you know if the dreams happen less frequently?"

"I don't want to put you through that shit."

"You're worried about having one while I'm here?"

"I'm not pleasant afterward."

"What if I promise *not* to kiss you and try to make it all better?" He frowned at her and she said patiently, "What if I just gave you your space and let you deal with it?"

"What if I don't want to have the dream at all?" he said roughly.

"Then take the pills."

And he did. That night. The next night, though, he didn't, half-afraid that the anxiety of not taking them would surely trigger a nightmare, but it didn't. He woke up with Shae curled up against him. He pulled her closer. The night after that was the same, but on the following night he woke up sitting up in bed, sweat beading his upper lip, his breathing hard and ragged. Shae was standing next to the bed, hugging herself, staring uncertainly down at him with Clyde standing beside her.

"I didn't want to leave," she said when he finally

focused on her, "until you knew that I was going. I didn't want you to wonder what had happened."

Jordan collapsed down against the pillow without answering, staring up at the ceiling. Shae went over to the lone chair in the room where they stacked their clothes and he heard her pulling on her jeans. He closed his eyes, focused on his breathing, fighting back the sensation of deep loss. Incredible loss.

He heard Shae walk to the doorway, pausing briefly as if waiting to see if he'd call her back. He didn't and a few seconds later he heard her cross the living room.

Was she also walking out of his life? His need to keep her there was suddenly stronger than his need to keep the aftereffects of the nightmares private.

"Shae." Her name came out on a hoarse whisper, spoken just as the front door opened, but she must have heard him. The door scraped shut and after a tense few seconds he heard her move. She was still there. Her footsteps sounded as she crossed back to the bedroom, where she paused in the doorway, waiting for him to make the next move.

"If you want to stay…"

She did. Her shirt fell to the floor as she walked back to the bed. Without a word she kicked off her jeans and slipped back into bed beside him, and when he put his arms around her, drawing her close against him, she let out a soft sigh.

"Sorry," he murmured in her ear.

She took what was left of his left hand and pulled

his arm around her more snugly, keeping tight hold as she whispered, "No worries."

The next morning Shae got up before him, just as the sun rose. She made coffee, fried a couple eggs and they ate breakfast on the porch as if it was a normal morning, even though they were both more than aware that it wasn't.

Jordan didn't feel like talking. He never did the morning after. He preferred to be alone, to let the feeling that he'd been beat up during the night dissipate before rejoining the land of the living, but he couldn't do that this morning. Shae was there and he felt uncomfortable now that they weren't quietly holding one another in bed.

Even though Shae didn't push things, he wanted her to leave, to allow him his time alone.

Instead she drank her coffee, stared out over the fields, a faint frown drawing her eyebrows together, as if debating how best to proceed. The air was thick with tension, with things unsaid, but Jordan couldn't bring himself to do anything to make things better. It was exactly what he'd been afraid of—that once the light of day hit, he would withdraw, shut Shae out. It was as if he couldn't help himself.

When Ashley's pickup came into sight, Shae got to her feet. "I'd better get out of here." She gave him a quick smile, then on impulse leaned down and lightly kissed his lips. "Can't help myself," she said before picking up his plate and disappearing into the house. She slipped out the back door as she did when Ashley arrived earlier than expected and he imagined she was now making her way unseen to the bathhouse, where she and Ashley were making big plans.

He reached down to stroke Clyde's curly head, then pushed himself to his feet, determined to meet the day.

He had horses to work.

And he had stuff to figure out, as in what he was and was not capable of in a relationship.

JORDAN WAS HAVING difficulty again with the palomino, who continued to live up to her reputation as a Claiborne horse. She was the last in the rotation that day and it was all Shae could do not to go down to the round pen and watch the proceedings as the mare tested Jordan.

Later that afternoon, after her alleged assistant had driven away, Shae did go to the round pen, where Jordan was standing with his arms on the rails, staring into space. Last night had been difficult, as had this morning. She'd wanted to break her promise, to force the comfort Jordan didn't want onto him. To tell him that yeah, he probably felt as if the dreams were a weakness but they weren't, so he should get over it, but she didn't. For once in her life she'd managed to see beyond her own needs, which were to get Jordan back to a place where he felt comfortable so that she could be with him. He needed to handle this his own way. Last night had proven to her that she could live with that.

And she could handle the aftermath, too, as long as he didn't totally shut himself off from her—which he pretty much had that morning. She told herself she could live with it as long as he eventually came back. The question now was, would he? And was she forcing the issue, which she'd promised herself she wouldn't do, by going to the round pen? A habit built over decades was not easily broken—even after one was aware of it.

When she leaned on the rail next to him, Jordan sent her a glance edged with self-consciousness. "I'm kind of a son of a bitch the morning after," he said, focusing once again on the horses he'd been watching.

"So is the palomino," she murmured.

"Yeah. I'm going to have to tell Claiborne that she's as good as she's getting. She's never going to be totally trustworthy."

Shae nodded, then shifted her gaze toward Jordan as he put a hand on the middle of her back. "You okay?" he asked.

"I could ask the same thing."

"No," he said honestly. "I'm all screwed up."

"Me, too." It wasn't the answer he was expecting. She could see it in his face. "But I think I'm improving and I can be patient while you do the same."

"Are you sure about that?"

One corner of her mouth lifted as she slowly nodded. "For right now I'm sure. I haven't seen anything that's a deal breaker."

"Even if I shut down? Afterward?"

"I'll just focus on myself," she said with a touch of amusement. "I'm quite content doing that. I have years and years of practice."

His hand slipped around her waist and he pulled her against him.

"I can live with the nightmares," she said softly, leaning her head against his shoulder, "and the moods that follow as long as you don't take it out on me. I can give you your space. And I think you'll get better."

"If I don't?" He hated feeling broken.

She reached up to kiss the underside of his jaw. "If it gets worse, we'll look at ways to deal with it. Just give *us* a chance."

HE WAS ALL about chances, because he wasn't ready to walk away from Shae. The one thing he wouldn't do, though, was put her in a position of having to deal with him if he slipped back into the depths of depression.

It struck him that night, as he lay holding her, that he hadn't felt depressed since starting the trip home. Angry, vulnerable, frustrated, outraged, yes, but not depressed. So why the nightmares? Why the sense of being overwhelmed followed by the deep sense of loss that had started permeating his most recent dreams?

He'd lost his fingers, the normal use of his arm. He'd lost his buddy. His military career, which he'd planned to leave anyway at the end of his current tour. And he'd lost his father.

Who'd sold him out. But he hadn't known that when the dreams had started again.

"What happens," he asked Shae softly, "when you're furiously angry at someone you love, and you never have the chance to make things better?"

"Maybe you have dreams about it," she said slowly.

His arm tightened around her. "Maybe."

Shae pushed up onto her elbow, brushing her hair away from her face. "How would you know if that's it?"

"I don't think there's any way to know for sure, but it's something to think about. I don't know if I ever grieved for my father. It all happened so fast. He died within days of my being hurt. And now I'm so damned mad at him for putting me in this position."

Shae settled back beside him, draping an arm over his chest. "That is something to think about."

ASHLEY SEEMED TO be arriving earlier and earlier— almost as if she suspected she could catch Shae coming out of Jordan's house. Well, so what if she did? Shae could have any number of reasons to be in there. But being there at 6:00 a.m. might be tricky to explain.

Ashley rolled in at six forty-five, earlier than ever, but Shae was already in the bunkhouse, dressing, and Jordan was in the north pasture, catching one of the fillies.

"I spoke to Miranda about Mr. Bryan's horses," Ashley said shortly after they'd started work for the day. "She says that she has no problem with him having horses, but they can't be dangerous. Not like the one he was riding the other day."

"She has to approve his horses?" Shae said on an amused note, but inwardly she was starting a slow burn. Miranda was now going to make certain that Jordan couldn't earn a living in the way he wanted. If he had to get a job elsewhere, it'd have to be on a neighboring ranch, which would pay next to nothing. Either that or he could drive to Missoula, maybe get on with a government office.

A government office had almost been his undoing. He'd talked to her more than once about slowly dying, doing mindless work alone in his cubicle.

"That's one way of putting it," Ashley said. "And the pig has to go, too, unless she's penned and stays off the leased land. No nuisance animals."

"I like her," Shae said.

"And that's not all you like, is it?"

Shae shot a sharp glance in Ashley's direction, but the girl refused to look her way.

Don't ask...don't take the bait.

Somehow Shae kept her mouth shut, didn't ask the question Ashley obviously wanted her to ask, saying instead, "When is the electrical contractor supposed to get here?"

"Early afternoon."

"Do you want to wait for the estimate, or get it tomorrow?"

"I'll wait," Ashley said with a touch of smugness.

"So when this is all said and done," Shae said casually, "do you plan on taking over operations here?"

Ashley didn't bat an eyelash at the candid question. "I have my studies to consider, but I hope to work closely developing this project."

"And what if I want the same thing?"

"I don't see that happening."

"Why?" Shae asked as a chill went through her at Ashley's confident tone. She'd realized she was getting sideways with Miranda, but had hoped that she'd played the game well enough since Ashley had arrived to redeem herself.

"Because you're sleeping with Jordan."

The chill turned into a freezing sensation that crept up Shae's spine, but she forced herself to impassively meet Ashley's superior gaze. "What makes you so confident of that?" Shae finally asked. It wasn't so much that she was afraid for her job anymore, but rather that if she stayed employed with Miranda she might be able to help mitigate the damages Jordan was going to have to contend with.

"You're not sleeping in the bunkhouse." When Shae just stared at her, Ashley finally said on a note of disgust. "I'm not stupid, you know. It's obvious there's something going on between the two of you and when I first started working here, the cot in the bunkhouse was never made. The blankets were always a mess. During the past week, the bed's been made and hasn't been disturbed."

"How do you know?"

Ashley smiled in a patently smug way. "I know," was all she said.

The electrician rolled in not long after that and Ashley went to meet him. Not caring one bit what Ashley thought, Shae marched down to the bunkhouse and went inside. Yes, her cot was neatly made and had stayed that way for many days as she'd shared Jordan's bed.

Shae blew out a breath and walked across the room. She might not have made up the cot after sleeping in it all that often since Ashley had started work there, but she had on occasion. How did the girl know that she wasn't simply going through a tidiness kick?

Reaching down, she pulled back the covers and then let out a low curse. There, lying in the middle of her bed on the sheet, was a nail from the bathhouse wall—no doubt exactly where Ashley had placed it many days ago. And the bitch had been checking daily—probably reporting back to Miranda.

Shae dropped her chin, pressing her fingertips against her temples.

Damage control. *Think, damn it, think.*

And…she could come up with nothing. Did she protest that she'd been sleeping in her truck as before? Oh, yeah—that made perfect sense with a perfectly good cot in her room and no mice. Or that she'd been going back to Missoula at night? That wouldn't wash, because Ashley got there so early. And she'd been leaving the truck parked next to the Subaru instead of by the bunkhouse, where she'd parked when she was sleeping in it.

What really struck her, though, was the fact that she was more concerned about what effect losing her job and leaving the ranch would have on Jordan rather than on her career.

After the electrician left, Shae walked with Ashley as far as her truck, getting a bit of grim satisfaction out of the fact that Ashley appeared slightly unnerved by Shae's escort. She waited until Ashley opened the truck door to say, "You've been tattling to Miranda, haven't you?"

Ashley went red. "Excuse me?"

"You know exactly what I mean."

The woman drew in a sharp breath through her nose. "It's in Miranda's best interest to know what's going on."

"Your best interest, too."

"I won't deny that," she said stiffly, getting into the truck. "I'm loyal to my employer."

"Who helps pay your tuition?"

Ashley pulled the door shut and started the truck.

Shae stepped back to stand out of harm's way as the woman put the truck in reverse, sensing that her days with Cedar Creek Enterprises were numbered by more than just the end of her contract.

CHAPTER FOURTEEN

THE FRONT DOOR banged open and Shae marched across the living room into the kitchen, stopping a few feet away from the table where Jordan stood folding the laundry he'd done on his last trip to town. "Ashley knows we're sleeping together."

"How?" he asked, putting down the T-shirt he'd been working on.

"She put a nail in my bed—quite a few days ago, apparently—and then checked to see if it was still there."

"Son of a bitch," Jordan said softly, impressed in spite of himself. He reached out to put a hand at her waist, his thumb smoothing over her lower ribs as he gently pulled her toward him. Shae took a half step forward, then stopped, her muscles taut beneath his palm. "What now?" he asked.

"We wait," she said. "Who knows how long that nail was in the bed? I haven't slept there in a week, so Miranda has known for at least a couple days. She hasn't done anything, so I'm not doing anything."

"I'm so damned sorry," he said. He didn't like Shae working for Miranda, but he didn't want his ex-stepmother plotting against her, either. And just on general principle he hated the thought of Ashley outmaneuvering them.

Shae smiled without humor. "I wish I had a clue as to how this is going to play out. I think my days of being able to run interference, as ineffective as if was, are over."

"They were over when Ashley showed up."

"I preferred to pretend they were not," Shae said wearily.

He pulled her closer and she tilted her face up before putting her hands around his neck, her fingers skimming over the scars as she pulled his mouth down to hers. It didn't take long for the kiss to deepen, to shift from consolation to heat.

"I hate waiting and wondering," she murmured against his mouth. "I'm the world's worst waiter."

"I can try to distract you."

She smiled. "I'd like that."

The distraction worked well for the next hour, but after that Shae disappeared down to the bunkhouse, leaving Jordan to wonder what he could do to make matters better.

Nothing. Shae had to work out her issues, just as he had to work out his. But he was finding that having company along the way wasn't a bad thing. He hoped Shae felt the same.

THREE DAYS PASSED, during which time Shae left the nail in the bed, right where Miranda's henchwoman had put it. She wished she could have come up with a way to replace it with something nasty, like a snake, but took the high road. Besides, she couldn't figure out how to keep the snake in the bed and she didn't want a snake in her headquarters, so that option was out.

She and Jordan debated about tactics while they waited for the other shoe to drop. Should she continue working until the end of her contract, knowing full well that Miranda would renege on her promise to reinstate Shae to her old job now that she knew she was sleeping with Jordan?

She already planned to send new résumés out, but was concerned about references. Mel was the only person she could count on and if Miranda decided to blackball Shae...

"Why am I saying *if* she decides to blackball me?" Shae asked Jordan as they sat on the porch steps, she on the step below his, drinking Bud Light and watching the sunset. "She's definitely going to do me some harm if I'm consorting with the enemy."

"Maybe you can convince her you're only using me for sex." He draped a hand over her shoulder, his fingers brushing lightly over her breast.

"It's more than sex," Shae said as she leaned back against his thigh.

"Yeah?" he asked softly.

She tilted her head back to look up at him. "You're also my sounding board."

"Is that all?"

Shae shrugged, once again looking out across the fields, but she felt the tension in his thigh muscles. He was waiting for an answer. An answer she wasn't ready to articulate. Somewhere over the past several days, she'd come to depend on his companionship. He was edgy and unpredictable at times, angry as hell at Miranda and defensive of his space, but there was also a steadiness about him where she was concerned. He was there for her, regardless of his mood, and that filled her with a type of tenderness she'd never experienced before.

She wanted to make Miranda back off, leave him in peace, but knew there was no way that was going to happen—just as there was no way Jordan was going to surrender his place to Miranda. The stalemate ate at her, because while neither of them would come out a winner as things stood now, Jordan would lose more.

His fingers smoothed over the sensitive skin at the side of her neck and Shae's mouth quirked up on one side. "No," she said softly. "That's not all."

"And we're going to leave it at that?" he asked several silent minutes later.

"For now."

"I'm good with that...for now."

That night Shae was jolted awake by Jordan thrashing around in the bed, and since she was sleeping against the wall, she was trapped unless she shimmied out at the foot of the bed. Instead, she hugged the wall until he suddenly jerked, then stilled. A moment later he exhaled as if he'd just come up from underwater, wiping a hand over his face.

She didn't touch him. Didn't make a noise, didn't move. She didn't know how long they lay there as Jordan gained control of his ragged breathing. Even though they weren't touching, she knew he was damp with sweat, could feel it on the sheets, smell it in the air. Finally he let out a long, long breath, then turned and snaked an arm over her, curling up against her. Shae lay still, letting him find his comfort with her on his terms.

AS DAYS PASSED, Shae came to the conclusion that Miranda was simply going to let her finish her contract and then cut her loose rather than confront her about consorting with Jordan. She sent out a slew of résumés on her last trip to Missoula and drove to the cattle guard each evening to check for email responses. Nothing favorable, but she told herself it was early. She was not going to dwell on the effect Miranda could have on her career in a small industry.

And then there was the matter of how she and Jordan were going to deal with living apart. What happened there was a wait-and-see kind of thing, mainly because she'd made a conscious choice to not think about it. To not try to force any issues, but to let things develop organically for perhaps the first time in her life.

Even Ashley seemed to accept that all she had to do was wait to get rid of Shae and take over the High Camp. She stopped arriving early, pulling in each morning at seven-thirty and then waiting for Shae down at the bunkhouse. Shae wondered as she walked to the bunkhouse with her cup of coffee if the girl still checked for the nail. When she let herself into the building, Ashley looked up from the samples of buffalo-plaid flannel she was comparing to say, "Miranda would like to meet with you this afternoon at three o'clock."

Maybe Miranda wasn't going to wait until the contract was done. Maybe she'd simply been busy messing up someone else's life and was now turning her attention to Shae.

Shae drove to the Cedar Creek Ranch from the High Camp, wearing jeans and a clean yet well-worn plaid work shirt—an outfit she wouldn't have been seen in public in a few months ago and never would have worn to a meeting. But she wasn't going to dress up to get fired again.

When she knocked on the frosted glass of the open office door, Miranda looked up from the papers she was reading, and Shae went inside, her heart beating fast with anticipation.

"Thank you for coming. Have a seat." Miranda waved at the padded office chairs that faced her desk and Shae took the closest one. This hadn't been a sure thing from the beginning. The only bad part was that it would be more difficult to see Jordan now that she wouldn't be living at the High Camp. But she didn't need to sneak around anymore.

She also wouldn't be able to afford to drive out all that often, either.

Miranda took her glasses off and tapped the bow on the desk. "Shae…"

Shae's spine automatically straightened. She knew that tone. Had heard it from Wallace not that long ago. "Yes?" she said.

"Looking over this—" she shook her head "—I think you've done all you can do on this property."

"What are you proposing?"

"That you go back to work at your old job."

Shae barely kept her mouth from dropping open. "What about the High Camp?"

"Ashley will take over. She's agreed to take a semester off from her studies. In the meantime, Wallace needs you. That bald man…Gerald…is giving him grief and may not be long for the company."

"This…is unexpected," Shae said.

"Why?"

"When you made Ashley my assistant, I assumed you were easing me out."

Miranda couldn't have looked more surprised. "You've done an excellent job there, Shae. Just coming up with the idea was brilliant. I admit I didn't like the tent-camp idea, but once we nailed down the difference between repair and capital investment and started to work on the cabins…well, I'm pleased."

Shae shifted in her seat. This was not playing out the way she'd anticipated and she wasn't quite certain how to take it. "Will I get the contract for my employment?"

"I spoke to Noel about that," Miranda said seriously. "He's of the opinion that we shouldn't set precedents…unless you'd settle for a six-month renewable contract. That he had no problem with."

"I'll, uh, think about it."

"Fine. In the meantime, you'll go back on salary as before. Starting Monday," Miranda said brightly. She stood and offered Shae her hand. "Congratulations on a job well done. You have more than proved yourself."

Shae walked down the stairs feeling numb. By the time she reached her car, she realized that she was shaking. She got behind the wheel, tried to jam the key into the ignition, missed and had to try again. If she hadn't been certain that Miranda was watching, she would have beaten her head on the steering wheel.

Well played, Miranda. She'd just effectively removed her as Jordan's ally—and she'd done it by giving Shae exactly what she'd asked for.

"WHAT HAPPENED?" Jordan asked as soon as he opened the truck door for Shae. He'd been waiting for her to get back to the ranch since putting the palomino away after her last official ride before he returned her to Claiborne.

"I'm going back to my old job on Monday."

"Monday?" Jordan's hand stilled on the door, then he pushed it shut. "Why would she give you your job back before the contract is finished?" he asked suspiciously.

"I had the same the question."

"Are you taking her up on it?"

"At the moment I don't have a lot of choice. I need a paycheck. Also, I might be able to keep apprised of what's happening here, which might be helpful in the future."

"Yeah. Maybe." But he doubted Shae would have access to information that would help him in any way.

He'd hoped that, despite her pessimistic feelings on the matter, she'd get another job offer before she left the High Camp—anything to keep her from continuing to work for Miranda. But she had to eat, and there were apparently tons of bills from her almost wedding that she was paying off in installments. Plus, she fully intended to reimburse her parents the money they'd lost.

Weddings done on a grand scale were apparently freaking expensive. Jordan was sorry that Shae was in the hole, in a position where she had to take work where she found it…but he was not unhappy that the marriage hadn't taken place. And neither, it seemed, was Shae.

The thought never failed to make him feel just a bit better about life in general. He didn't know where this was going, but he was glad to have the opportunity to make the journey.

Now all he had to do was to make certain that bitch Miranda didn't screw with Shae in any way.

It rained the day Shae left the High Camp. She kissed Jordan goodbye on the porch, then ran for her truck. She hated the thought of Jordan dealing with Miranda's crew without her, but knew in her gut this was a battle he needed to fight—or come to terms with—himself. She was almost home after a very long drive on rain-slicked roads when her phone rang. Even though she knew it wasn't Jordan, her heart skipped at the sound. She couldn't remember doing that when she'd first been dating Reed.

She reached for the phone on the seat beside her as she pulled off into the parking lot of a small convenience store.

"Mel?" she asked instead of saying hello. *My long-lost friend who hasn't contacted me in over three weeks?*

"Hi," Mel said. "Sorry about not calling sooner. I've been drowning in the studies."

"Ah."

"Working full-time, plus classes and studying... where are you?"

"Almost home."

"Can I come over? It doesn't have to be tonight, but—"

"Tonight's fine," Shae said. In fact, tonight would be a blessing. She didn't feel like being alone. "The sooner the better."

Mel arrived within minutes of Shae walking in her front door.

"Were you circling the block?" Shae asked, stepping back to let her friend into the apartment.

"Close. I was on my way home from a class when I called."

"I'm glad you did," Shae said casting a critical eye over Mel. Untidy wisps of black hair had escaped her ponytail and the hollows of her cheeks were more pronounced than usual, as if she'd lost weight. "Studies going all right?"

"I think I signed up for one too many classes," Mel said, dropping her coat on a chair and heading for the kitchen. "May I?"

"Pour one for me," Shae said, carrying her bag into the bedroom. "So how long are you going to carry on this overloaded schedule?" she asked as she came back out after dumping her laundry in the hamper.

Mel handed her a glass of white wine. "Today was my last day of the overloaded schedule."

"You quit school?" Shae asked over the top of her glass.

Mel shook her head and then took a drink. "Uh-uh. I quit work."

"No!" Shae set her wine on the bookcase.

"Okay, I didn't quit completely. I'm taking an unpaid leave of absence to focus on my studies. In this job climate, it seems wise to keep my toe in the door."

"But I'm starting work on Monday."

"I know," Mel said. "I heard today."

"Well, crap. You were going to keep me sane."

"Guess you'll have to depend on Wallace for that."

Shae snorted. "Somehow I don't think it'll be the same." She picked her glass back up and took a healthy sip before gesturing toward the sofa and the meaning of Mel's announcement sank in. "I'm basically taking your position, aren't I?"

"That's my guess."

"And when you return from your temporary leave of absence…" Shae made a slicing motion across her throat, which in turn made Mel's eyes widen.

"I don't think she'd bring you back just to—"

"I do." In fact, she was certain. Miranda had neatly filled Mel's position with an experienced employee while at the same time prying Shae away from Jordan. The woman was good.

Shae sighed. "I didn't plan on staying long, but I hate being played."

"I thought you respected Miranda. Why do you think she's playing you?"

"My eyes have been opened," Shae said bluntly. "She's not a nice woman."

"Really?" Shae nodded and Mel frowned as she said, "Because she fired you?"

"No. Because I got to know Jordan Bryan."

It took Mel a moment to say, "In what sense?"

"Biblical."

"No." Once again Mel's eyes went wide. "I mean…no."

"Yes." Shae understood her friend's astonishment. Mel certainly remembered the ass dumping as vividly as Shae did, having been privy to Shae's frequently verbalized views on what a jerk Jordan Bryan was for days after the event. And then there were the scars. Shae had always been about perfection and in that sense, Jordan was not perfect.

"He's the rebound guy?"

Shae leaned her head back against the sofa cushions. "No. He's not."

"So, you mean a serious hookup?"

"I think so," Shae said. "Not what I expected, but…the feelings are there. Now I just have to figure out what to do with them."

"Huh." Mel stared straight ahead, hugging a sofa pillow to her middle. "Crazy."

"What's so crazy?" Mel cocked an eyebrow at her and Shae quirked up one corner of her mouth. It was crazy, her and Jordan. But it didn't feel crazy. It felt right.

"Are you sure this isn't a rebound thing?" she asked suspiciously.

"If it is, then I'm a fan of rebound."

They sat in silence for a moment, Shae sipping her wine as Mel continued to hug the pillow as she stared into space and processed. "Other than drowning in studies," Shae said, needing to shift the subject away from herself, "and taking a leave of absence, how's life?"

"Good. Good." Mel still didn't look at her, and Shae knew from her tone that she wasn't being totally up front. Mel did prefer to hide her difficulties and deal with them herself—not that Shae had been all that helpful in the past. Oh, yeah. It'd all been about her. Time to change that if she could.

"Honestly?"

Mel looked at her then with a frown. "Good enough," she said matter-of-factly.

"Anything you want to talk about?"

Mel gave her head a shake. "Just…life. Small things adding up, but nothing major." She reached out with her glass to tap Shae's. "I'm confident that once I start getting some sleep, things will look rosy again."

"Wouldn't it be great if it was that easy," Shae said. If so, she'd start sleeping right now. "And if sleeping doesn't work…any chance you'd share?"

Mel gave her a slow sideways glance. "If I had something to share, yes."

"For real?"

"Yes. For real," Mel said as if it was a given. It wasn't, but Shae hoped she was telling the truth, because she owed her friend some payback.

SHAE ASSUMED THAT Wallace was expecting her at the office, but the stunned look on Risa's face when she walked in made her wonder. Surely Miranda had included Wallace in her plans.

"Would you please tell Wallace I'm here?" she asked Risa, who kept her heavily made-up eye on Shae while she picked up the phone and dialed Wallace, as if Shae was going to start riffling through desk drawers if Risa looked away.

"Go in," she said abruptly, dropping her gaze back to her computer screen. Wallace looked up from papers he had scattered across his desk when Shae walked in.

"You're back," he said and Shae could tell from his tone that he had indeed expected her.

"It wasn't easy," Shae replied, shutting the door. *And I know it won't last...*

"Your job will now have your full attention?" Wallace asked with mock sternness, leaning back in his chair, tapping his pencil on his palm.

"And then some," Shae said with a practiced smile, playing the game. She needed this paycheck and at least for now, until she found another position, this job was her life's blood.

"I'm sure your new manager will be happy to hear that. In the meantime, your old desk is waiting for you and Gerald has a project that he needs your help on. I'll send him by within the hour to discuss matters."

"New manager?" Shae asked, stunned.

Wallace laid his pencil on the desk. "I haven't announced yet, but I'm leaving. Just a handful of people know. Since you'll be directly affected, you're one of them."

Shae felt as if she'd just been sucker punched. "Where are you going?"

"I'm starting my own agency in Butte."

"Oh," Shae said hollowly. "Congratulations."

"Thank you."

"Does Miranda know?"

"Not yet. That's not a conversation I'm looking forward to, so I'd appreciate it if you didn't say anything."

"There's no winning with her, is there?" Shae said wearily, no longer seeing the sense in being politically correct.

"She's actually quite lovely," Wallace said, "as long as you do as she says and things go her way. I fought many battles on behalf of my staff that they know nothing about." Shae could believe that now.

"Why didn't you tell us?"

"Because it's my job to handle things like that. It

wouldn't have helped productivity to tell you guys about every run-in I had with the big boss. I wanted you to focus on your projects."

"I don't know how you've put up with working for the woman for so long."

"She paid me well to kiss her ass," he said matter-of-factly.

"Money talks," Shae said, still working to fully process Wallace's announcement. No Mel, no Wallace... Wow.

"You seem different," Wallace said.

"It's been one hell of a ride the last seven weeks." Were seven weeks enough to change a life? In Shae's experience, yes. Plenty of time. "My eyes have been opened to a lot of stuff."

"Such as...?"

What could she say? That she'd finally come to terms with just how self-absorbed she'd been and was working to change? That she'd met a man she could well be in love with who was too stubborn to stop poking the tigress? "What it's like to take on Miranda one-on-one." She hesitated for all of a second before asking, "She's using me to fill in for Mel and then she'll fire me when Mel comes back, won't she?"

Wallace didn't instantly endorse her theory, as she'd expected. "That probably depends on economics and how well you do Mel's job."

And whether or not she was still seeing Jordan—

apparently Miranda hadn't shared that tidbit with Wallace. "I guess I'll work extra hard, then."

Shae held out a hand over the top of the desk. "Good luck with your new venture, Wally." She smiled roguishly, even though she was dying inside. "I can call you Wally now?"

"No one calls me Wally and lives to tell about it," he said with a smile. "Good luck to you, too."

"Thanks." She started for the door, then stopped with her hand on the knob. "Any chance that you'll need a go-getter employee such as myself?"

Wallace shook his head. "I'll be a one-man band for a while."

"Just thought I'd give it a shot."

"Sorry, kid."

Work wouldn't be the same without Wallace and Mel, and life wasn't the same without Jordan in it full-time. In fact, it felt pretty damned empty.

THE PROBLEM WITH being on the ranch alone while the invaders worked around him was that he had no one to vent to, and after finally allowing himself to open up to Shae, he found he missed it. He, who'd kept everything bottled up for so long, had become a talker—at least where she was concerned. But she wasn't there and he did his best to keep his anger at what was going on around him contained. Not easy when Ashley had a small crew coming every day. For the most part he walked around the place as if he had tunnel vision. It was the only way he could function.

On Monday, Jordan delivered the horses to Claiborne with the help of Cole, who'd seemed more than happy not only to lend him a trailer and truck but to come along for the ride. The talk stayed general until Jordan once again apologized for sending Cole home after the cross-country flight and Cole told him that if he mentioned it again, he was going to have to do something about it.

Claiborne was happy with the horses, paid the money he owed, and then he and Jordan negotiated a deal for sixty days on three older mares. Cole told Jordan he was crazy for taking them on, Jordan agreed, then after delivering the horses to the High Camp, he and Cole bought a new stove for the ranch. Once the stove was in place, Cole took his leave, but not before suggesting that Jordan might want to invest in a vehicle more in tune with his lifestyle.

Jordan had to agree that the Subaru was close to the end of its usefulness, but it would take quite a few more colts before he had enough for a used truck. He could wait. He was patient…with everything except waiting for Shae to show up Friday night.

AFTER A LONG week working with Gerald on a publicity campaign aimed at getting buyers to invest in new guest-ranch properties, Shae drove past the exit to her apartment and straight out to the High Camp.

Jordan met her at the truck, wrapped his arms around her and kissed her deeply, washing away the last of her doubts about how she felt about the man. She loved him. Simple as that. She wouldn't have been so certain if she hadn't first thought she'd loved Reed. She had, but not like this. Not with the feeling that having him near made her complete. And she'd never before had a relationship with a guy who didn't eventually bend to her will when she got insistent—or at least bend to her will a couple of times before he walked away.

Jordan wasn't going to do that. He wasn't going to bend and she wasn't going to push things—not like she had with Reed.

"I missed you," she muttered against his mouth before starting to unbutton his shirt.

"Maybe we should wait until we get into the house?" he asked with a laugh.

"Details." But she patted his chest and allowed him to get her backpack out of the Audi, which had once again been punished by the High Camp road.

"I didn't know whether I'd see you or not," he said after ushering her inside.

Shae responded by backing him toward the bedroom as soon as the door was closed. He dropped her pack as she worked on his buttons while they moved down the hall. Clothing began hitting the floor and then the bed creaked under their combined weight.

"I *really* missed you," Shae said, clutching his head as he began a slow, sensual exploration of her body with his mouth.

"Me or my tongue?" he muttered.

"Don't make me choose," she said on a sigh.

For the next half hour, everything was right in her world. All the misgivings, all the worries, gone. Afterward, they didn't bother to get out of bed, but instead talked until moonlight spilled across the room and Clyde insisted that it was time for him to come in.

The weekend continued that way. There were signs of the renovation beginning, which Jordan pointedly ignored as they walked to the corrals where Jordan had a new crop of horses from Claiborne—and the palomino, which he'd agreed to put sixty more days on.

"Ashley told me to get rid of the horses. I told her to take a flying leap. I think I'm about to get a visit from that lawyer in the beaver hat."

"I'm sure."

It'd always been obvious to Shae that Jordan loved training, but he seemed even more satisfied now that he'd finished his first contract and had negotiated a new one at a higher rate of pay; it was evident in the way his expression lit up when he talked about his new charges and Shae found herself smiling as she listened to him. In that regard he was so different from when she'd first showed up. He now had a purpose—besides getting Miranda off his property—and training was something that he could do anywhere. He didn't need to be at the High Camp and, as Shae took advantage of Jordan's late-afternoon shower to assess the progress made on the buildings, she became convinced that he probably shouldn't be at the High Camp. Not unless he could get into the swing of having people coming and going, invading his territory, because the renovations were getting serious. She knew he still held out hope that something would happen. That maybe people wouldn't be interested in Miranda's unique experience and the place would fold.

Miranda would keep the place operational anyway. Shae was utterly certain now that the animosity between the two was so bitter that she'd run the High Camp guest ranch at a loss just to get back at Jordan.

Which made her uneasy.

Could she live with him fighting Miranda fulltime?

The woman was malignant and her poison would spread out, take over their lives…as it had already taken over Jordan's.

CHAPTER FIFTEEN

JORDAN MADE A grocery run on Wednesday afternoon, leaving the ranch fifteen minutes after the last of Ashley's crew pulled out. He would not have those people on the ranch when he wasn't there, so it was going to be a flying trip. There were several twenty-four-hour grocery stores, but he'd have to drive fast to get to the pharmacy before it closed.

The traffic was with him, so he made it with time to spare, hit the feed store before it closed for more pig mash and grain—one bag of each, since it was all he could carry in the Subaru—and then did his grocery shopping. It was almost nine when he called Shae. He'd hoped to take her out to dinner, but there simply wasn't time.

"Of course," she said when he asked if he could stop by. She gave her address and fifteen minutes later he pulled up behind the Audi at her apartment complex.

She greeted him with a kiss and smile, then ushered him into the apartment. Jordan stopped just inside the door, taking in the leather furniture, glass coffee tables, modern art on the walls. When he glanced over at Shae she smirked at him. "Hey, what can I say? I'm a conspicuous consumer," she said, closing the door. "But that doesn't mean I don't appreciate the charms of a bunkhouse with no plumbing."

"How about the cowboy that goes with the place?"

"I find myself appreciating him, too," she said with a smile before gesturing toward the other side of the room with her head. "I need to close down shop. Why didn't you tell me you were coming to town? We could have grabbed something to eat."

"I didn't want to leave until the crew was gone," he said, following her through the arched entryway to the dining room, where she turned off her laptop. Papers and a few aerial photos were scattered across the table.

"Pretty busy?"

"Yeah. My friend Mel took a leave of absence, so I'm doing her job."

"Along with yours?"

"No," Shae said, closing the lid of the laptop. "Just hers."

"So when she comes back…?" he asked darkly.

Shae leaned on the table, her shirt gaping at the neck, giving him a pretty good look at what he'd been missing since she left. "I'll be gone by then. I'm actively job hunting."

"Good. I hate you working for the bitch." Not that he was going to tell her what to do, but he did hate it and wasn't going to be shy about sharing his feelings.

"Working for her at the office is no different than me working for her at the ranch," she pointed out.

"It's different when you're with me. I know you're on my side."

Shae's eyebrows rose and for a moment he found himself facing the old Shae. The Shae who told you how it was going to be and if you didn't like it you could kiss her ass. "You think I'm going to change sides?" she asked.

"No, damn it. What I meant was that when you're with me I know..." He suddenly realized she was messing with him.

"What do you know?" she asked archly.

"Screw it." He reached out and took her face between his hands and kissed her, long and hard, trying to convey his feelings on the matter without words, which he had never been good at. He wanted her with him. While she was there, he felt...better. More whole. "I know that we care about each other," he finally said as he pulled his lips from hers. "That you have my back and I have yours. *That's* what I meant by being on my side." One corner of his mouth tightened ruefully. "I worry about all the shit Miranda might pull on you when we're not together."

"As opposed to the shit she pulls when we are together?" she asked with a hint of amusement. "I can handle it."

He'd debated on and off about asking her to stay there with him at the High Camp until she could find another job, but he knew her financial situation, knew that the wedding bills were killing her. And besides that, it was too soon, much as he would have loved having her there full-time.

"Can you stay the night?" she asked, flattening her palms against the front of his Carhartt jacket and leaning toward him.

"I'd have to leave early tomorrow. I don't want to be away from the ranch at all while Miranda's crew is there," he said. "I worry about my horses… the pig…Clyde."

There was more to it than that and they both knew it, but Shae was apparently going to take what he could give, because she took hold of the front of his coat and started backing toward her bedroom. She left the light off, so he wasn't able to gage the level of her conspicuous consumption in that room, but he did notice that the mattress was a shade better than his own and the comforter felt as if it was made of satin or silk. And after that he didn't think about much of anything except for Shae.

"Are you sure you have to go?" she asked sleepily several hours later as she escorted him to the door. "It isn't like you're punching a time clock."

Jordan leaned down to kiss her. "I'm territorial. I can't help it."

"Not a problem." She bit her lip, holding back whatever it was she wanted to say.

I love you, Shae.

He didn't say it. It wasn't time and he didn't want to complicate her life any more than he already was. Instead he kissed her again and then turned and walked down the hall.

JORDAN'S SELF-PROFESSED territoriality ate at Shae for the remainder of the week. What kind of life was he going to have living at the High Camp, defending his part of the property against Miranda and her minions? Surrounded by people who wanted him gone, or guests who would expect him to be friendly? Would the mental and physical toll be worth the satisfaction of standing up to Miranda?

Despite her workload, the days passed slowly, giving her too much time to think. She had to work late on Friday and when she finally arrived at the High Camp, close to ten o'clock, Jordan was waiting for her on the porch with the pig and the poodle.

"I was getting worried," he said, taking her bag before wrapping his arm around her and pulling her close for a kiss. The pig snorted at her leg and Clyde danced in front of her.

"Just a late workday," she said as they walked into the house. "We have a new property we're developing a campaign for and sometimes that runs into extra hours." She stilled once they were inside and she got a good look at him in the light.

"Damn, Jordan." She ran a critical eye over him,

taking in the taut lines around his eyes and mouth that showed even though he was halfway smiling.

"I'm no prize."

Shae shook her head, refusing to let him sidetrack her. "You look like you've been having nightmares on a regular basis." She narrowed her eyes at him. "Have you?"

"I'm living in a nightmare, Shae. Wait until daylight and you'll see."

"They're doing a lot?"

"They're building boardwalks, planting shrubs, doing all kinds of cutesy shit. The damned place is going to look like an Old West movie set when they're done."

"That wasn't part of the plan," Shae said.

"Well, it is now."

Jordan fell asleep almost as soon as they'd finished making love, his arm looped over her holding her close, but Shae couldn't relax, couldn't sleep. Determination was a wonderful thing—until it became obsessive and self-destructive. Jordan was stressed to the max, he was having nightmares and Shae had a bad feeling that this was only the beginning of the hell he'd go through if he continued to fight Miranda.

The next morning they walked to the corrals, past a group of men working on flooring in the cabins. Another man was tacking a facade onto the bathhouse.

"That's not a repair," Shae said.

"They can do anything they want that can be removed prior to my taking back the property," Jordan said sourly. "Emery checked into the matter."

"How can you stay here?" she finally asked. "With all this going on?"

"How can I not?"

She turned toward him, waiting until a contractor carrying a power saw walked by before saying, "As long as you stay here fighting her, you're never going to have any kind of life. You're going to have a vendetta."

His chin jerked up. "Bull. I'll make a life here. And I'll figure out a way to get her sideshow off my property."

"You haven't yet," she said reasonably. "Neither has your lawyer."

"What are you saying?"

Shae stopped walking and turned to put her palms on his chest. "I'm saying that maybe, at some point in the future, we should talk about an exit strategy."

"A what?" he asked.

Shae hesitated, which was so out of character for her when she had something important to say, but she had to tread lightly if she was going to get Jordan to listen to her. "I've been thinking about this for a few days now. Miranda has more money, a better lawyer, and a driving need to make you unhappy. Why subject yourself to this fight?"

"Because it's the right thing to do?"

"It might also be right to start a life somewhere else. Somewhere where every waking moment isn't overshadowed by 'beating the bitch.'"

"I'm not leaving, Shae."

"You'd rather have a vendetta than a life?"

"I'd rather keep what's mine," he said harshly. "I don't want to waste what little time we have together arguing about something that isn't going to happen."

They saddled Jordan's horses and rode the mountain trail in silence, Shae wishing the entire time that she had a way to make Jordan realize that protecting his ranch at all costs from a woman who had the resources to make him miserable for twelve more years was crazy. But one look at his tight jaw and the distant look in his eye told her that this wasn't the time to press the matter.

It was killing her not to. Only by conjuring up images of Reed, and every other guy she'd bent to her will when she really shouldn't have, did she manage to keep her mouth shut. She'd said her piece and now it was up to him...but that knowledge didn't keep Shae from riding home feeling as if she had a rock in the pit of her stomach.

What was he willing to sacrifice to stay on the ranch and show Miranda that she couldn't control him? His happiness?

Hers?

A question worth pursuing.

AFTER SHAE LEFT early Sunday afternoon, Jordan went into the bathroom to get the watch he'd left on the windowsill, catching a good look at himself in the mirror as he went by. He stopped abruptly and backed up to study his reflection for a moment. He'd gained weight since coming back to the High Camp and the good side of his face was tanned rather than pale, but his expression—holy shit. He looked as if he was about to murder someone. Stress, plain and simple.

All right, he admitted as he grabbed his watch and headed for the back door, Shae had cause to be worried, but she didn't need to push him to give up the ranch. He had no problem disagreeing or arguing or working out a compromise on any matter except this one. There was too much at stake here. His future, his pride. His deep, deep need to win somehow.

When she'd first mentioned an exit strategy, Jordan had been stunned. Hell, he'd felt betrayed until he managed to convince himself that she'd only broached the matter out of concern. She'd been unusually quiet after their argument, and when she left, they'd kissed goodbye, but it hadn't been with the usual passion or promise. The first rift had appeared and Jordan wasn't certain how to fix it, but he did know who was responsible.

Damned Miranda.

On Friday morning Jordan awoke to the sound

of a big diesel truck pulling up close to the house, followed by a knock on the door.

"Where you want me to start?" the burly man asked.

"Start what?" Jordan growled.

"The plumbing," the man said impatiently.

"I don't know anything about plumbing," Jordan said. "You need to get in contact with whoever hired you."

Ashley showed up shortly thereafter and Jordan did his best to ignore her as she flitted around, directing "repairmen" who worked on the plumbing in the bathhouse and continued to replace the floors in the cabins. He did exactly what he'd planned to do when this day came: live his life.

So much fricking easier said than done. There were people everywhere, banging and making noise, making it difficult to get his horses to focus on him and him alone. When the backhoe rolled in, he gave up and released the mare, then retreated to his house—where he had next to nothing to do. He was an outside guy. He worked horses. He did not do well trapped in a house with a poodle for company—even a good poodle like Clyde.

But he couldn't bring himself to go outside and face the mayhem. Every now and again he pushed the muslin curtain aside and looked out. The backhoe was ripping up the old septic area and Ashley was standing a good fifty feet away, calling directions the driver couldn't hear.

Disgusted, he walked back to his old leather chair and sat down, feeling very much the prisoner.

It was happening. Miranda was slowly but surely taking over his ranch, renovating under the guise of repairing and moving forward with her plans. He put up with two more days of the repairs that weren't capital investments, and therefore out of his realm of influence, before deciding that he had to take action. He couldn't let Miranda just waltz in here without challenging her.

And challenge her he would. Even if it got his ass sued.

IT WAS A LONG, stressful six-day week, but by late Saturday Shae was not only very close to nailing down the deal Mel had been working on before she left, she'd also gotten a call for an interview on the other side of the state. Miles City. A long, long way away from the High Camp.

At the moment she wasn't certain how she felt about that. She desperately wanted a job that wasn't connected to Miranda in any way. And as things stood, perhaps some distance from Jordan would be a good thing.

Yeah. That was why she had a bag packed and waiting in the car. She didn't know what kind of a reception she was going to get, but she was driving to the High Camp as soon as she got off work—even though she'd have to drive back the next morning. She hated the way they'd parted last Sunday and she needed to see if she could make peace with him—if the barrier that had risen after she'd mentioned giving up the ranch could be breached.

Her question was answered almost as soon as she parked her car. She'd barely opened the door when Jordan appeared. He stood before her, tense and uncertain, then opened his arms and she walked into them, pressing herself against him as she brought her cheek to rest against his solid chest.

"I missed you," he said against her hair.

"I missed you, too," she murmured, feeling his heart beat beneath her cheek. She eased out of his embrace and smiled up at him, glad to see that some of the tension had left his face. "Can we go to the house?"

Jordan reached into the Audi for her bag, then closed the door and followed her up to the house. Clyde's nose was pressed against the window and when Shae came inside he practically did a flip in his joy to see her. Shae laughed and knelt down to ruffle his fur. "Taking good care of the man?" she asked in a low voice as she dodged kisses.

"My turn," Jordan said, leaning down to put a hand beneath her elbow and helping her to her feet.

"I got an interview," she said with a smile. "Next week."

"Where?"

"Miles City."

A shadow crossed his face before he said, "How do you feel about that?"

"Hopeful," she said, smoothing her palms over his chest. "And how're things here?"

"I'm trying to focus on the positive," he said, his hands slipping down over her ass.

"Good plan," she murmured, pressing herself up against him. "I think you should make me feel very, very positive."

"I'll see what I can do to spread the joy," he said, swinging her up in his arms and heading down the hall. Shae squealed, her feet banged the doorframe, but Jordan didn't put her down until they reached the bed. And then, good as his word, he made Shae feel better than she'd felt all week.

She returned the favor and was just about to drift to sleep when Jordan eased himself out of bed. She didn't think much of it until the front door opened and closed. Shae pushed herself up on one elbow, then let herself back down on the pillow. Five or six minutes later the door opened and shut again.

Jordan got back into bed and dropped an arm over her. Shae snuggled closer to him and seconds later was asleep.

The next morning Jordan cooked her breakfast and they ate out on the back porch, where they couldn't see the abomination Miranda and Ashley were creating. Shae didn't want to leave without clearing the air between them. Yes, they'd made love and yes, it'd been good—makeup sex always was—but she wanted official closure...which didn't seem to be happening, since neither of them wanted to ruin the moment.

Finally Shae set down her cup and addressed the matter. Because that was what she did—addressed things that needed to be addressed. "About last weekend," she said.

Jordan's gaze jerked up. "Yeah?" he said cautiously.

"I know I have a rep for bulldozing over people to get my way, and I want you to know that I'm not going to do that with you."

"Good to know."

"However, I will let you know what I think."

"You've done that."

"And I'd appreciate it if you did me the courtesy of listening to my opinion."

"I will."

"But please…because this isn't easy for me… don't mistake my opinion for bulldozing. Okay? I'm still working all of this out." She shrugged ruefully. "Old habits are hard to break, so be patient with me, okay?"

"That goes both ways," Jordan said, smiling warmly.

Shae reached out and took his injured hand, her thumb smoothing over the damaged skin on his knuckles. "I've got to go," she said. "But I wanted that clear. I'm trying. I'm not going to do to you what I did to Reed."

"And probably a few others." Jordan smiled and Shae squeezed his hand before letting go.

"Maybe a few."

Ten minutes later Jordan set her bag onto the backseat of the car and then, instead of saying goodbye, told her he'd ride with her as far as the gate.

"It wasn't closed when I came through," she said.

"It's closed now."

Shae shrugged and got in behind the wheel while Jordan got into the passenger seat. If he wanted to open the gate for her and walk back, well, she'd happily take those extra moments with him. But he hadn't come along just to open the gate—he'd come along to unlock the big-ass padlock securing the chain around the gate. Shae's heart sank.

After taking the car out of gear, Shae got out and walked over to the gatepost. She lifted the heavy chain with one hand. He was locking Miranda out. One lawsuit, coming up.

"You don't expect this to work, do you?"

"I expect it to work for a while. The crew doesn't show up today, but sometimes Ashley does, and tomorrow..." He smiled in anticipation as the words trailed off.

"And what happens after a while? After she sues you for access and wins?"

"What makes you think she'll win?"

"Just a nasty feeling I have."

"If she wins this one, I'll think of something else."

For a long moment Shae stared at him. Nothing

good was going to come of this, but what could she do? Demand that he unlock the gate? Finally she simply took his face in her hands and kissed him long and hard before getting into the car. She drove through the gate, watching in the rearview mirror as Jordan closed and locked it behind her.

THE CHAIN WORKED for just about as long as it took Ashley to report back to Miranda that her access was blocked and for the burly cowboy to show up with bolt cutters. Jordan had expected no less. The small chain was his warning shot.

Ashley went to work as if nothing had happened and Jordan spent the day gritting his teeth and waiting for her to leave. When Shae had been working at the High Camp, he'd been able to go most of the day without seeing evidence of change, but Miranda was pulling out all the stops now and every day something new was done to one of the old buildings. The cabins had been gutted and new flooring had been laid over the old. Since there'd been an issue with rot, it was technically a repair. Miranda seemed able to twist everything around so that it was technically a repair. She could probably build a structure from the ground up and it'd be considered a repair. That was the way life worked for her.

"Excuse me." Jordan turned from where he was putting the buckskin through her paces in the round pen to find Ashley standing close to the gate. The expression on his scarred face must have been pretty damned spectacular, because she took a quick step back before she tilted her chin up and said, "We need to talk about the peacocks."

"What about them?"

"They need to go. They're encroaching on our property."

"And right now you're standing on mine. Get off."

She hugged her clipboard to her chest and then fled without another word.

Good. But he couldn't help thinking that Shae would have never backed down. She would have said her piece, listened to him and then told him where he'd gone wrong. And she would have looked damned hot while doing it.

He turned back to his horse, but his concentration was shot. He walked toward the horse, which met him halfway across the round pen, and rubbed her ears.

Damn it, Dad. Why did you put me in this situation?

After Ashley and her crew left, Jordan went to the barn and found the logging chains his grandfather had used. It was all he could do with his injured arm to get the damned things wrapped around the gate and gatepost.

Ashley and her crew weren't able to breach the new chain. The padlock was old and thick and beyond bolt cutters. A torch would get the job done, and it was probably coming soon. Then the flood of repairmen would start again. As it was, Ashley walked onto the property from where she'd parked her truck on the other side of the gate. She stalked up to him and said, "This isn't going to work."

"Seems to be doing okay so far."

She let out a huff of breath and pretended to go to work, but there wasn't much she could do with no crew to direct. The contractors were stopped at the gate and most likely went back home. That was probably going to cost Miranda a pretty penny for nothing and Jordan was going to see to it that it kept costing her. He had several lengths of logging chain.

"You can expect to hear from our lawyer soon," Ashley said as she started back down the driveway that afternoon.

"Can't wait," he replied.

But it turned out that he could wait, and he did. Ashley didn't show up the next day, or the following day, either. And the beaver-hatted lawyer didn't appear at his door with a cease-and-desist order. Jordan was starting to get edgy. Miranda hadn't gone away.

WITH WALLACE'S BLESSING, Shae took Friday off and flew to Miles City for her interview. She flew back with a job offer and two weeks to decide. Her flight got in early, and after loading her overnight bag in the Audi, she headed straight for the High Camp. Straight to Jordan.

It wasn't until she got to the gate that she realized

getting to the ranch was going to be more difficult than anticipated, primarily due to the presence of one very large chain holding the gate shut. Shae got out of the Audi and walked up to the gate, feeling a deep sinking sensation in the pit of her stomach. The battle of the gate had obviously escalated.

Shae shook her head and climbed through the fence, taking care not to snag her linen pants, and then walked the quarter mile to the house, her stomach knotting more tightly with each step.

Jordan was just coming from the corrals when he saw her and even at a distance she saw a wide smile form on his face. He met her before she reached the driveway, taking her in his arms, kissing her soundly.

"The first chain didn't work?" she asked as his lips left hers, resisting the impulse to lose herself in the moment and pretend all was well.

"No. This one is doing a better job. I hate to leave the property, because I don't know what to expect next. I have lots of chains, though, so I can keep this up as long as they can."

Shae took a small step back. "And what happens when you get the official notice to allow your lessees access?"

"I'll have to think of something else."

Shae framed Jordan's face with her hands. "Is this how you want to live your life? Thinking of something else? Fighting the inevitable?"

He broke away from her, frowning, and even

though Shae told herself to shut up, that this wasn't her battle, she couldn't stay quiet.

"Staying here, being bitter while Miranda builds her guest ranch around you is going to destroy you."

"So what am I supposed to do? Just…let it go?"

"Yeah. Let it go."

He stared at her, anger etching across his features. "And if I can't?"

Shae pushed her hair back from her forehead with both hands to keep from touching him again. "I know how much she's taken from you. I won't presume to know how devastating that was, but I can tell you that if you stay here, it will affect any chance we have to be happy."

"You're making me choose between the ranch and you."

"No." She blurted out the word, shocked. "The last thing I'd do is give you an ultimatum."

"You're asking me to give up the ranch. You're indicating that if I don't, we won't be happy."

She dropped her hands back to her sides. "You have to choose whether or not to ruin your life over a woman who wants to see you in hell. If you stay here, she gets her wish. You'll be miserable."

"And if I leave she gets her wish, too."

"If that's the case," Shae said, "then you have to choose the lesser of the two evils." He wore an expression of such utter betrayal that she knew it was useless, but she tried one more time.

"You don't have to sell the place—"

"I have no capital to set up anywhere else," he said angrily. "This is it. This is what I can afford right now, and this is where I have to stay."

For one very long moment, they faced off, Shae's throat tightening as she realized the futility of arguing further. "You might have to stay, but I can't."

"You're giving up on us." His voice was cool, bordering on icy, but there was no mistaking the flash of pain in his eyes.

"I can't stay and watch you destroy yourself."

"That's not what's happening."

"Yeah. It is, whether you want to admit it or not."

"And in your opinion, selling the ranch, will make things better."

"Getting *off* the ranch will move you out of Miranda's sphere of influence."

"I'm not giving up."

"Then…" Shae spread her hands in a helpless gesture.

"So my choice is to do what you want or lose you?" he asked in a deadly tone. "Sounds a hell of a lot like an ultimatum to me."

"Sorry you see it that way." Sorry enough that it felt as if her heart was breaking, but she'd told the stone-cold truth when she'd said that she couldn't stay and watch him destroy himself. It was now crystal clear that keeping his battle with Miranda was the most important thing in Jordan's life. He couldn't let go, and Shae couldn't live with it.

Shae walked back to the gate alone. Jordan had

coolly offered to go with her, but she'd turned him down. It was hard enough to walk away as it was. But walk she did.

What now?

She didn't know. The one certainty, though, was that if hating Miranda was more important than building something with her, then there wasn't anything she could do about it. Oh, she could try and everything in her gut told her to go for it, to not lose the best thing that had happened to her, but if there was one thing she'd learned over the past two months, it was that getting her way through strength of will didn't solve problems. It just changed them.

She couldn't have everything she wanted just because she wanted it.

CHAPTER SIXTEEN

SHAE DIDN'T COME back to the High Camp, didn't try to contact him. Jordan drove to the cattle guard several nights in a row and tried to call her, but she didn't answer. He was once again very much alone.

He hated it.

Hard to believe that his dearest wish a couple months ago was now the thing he hated most, next to Miranda.

Hating Miranda... He couldn't help himself, but it didn't seem to be getting him anywhere, either. The beaver-hat lawyer finally showed up a few days after Shae had left and personally handed Jordan a letter stating that he had to allow access to the lessee and if he did not comply in thirty days, he was liable for financial damages. Jordan stuck the letter back in the envelope and jammed it in his back pocket. The lawyer touched his hat and started walking back toward the gate, where his expensive truck was parked.

What did it cost to have an attorney hand deliver a letter?

Whatever it cost, Miranda apparently thought it was worth it. She was never going to stop.

And neither was he. A sobering thought.

Another week passed and still no word from Shae. Ashley didn't show up, either, not once, but Jordan figured it was due to some kind of legal maneuvering. He just didn't know what. Emery had several theories when Jordan called him while on a quick supply run, and all of them involved Jordan eventually losing. Before leaving Missoula, Jordan debated about trying to contact Shae, but abandoned the idea. She'd said that she wasn't going to force her will on him, and apparently the way she was going to refrain from doing that was by avoiding him. She wanted him to give up the ranch. He wouldn't do that. Stalemate. They were both stubborn, both certain they were correct.

Except that *he* was correct.

He drove over the cattle guard and on up to the gate, where he stood back and viewed his handiwork before taking out the key and unlocking the padlock.

The last stand of a desperate man.

Did he want to do this? Keep getting bigger chains and locking bigger gates?

Wasn't that what he'd done to his life before Shae had forced her way in?

He drove through and locked it back up before admitting to himself that Shae hadn't forced her way in. That might have been her modus operandi in most cases, but it hadn't been with him. He'd made the move. He'd allowed her in. And she'd waited for him to do that.

That wasn't at all like the Shae he'd known back in the day. That Shae had been real, but she was also a front for the Shae who had insecurities and fears just like everyone else.

Together they made for a complex woman, whom he missed.

Who was he kidding? She was a woman he was having one hell of a time living without, but he'd hit rock bottom before and lived to tell the tale. He could do it again.

SHAE HAD TWO legal pads sitting on her dining room table. On one she wrote pros of taking the job in Miles City and on the other she wrote cons as they occurred to her. At the moment her list was heavy on the pros, but she was still hesitant to pick up the phone and make the call that would separate her from Miranda forever.

The doorbell rang and Shae went to answer, thinking that it was a package she was expecting, but when she swung the door open, her stepsister, Liv, was standing on the stoop.

"What are you doing here?" Shae asked before she could stop herself. Liv never just popped in on her.

"Matt has an appointment with a knee specialist and I'm at loose ends." Liv's mouth twisted self-consciously. "And Mom wanted me to check on you. She's worried."

Shae looked at her in astonishment. "Why?" she asked, automatically stepping back to let Liv come into the apartment.

"Because you've been keeping to yourself and haven't asked for anything."

Shae pressed her fingertips to her forehead. "I'm done asking," she said. "In fact, I plan on paying them back for the wedding."

"Did you win a lottery?" Liv asked with a hint of amusement in her voice, and after a brief hesitation, Shae allowed herself a smile. Things had never been easy with her and Liv. She'd been jealous of her brainy stepsister when their parents had married, and half-afraid that Liv would steal the affections of her remaining parent. It hadn't helped that Liv was quiet and shy and Shae lived the high life. Polar opposites, she and Liv, and neither had tried hard to bridge the gap. But they had history and oddly, lately, Shae was thinking of her more as a sister than she ever had before.

"I didn't say I was going to pay it back soon, but I am paying it back."

"You'll have to fight them to do that."

"I've been working out," Shae said. "You want a beer or something?" Liv never had been a much of a wine drinker.

Liv started to shake her head, then said, "Why not?" She settled on the chair opposite the sofa, taking the beer from Shae as she walked by to sit on the sofa. "I also think that Mom wanted to kind of force us to meet face-to-face." She gestured with the beer. "Thinking that it was going to be awkward the first time after...you know..."

"I know," Shae said with feeling.

"I don't think she wanted to witness the first meeting," Liv said, the corners of her mouth lifting slightly before she took a small sip of beer.

"So how's it going, this first meeting?" Shae asked her sister.

"No more awkward than the average evening in our bedroom back in the day."

Shae laughed and then saluted Liv with her bottle. Liv smiled back and Shae had the odd feeling that a very old barrier had cracked just a bit. "How's married life?"

"I like it."

"And I'm really glad I didn't marry Reed."

Liv set her bottle down. "Really," she stated flatly.

"Really," Shae said. "It would have been a mistake."

"Reed was a good guy."

"But I was not good for him." Liv frowned, her expression one that Shae was rapidly becoming accustomed to as people realized she was looking beyond herself. "It was for the best." And her beer was disappearing rapidly as she debated whether or not to make a full confession. Yes? No?

Why not? At least Liv wouldn't feel weird about Shae's engagement ending at her wedding.

"I know it hasn't been that long…but I kind of hooked up with someone else. Briefly."

"Not…" Liv cocked her head and Shae nodded, guessing the direction of her sister's thoughts. "Jordan Bryan? The guy Mom thinks is going to murder you in your bed?"

"Oh, he's murder in bed, but in a good way," Shae muttered.

"Wow," Liv said, taking a long pull from her beer.

"But…we hit a snag."

"How so?"

"It's a long story."

"Matt has other business in town. Just let me text him and clear us a little time." She pulled out her phone and Shae went to get two more beers without asking.

Three beers in and Shae was getting the strong feeling that she and Liv should have started drinking together a lot earlier in life.

"So you gave him an ultimatum…" Liv said.

"No, no, no," Shae replied, waving a hand. "I did *not* give him an ultimatum. He made his decision and I made mine. I did not 'Reed' the guy."

"I'm proud of you," Liv said, glancing at her watch when Shae held up an empty bottle. "Better not. Anyway, Jordan chose to stay and fight, and you chose to…"

"Pretty much be miserable, but on my own terms. No one is going to win that fight between him and Miranda. She has more resources, but he won't back down. When he locked the gate with the logging chain—" A knock interrupted her and Liv got to her feet, frowning.

"Matt's early." But when she opened the door it was Mel standing there with her hand raised to knock again.

"Hi, Mel," Liv said with only a slight slur. "Long time."

"Want a beer?" Shae called from behind her sister.

"Uh…"

"Come on in, come on in," Liv said, guiding Mel into the room. "We're having a war council."

"Concerning?"

"A logging chain," Liv said, ambling back to her chair.

Mel caught Shae's eye and Shae shrugged. "Jordan locked Miranda out of the property by putting a logging chain on the gate."

"What happened next?" Mel asked, suddenly interested now that a legality was involved.

"I imagine he has received a letter telling him to open the gate or else," Shae replied. "But I don't know, because we haven't spoken in a while."

"She did *not* give him an ultimatum," Liv stated.

"I did not," Shae agreed.

"Maybe I'll grab a glass of wine," Mel said, heading to the kitchen.

"Water for me," Liv called.

"I'm good," Shae said.

Mel walked into the kitchen shaking her head.

A few minutes later Matt arrived to pick up Liv. She set her glass of water aside and smiled at him from across the room and again Shae felt a pang of jealousy. But it was good jealousy—the kind that comes from recognizing something worth having. Something she'd like to have but now realized she wasn't going to get only by wanting it…she was going to have to work for it. If only she knew where to begin.

"Are you sure you don't want some water?" Mel said after Liv left. "Or maybe black coffee?"

"My head's already clearing," Shae said. "It's just that we got talking and the faster we talked, the quicker the beer flowed."

"I bet Liv's head isn't already clearing."

Shae made a dismissive gesture. "Liv never was a drinker…but you know? I enjoyed talking to her today."

"Maybe you could do it again sometime," Mel said with a smile, settling in the chair Liv had just occupied.

"I think we're going to." And she liked the idea. "So how is life without work?"

Mel shook her head. "Different than I thought it was going to be."

Shae leaned forward, disturbed by her friend's defeated tone. Mel never gave up. "How so?"

"I just heard from my oldest sister. Her husband has left her, so she's leaving the ranch, going to school. She says she's done her time and either Jolie, Dani or I have to take over the place or we need to sell it."

"I gather that you're selling."

"The agreement is such that if the majority wants to sell, we do. The only one that wants to keep the place is Jolie, who is conveniently living in Alaska, so yeah, we're selling."

"Why don't you close down operations?"

"You know how well dead places sell."

"What are you going to do?"

"I'm canceling my fall classes and going home to oversee operations until the place sells."

"You have three sisters. Why does it have to be you?"

"Because I'm the smart one," Mel said drily. "What's going on with Jordan?"

She'd known the question was coming, but that didn't mean she wanted to answer it. "I haven't seen him lately."

"Because?" Mel asked with a lift of her eyebrows.

"He can't let go of this vendetta against Miranda. Maybe I should be there fighting shoulder to shoulder with him—" and frankly she felt guilty that she wasn't "—but I don't think anyone can win. I think it's going to end up destroying him and I don't want to be party to that." Shae sighed. "I don't want to watch the downward spiral." She gave Mel a searching look. "Is that too self-centered?"

Because she didn't know when self-preservation ended and self-centeredness began.

"I—" Mel started only to have Shae interrupt.

"Here's the deal," she blurted. "I promised myself I wouldn't try to force Jordan to do what I wanted as I've done with every other guy. That I would stand back and let him make his own decisions and live with the consequences, but this just isn't working for me. I see him beating his head bloody against the wall that is Miranda and I want to pull him back and demand that he stop."

"Will he?"

"No."

"Then you've done all you can do."

"Maybe," Shae said, focusing her attention on her new manicure because she didn't want to look at Mel, "But, in a way, I did give him an ultimatum. I want him happy and stress free, because if he's not happy, then it's hard on me." She bit her lip. "As always, it's all about me."

Jordan put the palomino through her paces, then released her into the field. Finally, after more than ten weeks of constant work, she was starting to show signs of settling. A victory. One of many in recent weeks.

So why didn't he feel more victorious?

Because it could all go to hell at any moment. Even though he no longer had Ashley and her crew invading his space and could work his horses in peace, it was a peace that could rupture at any moment. He felt as though he was living on a steep hill in a house with a crumbling foundation. Eventually something was going to give and then he was in for one hell of a ride.

Something was going to give here, too. He just didn't know when.

As it turned out, the giving point occurred that afternoon, when Ashley came walking up the drive as he was sitting on the porch cleaning the .22 he'd been using for target practice. When she saw the gun she stopped abruptly. Rolling his eyes, Jordan carefully set the weapon on the porch and walked out to meet her with both hands where she could see them. He didn't want her having a heart attack or accusing him of assault or anything.

"You're on my property," Jordan said.

"Miranda wants to see you."

"Where is she?"

"She wants you to come to the ranch."

Jordan simply smirked at her and walked back toward his house with Clyde trotting beside him.

"It would be to your benefit to go."

Jordan kept walking.

"If you don't, she's firing Shae."

"Shae has a new job."

"No, she doesn't."

Keep walking. He couldn't. He turned back. Ashley raised her chin. She never appeared comfortable facing off with him, but she did her best.

"I'm not saying anything else," she said, the quiver in her voice convincing him that she was speaking the truth. "If you want to hear more, meet with Miranda at the ranch."

FOR THE THIRD TIME—and he promised himself the last time—Jordan parked behind the Cedar Creek Ranch house and got out of the Subaru. This time he wasn't going to lose it. This time he'd remain in control.

This time he had nothing to lose, but it sounded as if Shae did.

A new girl was behind the reception desk, a cool blonde who must have been warned about his scars, because her face remained a blank slate when he walked in the door and they made eye contact.

"Miranda is waiting for you upstairs, Mr. Bryan."

He shook his head. "I'll meet her out back by my car. I'll wait for ten minutes, and then I'm leaving." There was no way he was going back up into her lair.

"But—"

"Ten minutes." He checked his watch, then walked back out the door. He only had to wait five before Miranda sauntered around the corner of the building and came to stand a few feet in front of him.

"This is all very dramatic," she said.

"You like drama," he replied, folding his arms.

"I've spoken to my lawyer and they assure me that the gate will be opened. *That's* a given. All I have to do is wait." Jordan shrugged carelessly, his arms still crossed over his chest. "All you're buying is a few weeks' time and then I'll once again have access to the property. And at that point I will do everything in my power to make your life a living hell." She smirked up at him. "I'll do the same for your girlfriend."

"Ex-girlfriend."

"Then I guess you won't care."

"I'm not going to be manipulated by you."

She took a step forward, smiling smugly up at him. "So you're opting for living hell? Have you ever known me to bluff, Jordan? Haven't you had enough experience with me following through to believe that I don't bluff?"

"I don't bluff, either, Miranda."

"Meaning?"

He took a step closer. "Meaning bring it on."

"You really don't care that much about Shae, do you? Were you just screwing her to pass the time?"

"Jealous?" he asked.

Her hand snaked out and slapped him soundly across his scarred cheek, then she took a quick step back, swallowing drily. It was the first time he'd ever seen her lose control. Even when he'd sent her from his bed, she'd been calm and icy, telling him his father would never believe him if he said a word about it.

"I realize that in your current mental state, it might take you some time to make a well-thought-out decision. You have one week. If the gate isn't opened by that time, I'll send a bulldozer through it and I'll fire Shae's ass. And yes, I know she has a job offer. That won't last, either."

She drew a sharp breath in through her nose, then pivoted and stalked around the house.

Jordan leaned back on the hood of the Subaru, idly rubbing his hand across his still stinging cheek. Was this really how he wanted to live the next eight years of his life?

And what about Shae? What had he done to her?

SHAE HAD PROMISED herself and Wallace that she would put every bit of her focus on her work if she got her old job back, and she was trying, but it was damnably difficult when she couldn't get Jordan off her mind. For all of her talk about not giving him an ultimatum, she'd forced him to choose and he'd chosen to continue fighting the battle he'd needed to win.

He'd tried to call twice the previous day, but her phone had been off as per her promise to Wallace. By the time she'd gotten his message—a warning that Miranda once again had her in the sights—it was well after 10:00 p.m. and she couldn't bring herself to drive to the ranch and confront that chain and padlock again to discuss matters.

Liar. She couldn't bring herself to face coming in second to a vendetta. That hurt. Bad. Worse than the knowledge that she was on shaky professional ground. She had to take the Miles City job before Miranda ruined the deal, but she couldn't quite bring herself to make the call.

Shae leaned back in her chair, pushing her hair back, and closed her eyes.

"Headache?" Gerald asked in his snotty voice as he walked by.

"Nasty one," Shae said.

"Coming to lunch? It's two-taco Tuesday."

"I have some stuff to catch up on."

"Oh, really?"

"Yes, really. I have to investigate some access issues prior to recommending a property for purchase." Access issues were making her crazy lately, what with people assuming matters and not putting them in writing. Their extreme carelessness was making her job a nightmare.

Shae suddenly put a hand on her forehead.

What if…

Fifteen minutes later Shae walked into Wallace's office and set the lease agreement she'd pulled up on the computer on his desk.

"Is this one of *our* projects?" he asked pointedly.

"It's my lunch hour," Shae replied. "And you're

only here for three more days. Would you please take a look at this and tell me what it says about access?"

Wallace slipped on his reading glasses as he pulled the lease agreement closer. He read silently for a few minutes, then shook his head. "I assume you mean access to the land itself and not the buildings."

"Yes."

"It says nothing."

"So let's say the lessees have to cross property they have not leased to get to the part they have leased. And let's say the owner of the land they cross locks a gate on them…then what?"

"Sounds like he's asserting domain."

"That's what I thought."

"Why didn't he assert domain earlier?" Wallace asked, looking over his glasses.

"Because we—" Shae cleared her throat "—he probably assumed access was granted. And when he'd had enough…"

"He accidentally asserted domain." Wallace smiled a little. "I sense a storm moving in."

"Yep," Shae said as she picked up the lease document. "After I get off work, of course."

"Of course."

She nodded her thanks and headed for the door, stopping when he said her name. She looked back curiously and Wallace said, "Why don't you take the rest of the afternoon off?"

SHAE TOOK THE afternoon off and drove to the High
Camp, stopping at the gate with its heavy chain and
sturdy lock. Not the way she'd want to live, but the
chain and lock might well give Jordan exactly the
life he was looking for. Not that he wasn't in for a
long legal battle, because there was no way in hell
that Miranda was going to give up just like that. But
at least now Jordan would have some ammunition.

Jordan, who was nowhere to be found. The dog
and the pig were both gone and the peacocks…
where were the peacocks? Did Jordan even live
there anymore?

He had to, because the yellow Claiborne horses
were still in the north pasture. So where were the
other animals?

Shae walked to the empty round pen, then on
to the barn. The boardwalks were all finished and
the shrubs had been surrounded by rounded river
gravel. She resisted the temptation to peek inside the
buildings and see what Ashley had accomplished.
She didn't know if her stomach could take it.

The barn was as empty as the round pen. No Jordan. Just a Subaru and some ornery yellow horses.
Finally, after checking the ponds, she let herself
into the house and wrote out a note asking him to
call her as soon as possible and telling him to keep
the gate locked. She figured that last part was in-
triguing enough to make him call regardless of his
feelings toward her.

He did. She was driving across town to meet Mel when her phone rang.

"When were you here?" he asked after a quick hello.

"A few hours ago. Where's the pig?"

"I took her home to Claiborne."

"And the peacocks?"

"Went to some starry-eyed California transplants."

Shae felt a ridiculous pang. She'd grown to like those noisy birds and the pig…she drew in a deep breath. "I've been doing some research," she said, "and when you locked that gate, you asserted domain."

"How's that?"

"Miranda doesn't have right-of-way across your property to access hers. There's nothing in the agreement that Emery drafted for you and your father that spells out right-of-way."

"It wasn't Emery. It was his assistant. He's the one who screwed up and made it possible for her to start a guest ranch instead of farming."

"Well, he may have also saved your ass. By closing that gate and stopping Miranda's access, you're asserting your right to keep her off your property. If you don't continue to stop her, she could get access by default. You have to keep that gate locked."

"I never thought I'd hear you say that."

"Yeah. Well, this doesn't automatically mean that Miranda will go away. In fact, I'm pretty certain she'll continue to harass you for some time, but legally you might have the upper hand."

"Shae—"

"So you need to go and see—"

"I've been doing a lot of thinking, Shae," he interrupted, and there was something in his tone that kept her from reiterating the importance of seeing Emery as soon as possible. It also kept her from breathing correctly. "I'm going to sell the ranch. I have to if we're going to have a chance at anything."

"Do you *want* to sell the ranch?"

"I want to have a shot at a future with you, and if that's what it takes…"

Her throat felt as if it was closing. She wasn't going to have this happen, to have him sell the ranch because of her and resent her for it later. What if things didn't work out between them? He'd have lost his last link to his father. "You can't sell the ranch because of me."

"I thought that was what you wanted."

"No. That's not what I want," she said.

"Then I must have been talking to some other dark-haired woman, because I'm pretty damned certain that was what I was hearing before I got you fired."

"What I wanted…was for you to give up the vendetta."

"Then I have to sell the ranch."

"Not because of me," Shae said.

"Then why the hell should I do it?"

"Exactly. If you don't have a reason other than me, then don't do it."

There was a very long moment of heavy silence and then Jordan said, "What the hell do you want, Shae?"

She wanted to know how to walk that thin line between compromise and control, and right now she had no faith in her ability to do so—or to even recognize when she strayed too far one way or the other. Yes, she wanted him to leave the High Camp because he'd be free of Miranda, but what if he hated his life away from the ranch that he could now possibly make his own? She didn't want to be the cause of that.

"Shae?" he asked with an edge to his voice. A justified edge, really.

"I want...I want time to think," she finally said. And then she hung up.

EVEN THOUGH SHE wanted nothing more than to be alone, Shae met with Mel as planned for a Friday night drink at a small bar a few blocks from the Cedar Creek Enterprises offices—a place with decent burgers and a jukebox, which didn't attract a crowd until the later hours of the evening. They sat in their usual booth and then Shae went to the bar to give their order, since the bartender was also the waiter for the first part of the evening.

"So when do you think Miranda is going to lower

the boom?" she asked Mel, who was eyeing her with an I-know-something's-wrong look.

"She may be bluffing. Take the Miles City job."

"The one that she's supposed to ruin for me?" Shae said with a cocked eyebrow. "I'm beginning to feel like Jordan," she said, satisfied with how casually she'd said his name. "No matter what I do, there she is."

"How are things with him?" Mel asked. So much for sidetracking her friend.

"We parted ways."

"Why?"

Shae cleared her throat, which seemed to be closing on her for the second time that evening. "It's not working out."

"Are you in love with him?"

"Unfair question," Shae said, reaching for her drink.

"How so?"

"Because I want to say no, but I can't."

"Then…?"

"I can't be in the middle of this thing with him."

"Why? Afraid you'd fight too hard?"

"Afraid that I'll take over his life."

Mel cocked her head as she slowly stirred her drink. "Have you controlled anything about his life yet?"

"I'm a strong influence," she said darkly.

"What if he needs you?"

Shae frowned at Mel. "Aren't you supposed

to make things easier for me? You know…best friend…shoulder to cry on…moral support?"

"All I'm going to say is that there's nothing wrong with being a strong influence with a person strong enough to stand up to you."

"He just told me he's selling the ranch—because of me."

Mel was silent for a moment. "That's big."

Shae nodded without looking at her friend. "Yeah. Remember how Reed kept changing to make me happy…how that ultimately turned out?"

"Not well," Mel conceded.

"I don't want Jordan to come to resent me."

"I see your point."

"Exactly." And if Mel wasn't going to argue with her, then Shae was pretty damned certain that her fears were well grounded.

SHAE PASSED ON a second drink, pleading a headache—which was no lie—and drove back to her apartment. Her parking space was taken by a strange car, as were all of the other available spaces. Great. Her neighbor was having one of his parties, which meant no sleep for her—as if that was going to be a possibility in the first place. She finally found a spot two blocks away and walked back to her apartment, nodding at the people standing in her hallway, drinks in hand. Maybe this was for the best—it'd give her something to think about besides Jordan.

Someone knocked on her door and she pulled it open a crack, leaving the safety chain in place. "Hey, Brad," she said to her party-giving neighbor.

"We'll be done by midnight," he promised, raising his drink. "As per apartment regulations. Want to join us? There's always room for one more and we have plenty of beer."

"Thanks, no," Shae said with a tired and totally fake smile. "Maybe next time."

"Well, if you change your mind..."

"Thanks." She pushed the door shut, then wandered through her living room before finally settling on the sofa with the lights out and listening to the muffled voices of the partygoers. When her doorbell rang, she ignored it the first time, but after three rings, she got to her feet and once again pulled the door open as far as the chain would allow.

Then she almost closed it again. It was Jordan, and she was so not ready to face him.

"Can I come in?" he asked just before a guy stumbled sideways in the hall next to him. Shae undid the chain and allowed him in, closing the door behind him, shutting out the party.

"I told you I wanted time to think," she said.

"I gave you time—"

"Two hours?" she asked on a note of outrage.

"I waited an hour before I started driving," he said. "I couldn't wait any longer. I've been going through hell alone and I just want to know...what do *you* want?"

You. With no complications.

As if.

Shae forced herself to meet his very blue gaze and stay strong. "It's what I don't want, okay?"

"You're going to have to explain that."

"I don't want you to resent me later for forcing you into choices you didn't want to make."

Jordan shifted his weight and she had to give him points for taking time to process her words before saying, "Okay. We know what you don't want. Now…what *do* you want?"

Shae took a couple agitated paces toward the window, then turned back and pushed her hands through her hair in a gesture of frustration. "I want you to not be eaten alive by your hatred of Miranda."

"What else?" he asked patiently.

"I want you to be at peace. I want you to train your horses and enjoy life and not…be angry and stressed all the time." She sank down onto the sofa, staring straight across the room at the ornate hook on the wall where her wedding dress had once hung. "And I don't know that selling the ranch would give you those things."

"It might."

"Yes. If *you* wanted to sell." She rolled her head on the sofa cushion to look at him.

"You're not forcing me to do anything, Shae, except to come to my senses. You were right. I can't live like this." He sat down beside her, but he didn't touch her. "Locks. Chains. Headaches from stress."

"Nightmares?"

"A few. Less since I started forgiving my father and dealing with grief."

Shae felt her expression soften. "How's that going?"

"I'm making some progress," he said, reaching over to take her hand in his. Automatically she threaded her fingers through his, needing the connection even though she didn't know where this conversation was taking them.

"You could sell the ranch." It was more of a question than a statement.

"I think so."

He sounded as if he meant it, not as though he was making a concession. But the ranch was such a part of him, and he seemed such a part of the ranch—the old ranch, pre-Miranda. She hated what had happened to his sanctuary…to him.

"What if you could win?" Shae finally asked in a soft voice. "With locks and chains and asserting domain. What if you won?"

"Meaning?"

"If you won, by locking the gate, would it be enough? Would you be able to let go of the Miranda thing?"

"I think the question is…would she be able to let go? Because one thing I've become pretty damned certain of over the past few days is that you're the best thing in my life. But Miranda…she's never going to stop, and that's why I decided to sell." He squeezed her fingers. "It's not because you're forcing me to do anything."

"Could I?" she asked.

"I'm more of a joint-decision kind of guy."

"So if I pushed really hard?"

"We'd talk…like you tried to talk to me before. Negotiate, like you were trying to negotiate with me before."

She smiled a little. "I was negotiating?"

He smiled back, lifting their joined hands and setting them on his hard thigh. "I know this is all new to you, give and take," he said with just enough good humor that she didn't get her back up, "but yes, you were negotiating. And we were talking."

She closed her eyes, leaning her head back against the cushions again, the smile still playing on her lips as she held his hand just a little tighter. Someone stumbled against the wall in the hallway, but Shae barely noticed.

"That's what this is about?" he asked in a low voice. "You being afraid of pushing me around?"

"You can see where it's a concern…right?"

"Yes, but you weren't forcing your will on me. You asked if I wanted to live my life the way I was—with bitterness, locks and chains. And I realized that I didn't." Their shoulders were touching now and Shae leaned into him. He was so warm and solid and…there. Jordan was there for her.

She wanted to there for him, too. Her mouth quirked sideways. "I hate to give up the fight, too. But Jordan?" He turned his face toward hers and it was all she could do not to give in and kiss him. "I can't stand by and watch you destroy yourself. That was why I had to leave."

"You're more important to me than any damned vendetta." He lifted their hands, kissed her knuckles, and Shae found that she couldn't look away from his intense blue gaze. "I can't let go of my feelings for Miranda just like that...but—" he let out a breath "—maybe with some assistance, I can learn to manage them."

Assistance. Shae liked the sound of that.

"If you choose to not sell, to stay at the ranch, fight the good fight, I guess I want to be there with you. I have a thing or two I'd like to impart to Ashley if I ever get the chance," she added in a low voice.

"What about your job?"

"I need to leave before I get fired again. But I don't want to go to Miles City."

"Then what will you do?"

"Whatever I can. If I have to leave real estate, I will. It doesn't have to be forever."

"Just until someone throws a bucket of water on the wicked witch?" Jordan muttered.

A smile wavered on Shae's lips, then faded. "Finding a new job won't be easy, but I could move into a cheaper apartment, or maybe get a roommate. I want to pursue this, Jordan. To see if it works."

A corner of his mouth curved up and he caressed the side of her face with the back of his injured hand. "It works."

"Excuse me?"

Shifting his position so he was half facing her on the sofa he said simply, "It works."

He took her face in his hands and kissed her, a deep, sweet kiss, so full of promise that she almost forgot what she was about to say. "We'll make it work wherever we are," he said against her lips.

"I was talking about the ranch," she said faintly.

"I was talking about us."

She leaned back a little, arching an eyebrow. "It's that easy?" she asked.

"Oh, yeah," he said. "So easy. Let's see. I had to make mash for a toothless pig, endure weeks of invading workers, risk a lawsuit, go toe to toe with a woman I hate, get the woman I care about—who wouldn't talk to me—fired…yes. It was that easy."

Shae raised her lips to touch his. "We're still going to go see Emery, right?"

"Yes," he said. "But before we go, I need you to know…you're more important to me than the ranch. Much more important to me than beating Miranda. She wins. She can have the ranch. I just want you."

"That's maybe the best thing anyone has ever said to me."

"I have better stuff that I'm saving for later," he said.

She couldn't help but smile. "I hope so."

He took her hands in his, his expression solemn as he said, "I promise that if you give us a chance I'm not going to let you push me around."

"As if I'd try." She held his fingers more tightly. "In return, I'll give you your space when you need it...and I'll be there when you need me."

"A fifty-fifty deal."

"Do we need to sign something?"

He let go of her hands, held up his little finger and a moment later Shae solemnly linked her pinky with his. "I love you," she whispered.

"I love you, too. And I think this fifty-fifty thing is going to work just fine."

EPILOGUE

"You're not supposed to cry, Mom!" Shae crossed the room to where Vivian was losing the battle as she tried to blink back tears.

"They're tears of joy," Liv murmured just loud enough for Shae to hear, bringing a smile to her lips as she hugged her stepmother. No doubt they were after Shae's last wedding fiasco.

"You can't elope," Vivian said. "I mean...you *can't!*"

"The marriage is the important part," Shae said soothingly. "Not the wedding."

"She has a point," her father said. "We had a small wedding and look at us."

"It was our second wedding." Vivian sniffed. She stepped back to take Shae by the shoulders, carefully scrutinizing her. "Are you sure?"

"Positive. After the last time...let's just say that I still have bad dreams where I'm being wrapped in tulle and chased by wedding planners through wedding-cake obstacle courses."

"While wearing a six-thousand-dollar dress?" Liv asked innocently.

"Exactly." If Liv hadn't helped her find a buyer

who'd paid nearly that much for her pristine dress, she might have resented the reminder, but the truth was that she and Liv were doing well together. Something about no longer having anything to prove. Or needing to have every little thing go her way. Not that she didn't have her moments, but all in all…she glanced over at Jordan, who gave her a quick nod, indicating that his part of the Sunday-afternoon mission had been accomplished. Shae had asked that he quietly give her father her check for the first of many wedding reimbursement payments after brunch and insist that a) he take it, and b) he put it into their retirement fund quickly so that Vivian wasn't tempted to try and give it back to Shae for the wedding.

Her father beamed and winked at her and Shae gave Vivian one last hug. Her new job at the county assessor's office wasn't as dynamic as what she'd done before, but it paid the bills and eventually she planned to go back into real-estate procurement. No hurry, though. The important thing was getting the ranch back…and forging a new life with her new husband-to-be.

"Thank you," she said, looking her stepmother in the eye. "For everything."

"Oh, Shae."

David stepped in then and put an arm around his wife, who nestled into him. "When's the big day?"

"Tomorrow," Shae said. "In the backyard, here at the house, if that's okay."

"Fine with me," David said with a shrug.

Vivian's eyes widened in shock, but Liv went to the rescue. "It's tomorrow, Mom, because Shae and Jordan want you to relax and enjoy the event. And since it's just me and Matt and Brant and Sara and Cole and Mel…well, no commando house cleaning necessary."

"We're going to dinner afterward," Jordan said. "The reservations are made and the dress code is casual. Jeans and boots."

"Which Matt is going to love," Liv said. "And speaking of Matt, I need to get going. We'll see you back here at noon, right?"

"High noon," Jordan said, walking over to put his arm around Shae. "And we need to get going, too. We've yet to pick up the rings."

David glanced down at Jordan's left hand, which wouldn't be wearing a ring, and Jordan said, "I'm thinking a chain around my neck."

"Russians wear their wedding rings on their right hands," Vivian said helpfully.

"We'll consider all the options," Shae said as they headed for the door.

"I like that right hand idea," Jordan said a few minutes later as they walked hand in hand to the car.

"Me, too," Shae said lightly. She squeezed his hand, then glanced sideways at him. "I told you the only way to do this was by kamikaze attack."

"It seems to have worked," he said. "Although I

still have a strong feeling that we might be greeted by a houseful of flowers or balloons or something."

"But nothing outrageous due to time constraints." Shae smiled with satisfaction as Jordan opened the door for her. Figuring her way around Vivian had been easy once she realized that all she had to do was make sure there was just no time to pull together anything extravagant. Score.

"I forgot to tell her Emery was coming." Officiating, in fact, in his role as justice of the peace. "I just hope he found a suit that he's okay with," Shae muttered. He'd been pulling suits out of closets and trunks for the past day and a half.

"We'll find out when we get back." Jordan had been living with Emery for the past nine months while the lawsuit was in full swing, training his horses there, living in a travel trailer behind the house, helping the aging lawyer manage his livestock. It had worked so well that Shae hated to leave the old man alone again.

"He'll be fine," Jordan said when she voiced the concern for the third time that day. "Macy—" Claiborne's son's girlfriend "—will take good care of him."

"As long as we get the pig, I guess I'm okay with her taking over Emery."

"We get the pig." He pulled the car over to the edge of the road.

"What?" Shae asked, craning her neck to look at the gauges. Everything seemed fine.

He smiled at her, that rare, devastating smile that had sent her hormones into overdrive back in high school and did the same today. "We get the pig, the ranch, each other." He put a hand behind her neck and pulled her lips to his for a hot, hot kiss. "It couldn't get much better."

"Miranda could move to the East Coast," Shae murmured, pulling his mouth back to hers. The woman had backed off once she'd officially lost access to the property, but Shae didn't for one minute believe she was gone.

"We can deal with Miranda," Jordan said, nipping her lower lip before he settled back behind the wheel. "Just like we deal with everything."

"As a joint force to be reckoned with?"

"Exactly."

Shae leaned her head back against the seat and smiled to herself as Jordan put the car into gear.

Oh, yeah. They could handle anything.

* * * * *

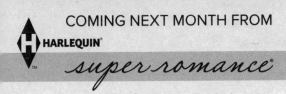

COMING NEXT MONTH FROM

HARLEQUIN®

super romance®

Available July 1, 2014

#1932 COP BY HER SIDE
The Mysteries of Angel Butte • by Janice Kay Johnson
No way is Lieutenant Jane Vahalik giving Sergeant Clay Renner a second chance.
Their brief romance is history! But when her niece is kidnapped, suddenly Clay is
the only cop Jane trusts to solve the case. And being this close to him shows Jane
another side of the man....

#1933 CHALLENGING MATT
Those Hollister Boys • by Julianna Morris
For Layne McGraw, clearing her late uncle's name is all-important. Proving he wasn't
an embezzler isn't easy. Especially when Matt Hollister gets involved. The former
playboy has his own reasons for helping her—and the attraction between them
could derail everything.

#1934 HEARTS IN VEGAS • by Colleen Collins
When former jewel thief turned investigator Frances Jefferies is sent to retrieve a
stolen diamond, one thing stands in her way: bodyguard Braxton Morgan. She has to
succeed to clear her record, which makes him a sexy distraction she doesn't need.

#1935 A SINCLAIR HOMECOMING
The Sinclairs of Alaska • by Kimberly Van Meter
Wade Sinclair has finally come home to Alaska after his sister's murder eight years
ago. His family is struggling. When psychiatrist Morgan O'Hare is called in, Wade
and Morgan can't fight the attraction between them. With Morgan's help, Wade can
finally move on and embrace the future—with Morgan.

#1936 A PERFECT TRADE
by Anna Sugden
Should she make a deal with a man she no longer trusts?
With her life in shambles, Jenny Martin doesn't have
much choice. Professional hockey player Tru Jelinek has
the money she needs and he owes her. It's a good trade
as long as their attraction doesn't interfere!

#1937 DATING A SINGLE DAD
by Kris Fletcher
Brynn Catalano is everyone's rock. She doesn't think
twice about taking a temp job to help her cousin in crisis.
Before she knows it, though, gorgeous Hank North and
his sweet little daughter make her feel like staying...and
putting her own happiness first, for once.

**YOU CAN FIND MORE INFORMATION ON UPCOMING
HARLEQUIN® TITLES, FREE EXCERPTS AND MORE AT
WWW.HARLEQUIN.COM.**

HSRLPCNM0614

SPECIAL EXCERPT FROM

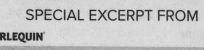

HARLEQUIN®

superromance®

Cop by Her Side

By Janice Kay Johnson

When Lieutenant Jane Vahalik met
Seargent Clay Renner she thought she'd
finally found the one man who could accept that
she was a cop. Too bad he proved that wrong.
So why does she get a thrill when he calls out
of the blue? Read on for an exciting excerpt of
the upcoming book **COP BY HER SIDE**
by Janice Kay Johnson, the latest in
The Mysteries of Angel Butte series.

Jane felt a weird twist in her chest when she saw the displayed
name on her cell phone. Clay Renner. Somehow, despite the
disastrous end to their brief relationship, she'd never deleted
his phone number from her address book. Why would *he* be
calling in the middle of the afternoon?

"Vahalik."

"Jane, Clay Renner here."

As always, she reacted to his voice in a way that aggravated
her. It was so blasted *male*.

"Sergeant," she said stiffly.

"This is about your sister." He hesitated. "We've found
Melissa's vehicle located in a ditch. She suffered a head injury,
Jane. She's in ICU. But I'm focusing on another problem.

The girl, Brianna, is missing."

Of all the things she'd expected him to say, this didn't even come close.

"*What?*" she whispered. "Did anyone see the accident?"

"Unfortunately, no. Some hikers came along afterward."

"If another car caused the accident and the driver freaked…?" Even in shock, she knew that was stupid.

"A logical assumption, except that we've been unable to locate Brianna. We still haven't given up hope that your sister dropped her off somewhere, but at this point—"

"You have no idea where she is." Ouch. She sounded so harsh.

"Thanks for the vote of confidence, Lieutenant."

She closed her eyes. As angry as she still was at him, she knew he was a smart cop and a strong man. He didn't need her attitude. "I'm sorry. I didn't mean…"

"We're organizing a search."

She swallowed, trying to think past her panic. "I'll come help search."

"All right," Clay said. He told her where the SUV had gone off the road. "You okay to drive?"

"Of course I am!"

"Then I'll look for you."

Those were the most reassuring words he'd said during the entire conversation. And as Jane disconnected, she didn't want to think about how much she wanted *his* reassurance.

Will this case bring Clay and Jane together?
Find out what happens in COP BY HER SIDE
by Janice Kay Johnson, available July 2014 from
Harlequin® Superromance®.
And look for the other books in
***The Mysteries of Angel Butte* series.**

Copyright © 2014 by Janice Kay Johnson

HSREXP0614

LARGER-PRINT BOOKS!
GET 2 FREE LARGER-PRINT NOVELS PLUS
2 FREE GIFTS!

HARLEQUIN®

super romance®

More Story...More Romance

YES! Please send me 2 FREE LARGER-PRINT Harlequin® Superromance® novels and my 2 FREE gifts (gifts are worth about $10). After receiving them, if I don't wish to receive any more books, I can return the shipping statement marked "cancel." If I don't cancel, I will receive 6 brand-new novels every month and be billed just $5.69 per book in the U.S. or $5.99 per book in Canada. That's a savings of at least 16% off the cover price! It's quite a bargain! Shipping and handling is just 50¢ per book in the U.S. or 75¢ per book in Canada.* I understand that accepting the 2 free books and gifts places me under no obligation to buy anything. I can always return a shipment and cancel at any time. Even if I never buy another book, the two free books and gifts are mine to keep forever.

139/339 HDN F46Y

Name   (PLEASE PRINT)

Address   Apt. #

City   State/Prov.   Zip/Postal Code

Signature (if under 18, a parent or guardian must sign)

Mail to the **Harlequin® Reader Service:**
IN U.S.A.: P.O. Box 1867, Buffalo, NY 14240-1867
IN CANADA: P.O. Box 609, Fort Erie, Ontario L2A 5X3

Are you a current subscriber to Harlequin Superromance books and want to receive the larger-print edition?
Call 1-800-873-8635 today or visit www.ReaderService.com.

* Terms and prices subject to change without notice. Prices do not include applicable taxes. Sales tax applicable in N.Y. Canadian residents will be charged applicable taxes. Offer not valid in Quebec. This offer is limited to one order per household. Not valid for current subscribers to Harlequin Superromance Larger-Print books. All orders subject to credit approval. Credit or debit balances in a customer's account(s) may be offset by any other outstanding balance owed by or to the customer. Please allow 4 to 6 weeks for delivery. Offer available while quantities last.

Your Privacy—The Harlequin® Reader Service is committed to protecting your privacy. Our Privacy Policy is available online at www.ReaderService.com or upon request from the Harlequin Reader Service.

We make a portion of our mailing list available to reputable third parties that offer products we believe may interest you. If you prefer that we not exchange your name with third parties, or if you wish to clarify or modify your communication preferences, please visit us at www.ReaderService.com/consumerchoice or write to us at Harlequin Reader Service Preference Service, P.O. Box 9062, Buffalo, NY 14269. Include your complete name and address.

HSRLP13R